The Diaries of Velvet Brown

Also by Myra King and published by Ginninderra Press
City Paddock
The Journey of Velvet Brown

Myra King

The Diaries
of Velvet Brown

The Diaries of Velvet Brown
ISBN 978 1 74027 301 9
Copyright © Myra King 2017
Cover: Martin Gerritsen

First published 2017 by
GINNINDERRA PRESS
PO Box 3461 Port Adelaide 5015
www.ginninderrapress.com.au

First Diary

Tuesday 2 October

I've dug up my time capsule. I need to read again what I wrote about Willem. It's only been buried for six months, but my journal, which was inside, has already got damaged. The print is still sort of readable, thank God – it would be impossible to remember it all. I don't have it saved anywhere else. I'm copying the main points into this new notebook, a diary actually, which I got for Christmas. Not an electronic one, a retro one. Like people used in my Mum's day. You actually write everything in this diary by hand.

Kaleen and I buried the time capsule in my garden in the middle of autumn. It was shortly after the love of my life, Willem Van Den Hoven, an exchange student, had to return to Holland. I only wish I could have gone with him.

I see monsters. I'm a bit like the boy in that famous movie who sees dead people when nobody else can, except I'm a fourteen-year-old girl (almost fifteen) and I see monsters when nobody else can.

One day, when I was about three, I looked at this photo my mother was holding, pointed and asked, 'Who's dat one, Mummy?' I wondered who that man was, with the smiley mouth and laughing eyes.

'Why, Velvet, that's your dad.' I can still recall my mother's face as she said that, all screwed up like the orange we'd left out in the sun after picking up the summer fall.

My father was sitting in his chair, and I remember going over to him and peering around the paper, to check whether he had changed since I'd last seen him. But he still looked as he had on the morning before.

I came back to my mother and traced my finger around his face on the photo she held. I had seen other photos before this, but I'd only recognised Mum and myself and I'd been too young to wonder, or question. Now, looking closely at the photo, I could see the body shape was my father's, the hair was his, and even the clothes were familiar. But his face was different.

'Where's the wavy bits and the horns, Mummy?'

Along with a fuzzy outline, Dad had horns like my pet goat, Sebby. I mean, I knew they weren't solid like Sebby's. I had tried grabbing Dad's horns before and my hands had grasped air, but in the photo they were missing. I'd glanced over at my father again and there they were, pointing above his paper like sharp grey wings. I realised then that I couldn't 'see' in photos everything I saw in reality.

My mother said, 'Monsters have horns, Velvet. People don't.'

I noticed, not for the first time, her colour change from a light yellow to a dim red, making her look even more like the orange.

Obviously, a monster wasn't a nice thing. So did that mean my father wasn't good? Or my brother? He looked similar, but with only one horn.

I wanted to ask, 'What about Sebby, then? Is he a monster too?' But my mother's complexion was deepening, and her eyes were squinting at me in that weird way they did when I asked her things which she didn't have an answer for.

My parents named me Velvet, after the heroine in the film *National Velvet*. That Velvet Brown wins a horse in a raffle and trains it to come first in the Grand National in the UK. Me, I was horseless up until the beginning of this year when Spirit, my beautiful Cremello quarter horse, literally galloped into my life. My best friend, Kaleen Pingelly, had a lot do with me getting him. Everything actually. Her father bought Spirit for her birthday, and then she gave him to me. The biggest re-gift in history. My parents don't know about it as they still think he's Kaleen's. (Spirit stays at Kaleen's property – Dad won't have a horse on our place.) But Kaleen gave me Spirit's registration papers, and ownership, for an early birthday present.

I was born fourteen years and nine months ago, fifteen seconds before midnight on New Year's Eve, so that makes it still last year. I used to wonder if all those fireworks had anything to do with my ability, but now I think it might have something to do with my great grandmother, who was Pitjantjatjara. Something I've inherited.

Kaleen Pingelly is the only one I trust to tell about the monsters. We've grown up next door to each other, from when we were both four years old. Next door is a relative term as we live in farmhouses four kilometres apart, although most of those kilometres are on her side of the fence. Our property is small, but large enough for Sebby and Dad's six merino sheep. He says he's a shepherd and house husband now. I wish he'd get a paying job again, but he reckons he's inherited the walkabout gene from his Aboriginal grandmother. She was from the north-west of South Australia – desert country, but beautiful for it.

Kaleen has a theory about what I see. She says it's the people's real selves showing through their bodies, revealing the mind-shape of who they really are. Their true characters.

There's a sort of garden around the back of our farmhouse where Dad's prize merino sheep, all six of them, can't get through the fence. It didn't stop Sebby, though, getting in and eating all of the black Mondo grass we'd planted to mark where the time capsule was buried. I made quite a few holes this morning before I got lucky and dug it up. Our garden looks a bit moon-scapey now, but I'll fill it in later. I've been up since five a.m. and I still have to get ready to catch the school bus.

Tuesday 2 October – late afternoon

Earlier this year, Kaleen and I went on a quest. We rode all the way to Adelaide (TAOB – To Adelaide Or Bust), an almost two-hundred-kilometre round trip. We met up with the publisher, Tarrant Moselle, of Wanda-Willow Press, who'd just accepted Kaleen's first novel *Death Does Not Innocence Make*. Even though she's my age, she's a brilliant writer. Our parents didn't know about TAOB and we got into so much shit. Well, I did, more than Kaleen, but it all turned out okay in the end.

You know how they always say fact is stranger than fiction? Well, Kaleen and I have had first-hand experience with real murder. Two murders, in fact, and that was after she wrote her crime novel. Her mother's gardener, Jim, and one of her father's factory workers, Chocka, were murdered.

Tarrant Moselle hasn't done anything to promote the book. And as Kaleen's sort of agent, I need to talk to him about that.

We're in the last term of the year, and in a few weeks, Kaleen and I are off to Adelaide again, this time with the parents' permission, to see the Agatha Christie play *The Mousetrap*.

I wish Willem wasn't in Holland. He could have come too. Maybe I should have hidden him like an illegal immigrant.

Something which hasn't happened since we buried the time capsule is me riding Zeus. Zeus is the young colt belonging to Old Ma Izzy, the horse lady. Her proper name is Rosalie Islington-Prior and she's amazing. What she doesn't know about horses isn't worth knowing.

Zeus got a paddock injury, a bad gash and hairline fracture of his nearside foreleg. It was put down to another horse kicking him. The pecking order thing. Anyway, Zeus is fine now and almost ready again for backing. That's mounting the horse for the very first time in its life. In your life too, actually. You will always be its first rider. Old Ma Izzy says it's a sacred moment. An anagram of 'sacred' is 'scared', which is more like it. I've never done this before. I mean I've ridden heaps of horses, Kaleen has lots of stock horses on her property, as well as her own horse Watson, but I've never ridden any of them for their very first time. Their virgin ride.

Old Ma Izzy says Zeus should be ready soon. We've been doing lots of long reining and leading him off Spirit, who's bombproof. And he's fine with the girthing up and wearing the bridle. It's a bitless one, which makes it easier for him to have on, and for us to put on. Well, that's about all for the update – Kaleen would call it a prologue, the unkind may call it info dumping.

Yay. Willem's Skyping me – I have to go. (We talk every morning my time, which is every evening his time.)

Friday 5 October

After school I stay on the bus and travel to Kaleen's place. She's not expecting me, but even if she isn't home I can still take Spirit out for a long ride. I really need to.

Willem wasn't on Skype today, yesterday or the day before. The last time I talked to him was on Tuesday morning when I first wrote in this new diary. He hasn't been in contact with me now for three days. And that's even allowing for the time difference between here and Holland. No texts, no emails, no calls.

To make it worse, all day Clarissa 'Kiss' Rothchile, a Category Three Away in the Clouds Monster (I have four different categories for my monsters) with a mouth like a razor blade, has been cutting me with her crap.

Kaleen's not at school today and Kiss has only me to slash out at. Kiss hates Kaleen, but she despises me in a condescending sort of way, always calls me Velveteen. Or Half-caste. She must have noticed I was feeling down and just before the bus came, she'd gone in for the kill. Her last statement still lingers in my mind, like a badly draining sewage pipe.

'Oh, here's poor little Velveteen…Rabbit,' Kiss had said, twisting her inwardly twirling mouth and barring my way with jutted arms.

Her friend, Cheryl, dug her in the ribs when she added 'rabbit'. Their laughter mingled, gurgling up their disdain.

'Poor Velveteen,' Kiss said again, 'Are we missing someone special? Your little Dutch boy, perhaps?' Then her aura merged to the dark hue of a stagnant swamp. 'Stupid slut,' she'd hissed. 'Don't you know long-distance relationships never work?'

They'd clutched each other then, her and Cheryl, stumbling in their shared mirth before getting onto the bus.

I never said a word or flicked an emotion – it doesn't do to let a Category Three know they've hurt you. It's what they strive for. But inside I was stomping her face into mud.

When I get to Kaleen's place, Mrs Pingelly answers the door and tells me Kaleen is at the dentist's and that Mr Pingelly will be bringing her home after work. She says I can still go for a ride if I want to. (She doesn't know Kaleen gave me Spirit, just the same way my parents don't know.) I thank her politely and go and catch him. Actually he trots up to me with 'expectancy of carrot' in the shine of his blue eyes. He's not disappointed and takes the treat after I've bridled him, finishing it in a couple of crunches. He has a bitless bridle too, like Zeus, so there's no steel bit to get in the way of eating.

I'm ready now. I don't want to waste any more time, so I don't bother with a saddle. I've learned to get aboard by grabbing a bit of mane near the withers and swinging on. I'm still clumsy at it, though. Spirit's not huge, only fifteen hands, but he's quite wide and I usually only manage to hook my foot over his rump and scramble on. I often check that no one's watching, but not today.

Watson, Kaleen's gelding, doesn't even stop grazing as we ride off. And he only neighs out once as we reach the outer gate. Spirit looks over his shoulder, but doesn't slow down. They're great paddock mates but once the bridle is on, Spirit is mine. I've ridden out lots of times on my own and Kaleen has done the same with Watson, so they're used to it. Two of the stock horses, Ganymede and Topper, always worked together and became quite dependent on each other's company, until Donovan, the head stockman, did a runner and left Ganymede here. (Now Ganny's in a paddock on his own.) Topper jumped out and followed us when we were on our Quest to Adelaide and, later, Ganymede, who was our packhorse, had to be left at Brandon Quinn's place with him.

Willem and Brandon are best friends. Like me and Kaleen.

OMG, I miss Willem so much. Why hasn't he called me? Three days. It's Been Three Days! It's never been this long before. We've been in contact every day, in some way, for the last six months.

I touch my beautiful golden necklace locket pendant. It's Steampunk, a handcrafted golden sun on a copper background, and it contains some of Spirit's mane, entwined in a silk blue ribbon the colour of Willem's eyes. Willem gave it to me just before he went back to Holland.

I catch back a sob, swallow hard, and push Spirit from a walk into a canter – no bouncy bits. The fast trot is the most difficult to sit when bareback. Kaleen tells me it's all about keeping the bottom of your spine in line with your horse's backbone. Trouble is it's hard to feel Spirit's. He's in such good condition.

Soon we're out in the forest, Spirit's ears are forward and I think he thinks we're heading to Old Ma Izzy's, but I don't want to go that far. Even though it's spring, and the days are longer, it'll be dark in a few hours.

I stop at the clearing where Jim's and Chocka's bodies were found. The police tape is gone and now, where the ground had been disturbed, there's a tangled carpet of weeds, covering the gravesite. I lean forward, taking some of the pressure off my bum. I welcome the pain, as the recirculation kicks in, hope it will keep my mind from thinking. But it doesn't.

What if Willem has found someone else? Plenty of 'ladies', as he calls them, in Holland. I know I'm not his first girlfriend. And I know Willem's not a virgin, although I still am. He was never pushy. But he did want me, if you know what I mean. Perhaps I should have been more insistent.

I think back to the night we spent in Adelaide, at the saleyards (in different tents of course). I wonder if Kaleen went all the way with Brandon? I never did ask her, and they were alone together half the night, keeping watch on the horses. She wasn't mad crazy in love the next day, like I was, though.

I look around, try and fill my thoughts with other things. Directly in front of me, at the other side of the clearing, a five-foot emu with two chicks knee-high to their father (all emu chicks are raised by their dad) are high-stepping into the sunlight. The father emu scratches up the brackish undergrowth with his thick, three-toed feet. Then he stands back. The chicks in their striped brown and cream feathered suits dive in and start pecking up the uncovered tidal wave of insects.

It hasn't helped, I'm still thinking of Willem. I turn Spirit away and we forge another path, one I haven't gone along before.

Love hurts. Actually it bloody sucks.

I don't think I can take any more of this separation. It's like I've become incomplete. The Skyping and texting held me together, but now I'm unravelling.

We canter on and on. I don't watch the track, but Spirit has lowered his head and is looking out for us, for the knotted tree roots that snake across the path, or the shallow pockets of sand which could give way beneath a hoof placed wrong. He's so sure-footed; I wish I could be as certain as he is.

It gets darker the further we travel. I glance at my watch. It's not late, not late enough for such gloominess. I take a deep breath and lean back. Spirit slows to a walk. I let him. I'm breaking the rule of the rider always asking, but I can't think beyond this haze of hurt. It's then I realise I'm lost. In so many ways. And the thing is I don't even care. Let me stay lost. I'm so sick of the Kisses and Cheryls, the bloody bullies of this world, who never worry what they say, what they do. How close they slipper-foot to the truth, my mind whispers.

I allow Spirit to get slower and slower until eventually he stops and shakes his mane, like a question. 'Where to now?' he seems to be asking. I feel a sudden urge to talk to someone, anyone, but I want answers too. And then, just as suddenly, I don't want to see anybody.

I slide off Spirit's back and let go of his reins. 'Off…you…go,' I say, soft slapping his rump. My throat seems to be closing off my words.

He goes a few steps and, dog-like, turns towards me and stops, head and neck on an angle. Then he looks up and his halt becomes a freeze. Someone is approaching.

A familiar voice rings out. 'Odin, where are you, lad? Time to be going home.'

Old Ma Izzy materialises from behind a lone pine tree and

then Odin springs up and rushes across the path towards her, with something in his mouth. It's a rabbit. Involuntarily I think of Kiss and what she'd called me that afternoon – 'Velveteen Rabbit', like the kid's storybook. I smile wryly. At least it's a top seller.

Old Ma Izzy doesn't seem surprised to see us, but she only addresses Spirit, laying her cool brown hand on his cream-white shoulder. 'Ah, now, my wondrous Spirit. Wandering free, then, like your name?'

I know she can see me; I'm only a few steps behind. But she walks off and Spirit and Odin follow her. I do too.

Soon she stops, sweeps a hand over a fallen log in a sit down gesture, and speaks. 'You are worrying then, Velvet. Come, sit here. Do you need to talk? Is it the Odyssey of Zeus that's giving you anguish?'

'Odyssey?' I croak, my voice rising.

Leaning forward on the log, Old Ma Izzy strokes Odin's large muzzle. My breath catches as he lets go of the rabbit, which then dashes off into the scrub. Apparently unhurt.

I stare at Odin who, I swear, seems to be grinning at me.

'Ah, Odin, my lad,' says Old Ma Izzy, 'what are they teaching these children now? Oh, but not the old ways…I suppose…' She pauses, looks at me.

I try and scrape some facts from the edges of my brain. Homer? Greek philosophy? The Odyssey of Zeus? Is that right? For a moment, my mind has cleared all thoughts of Willem. It feels like balm on a bruise. It's fleeting, though. I shake my head, pull myself to the present and with fingers which seem numb, take hold of Spirit's reins. What was I thinking? He would have headed home, but anything could have happened to him on the way there.

I sit down on the log next to Old Ma Izzy and sink my face into my hands. Through my rein-laced fingers I can smell the leather and then through that, the aroma of the forest floor, its perfume of pine needles and earthiness. Silence here is complete, the darkness less intense, the trees more sparse, their ragged thinning tops letting in the evening sky, still blue but scalloped with pink.

'Lightning strike, Velvet,' Old Ma Izzy says, indicating the damaged treetops with an upturned glance.

Once more, as I look up. I feel disconnected from the pain of missing Willem. This time the sensation lasts a few minutes longer.

'Velvet, this isn't about you riding Zeus for the first time, is it?' She doesn't wait for an answer, but continues. 'And he fast is approaching his time and yours. His accident a mere set-back. Only six months, 'tis nothing. And everything for his healing. Ah yes, he's almost ready. But you, Velvet.' Old Ma Izzy lifts my chin with a finger. 'Must be ready also. No doubts.'

She stops and I know, without asking, that she expects me to talk. I take a deep breath and, as I exhale, find my voice. I tell her about Willem, everything. What I feel for him, and how I've never felt like this before. I even tell of his aura with its rainbow myriad facets. I don't tell her about my monster-seeing ability. It doesn't count to the sum of Willem and me. I say how I haven't heard from him for days. That it's not like him. He's always kept in touch.

Old Ma Izzy listens and all around us seems to grow lighter with every sentence travelled, even though the day is older.

At last there's no more I can say. Old Ma Izzy gets up and we – Spirit, me, and Odin – follow her. When I come up alongside, she speaks, her voice quiet, straight and clear, and I know now what I have to do.

Spirit and I get back to Kaleen's in time to see Mum's old Holden pulling up into the driveway.

Kaleen comes out of the house and waves. 'I knew you were coming, Vel,' she says, pointing at Watson. 'Look at him. He's been like that for the last half hour.'

Watson's leaning over his stable railing, neck and head outstretched in our direction. He whickers out softly as we ride up.

Later, as Mum and I drive off, I call out to Kaleen through the car window. 'See you at Old Ma Izzy's tomorrow.'

She nods and waves again before disappearing back into her house.

Saturday 6 October

We seem to be plugged back into winter, the wind is screaming through the eaves like discordant panpipes and rain batters our tin roof like it's trying to get in.

The electricity keeps going off and coming back on, so Dad's turned off the main computer, in case we have a lightning strike. I think of the pine trees, their tops sheared off as if by a giant scythe, and Old Ma Izzy listening to me until all my words ran dry. Then I remember what she'd said. It was quite obvious, and I had thought of doing it before, myself, but I hadn't been sure how to go about it.

I had to ring Willem.

Of course I'd tried calling his mobile and ringing on Skype too, even though over the past six months he'd been the one to call me on there. Old Ma Izzy had said I should ring his landline, but I don't have that number. Yet.

Later in the day, when the storm has ridden over, probably looking for other parts of the country to trample, Dad puts the modem back on and I boot up my laptop. I search on Google, but either Willem's number is unlisted, or I'm not looking it up properly. It makes it bloody difficult that I can't read Dutch.

I log onto Facebook. Willem added me as a friend way back when we'd first met, but we haven't kept in touch on there. We much prefer to see and talk to each other on Skype.

I look up his page. There's been no activity for ages, except for a few posts to a pretty girl called Rita (he told me he had a sister called Rita) and some photos of her birthday party two weeks ago. He must have taken them. One pic stands out: Rita sitting at a table full of plates of snacks in varying heights of yumminess. Placed in front of her is a cake. A large fifteen in its centre, written in gold, contrasts with blue icing and a circle of orange candles. Rita's blonde, with oval features unlike Willem's.

For many moments I sit staring at her face, juxtaposing it with his. There doesn't seem to be a family resemblance, but she's hot, though, like him, and only a year younger.

I look through one of his photo-folders, entitled Boxing. The first pic is of Willem in the boxing ring, the referee holding up his arm in victory, Willem's face split in that sexy grin I remember so well.

I forward through dozens more photos. He hadn't told me how good he was. He'd said his boxing was just for fun, but going by these photos, along with the pic of his trophy cabinet, shining silver and gold like a king's treasure, it's way more than that.

I go back to Willem's home page and send him a message. I keep it short and try not to sound hyper, ask him to get back to me ASAP. Then I go to Rita's page and send her a friend invite. I also add a small note saying who I am.

I try Skype once more, hear the lonely echo-sounds of ringing at his end, but no one picks up. No image comes up on the screen, just his Skype name, Willdo4eva, and the little phone symbols. Then I send him a text message: where r u? It looks as pathetic as I feel.

Sunday 7 October

The storm's returned; must have enjoyed terrorising the trees. I wonder if there's anything left of those the lightning struck in the forest?

Kaleen rings me early and tells me about the call she's received from Old Ma Izzy – it's a repeat of yesterday's phone call. No riding today.

Even though I'm not sure if I was supposed to ride Zeus this weekend (if he was ready), I feel a curious mixture of relief and fear. I just want to get it over with. I realise this is not the mind-set Old Ma Izzy needs me to have. It's probably just as well that riding Zeus for the first time has been postponed.

Old Ma Izzy doesn't have an undercover riding arena like Kaleen has, or it might still have been on. She doesn't have a horse trailer either, and neither does Kaleen, so we couldn't float Zeus to Kaleen's place. Kaleen got rid of her trailer after her first horse, Holmes, or Holmesy, as she called him, was killed in a terrible accident on the way to a jumping event two years ago. Early this year, Old Ma Izzy helped Kaleen come to terms with his death. I don't think Kaleen will ever get over it completely, or do the show scene again. And the Pingellys will probably never get another horse trailer.

I open up my blind and scan our yard. The Mondo grass is regrowing and a faint grey X marks the spot where I dug up the time capsule. That hole and all the others I'd made trying to find it are now full of rain.

Sebby's peering out of his shelter, his furry upper lip curled in a little twist, his goatee beard dripping water to its point. He lets out a feed-me bleat.

When the heavy rains lighten to a shower, I don't my wet-weather clothes, slip into my rubber boots (after checking them for spiders) and head outside. After I feed Sebby his hay, I dig a trench away from his shed, to help drain the puddles. I bucket out water from the holes in the garden and start to fill them in. I wish it was as easy to fill in the holes in my life. Oh shit, I'm starting to think in metaphors, like Kaleen does.

The exercise lifts and warms me and by the time I've finished I'm smiling at the greyness of the day, at Sebby scoffing down his feed, and even at the birds feasting on the poor little drowned insects.

I breathe in the freshness of the air, wipe the sweat from my face and pat down the last of the holes with the back of my shovel. Willem will be on Skype tomorrow. I'm sure of it!

Monday 8 October

Willem was not on Skype this morning and Rita still hasn't joined me up as a friend on FB either.

The bus is ten minutes late, but it's not because of the bus clown, Spider Johnson, it's because we have a new driver and he's learning the route.

Our last bus driver, Mr Tangelo, has retired or something. I think it's more the something, but no one seems to know what that 'something' is. If he's gone nuts, it's more than understandable. Spider Johnson is just that bad. Spider's not on the bus this morning, though, thank goodness.

The new driver, who hasn't introduced himself, seems okay. He's mid-old, brown hair, nothing distinguishable. And no monster signs, no weird auras or jagged lines. Seated behind him, across two of the seats, are three kids I haven't seen before. His relatives? When I hear one of them call him Father, I realise I'm right.

From where I'm sitting, I try and guess their ages and genders. I didn't look at them when I was getting on the bus, and they all have short hair. I can't see if any are wearing school skirts or shorts or monster auras either.

Kaleen sees me staring. 'That's the family who's moved into the Thomsons's old place,' she whispers, hand around her mouth. 'The Moonstones. I think they're renting but, as Mother said, "with an option to buy".'

I see the tallest of the trio stiffen its shoulders and then glance around behind. It turns out to be a boy about Willem's age. Could he have heard Kaleen? I could barely hear her myself. There's something really odd about him. But not…monsterish. Although from this angle I can't really tell for sure.

We arrive at school and the Moonstone kids get off almost before the bus has screeched to its stop. When we go into class, one of them, a girl this time, is already seated at the back of the room. She's bending over, getting something out of her bag when I come in, so I can't see her face, only her hair, the same length and colour as her siblings'. When I sit down, she's still up to her elbows, scrabbling around in her bag. Looks like she hasn't been given a locker yet.

Kaleen is allotted to be her school buddy, take her around, orientate her to where everything is. Toilets and stuff.

I can't find Kaleen at recess, so I sit alone at our favourite spot under the cedar trees which surround the oval. I do catch a glimpse of her with the new girl, whose name is Celestial, crossing over to the Rec room. Their heads are bent together and Kaleen's swinging her hands like she does when she wants to emphasise a point. Even from this distance, I can see Kaleen's aura is glowing the soft yellow of happiness. I feel jealous…no, envious – better word, not such a strong feeling. I tell myself this is natural, I'm only human and Kaleen is my best friend. With this thought, I feel sort of okay. But then a twinge of abandonment tightens my throat – first Willem, now Kaleen. I try to shake away the thought as I bite into my apple. Next minute I'm choking and spitting. The apple has codling moth and, like that old joke, I can only see half the worm. Gross!

I turn around. Kaleen and Celestial are coming over. I wipe the back of my hand across my mouth and kick what's left of the apple behind the bench.

Celestial narrows her eyes. 'One should not litter, er…Velvet Brown, isn't it?' she says, drawing out the 'Brown'.

OMG, she sounds more posh than Kaleen's mother. For a second I'm choking again, but this time on words. I clear my throat. 'It's orgasmic,' I splutter. Shit, I meant organic. I'm hoping she won't notice. But the look on her face says she has.

Kaleen is staring at me too, eyebrows set at quizzical. Not judgemental exactly but I see a glint of something there.

We go back into class. English Lit is up next, and Kaleen moves her desk over to Celestial's. The lesson we've been set is a pair-up project thing. I was going to ask Kaleen, but she's already asked Celestial, by the look of it.

Rosemary Pooter, the most unpopular girl, and I end up being the last two without partners, so fate's decided for us. She's nice enough, but a bit of a nerd and very quiet.

Now I'm definitely jealous of Kaleen and Celestial buddying up. Nothing good about this feeling, and there's no way I can sugar-coat it, or downgrade it to envy. To make it worse, Kaleen and Celestial seem to be getting on like a bushfire on speed. Even though they're at the back of the room, I can hear Kaleen laughing and whispering. It's almost like she's on a drug. She seems a bit manic, actually, even for her. I can't hear Celestial, but I can see her. She's waving her arms exactly like Kaleen does, which is sort of odd, and her mouth is moving, so she is talking.

We have to do research on nineteenth-century poets. I choose Emily Dickinson, and Rosemary Pooter chooses Byron. Funny how I thought she would. We have to Wiki them and compare the differences in their work.

Byron is a romantic and his poems are flowery and full of love and beautiful women. Emily is dark and deep. Her poetry asks questions you'd never think of asking, and sets the answers spinning in your mind.

I'm interested in it all, but my eyes keep wandering over to Kaleen and Celestial. They've stopped talking and are busy on their laptops. I wonder who their poets are? I know Kaleen adores Noel Coward, but I don't think he's nineteenth century.

The next lesson is PE, if you can call physical education a lesson. Our PE teacher, Mr Hanker, AKA Hanker Wanker, is a Category One, Up Your Own Arse Monster. That category is how it sounds, with the added danger of no compassion thrown in, making it the most dangerous of monster types. Evil sometimes lurks where empathy doesn't.

Hanker Wanker is always preening himself (some say he even wears make-up) and combing his hair, or flexing his muscles, especially in front of the female student teachers. There's one of them with him today; she reminds me a lot of Willem's sister, Rita. Similar colour hair and features. Gorgeous.

Rosemary Pooter ends up with me again, playing volleyball. She peers at me over her glasses, her eyes half-mast. It's a look she often gives, adding a closed-eye interval like a long blink, especially if she's telling you some fact she's just learned.

'It's your serve, Vel,' she says quietly, but sounding all chummy.

I close my lips tightly. Only Kaleen calls me Vel.

Our game is a disaster. I keep hitting the net. I'm not usually this bad. When I glance over, I see Celestial staring at me. No blinking there. It's almost preternatural.

After the game, I try and get near her again. I'd been so distracted the first time she'd come up with Kaleen, with my 'it's orgasmic' speech malfunction, I hadn't really got a good look at her. I smile despite myself. Speech malfunction. I'll have to tell Kaleen that one. If I ever get to talk to her again, that is.

Celestial keeps moving away as I get closer. I'm behind her, but it's as if she can sense me following. Finally she spins around and glares at me. She doesn't say anything. And then I gasp. Her aura's mirror-like, but all glass without reflection. Her eyes are small, the irises black, depthless, and faceted like flies' – a honeycomb of shapes like those I'd seen under the microscope in our science lab.

Celestial smiles as if she sees my confusion, but says nothing.

Is she a weird type of monster? One I haven't seen before? I take a step back and she takes a step forward into my personal space. I counteract and take a step forward too, so now we're face to face. So close we can feel each other's breath. After what seems like ages, instead of backing up, she turns round and walks over to Kaleen, who's tossing the ball in the air, catching it and trying to balance it on her little finger.

I'm trembling, quivering. There is definitely something odd with Celestial Moonstone. A not-quite-rightness. But I have no definition, no category. She certainly doesn't fit any of my four monster types.

The student teacher is flicking her hair and laughing. Hanker Wanker has the serious look he has when he's trying to convince someone that he cares about them. It doesn't fool me. Category Ones only care about themselves. But even though they're the worst one of my monster categories, at this moment I'm way more frightened of Celestial. And I'm scared for Kaleen too.

Inwardly I grimace. At least fear's cured me of my jealousy.

Friday 12 October

For the past week, Kaleen and I have hardly talked to each other at all. She only caught the bus into school on Wednesday, and then she was already sitting with Celestial when I got on. Their stop's before mine.

I still haven't heard from Willem, or his sister, Rita. Now I'm wondering all sorts of things. And to add to the chafing of my soul (sorry, it's all this poetry we've been doing), Kiss has been in my face almost daily. Keeps asking about Willem and stretching my self-control to breaking when she goes on about Kaleen and Celestial getting on so well. 'Oh, how sad,' she keeps saying, her voice sneering through her teeth, 'poor Little Velveteen Rabbit has lost her bestie as well.'

God, I could kill her. If only she knew how she looks through my monster lens, it would probably do her head in. Well, I hope it would. Maybe make an improvement. I smile; it's the only way I can stay sane, making these inner jibes. Outwardly I'm as cool as clouds. As I said before, Category Threes, like Kiss, are looking for reaction.

I've been told by my brother, Danny, that Kiss is seriously hot. But through my monster sight, Kiss is anything but. Her aura is the colour of ditchwater and her features so swirled and fractured she looks like an extremely bad Impressionist painting. She doesn't have a mouth, which makes her nickname to me such irony. Sorry, couldn't help rhyming those few last words.

I absolutely love Emily Dickinson. I'm not as rapt in Byron, but he has his moments of brilliance too. The poetry is helping to soothe me a bit, even though Emily Dickinson can get morbid sometimes. Guess I like the mirroring of our moods.

Mirror makes me think of Celestial. I keep trying to bump into her to get another look, but she's expert at avoidance. It was so weird, her looking-glass facade. And I'm no stranger to weird. With one out of every forty people superimposing a monster to me, my weirdo-benchmark is really high.

As far as school work goes, though, I have to hand it to Celestial Moonstone: she's incredible with computers, and not nerdy with it, like Rosemary Pooter. She also has an amazing general knowledge and is tops at maths. Strangely enough, Kaleen is doing well in maths too now; got an A on our test yesterday. She's never got one of those before, mostly she scrapes through with Cs. I know she's not cheating; Kaleen would never cheat. It's not in her character, just like she doesn't swear, unless it's a totally extreme situation. She did swear when we were being chased by a four-wheel drive vehicle on our riding quest to Adelaide. But that was only the second time in the ten years I've known her.

Our last lesson for the day is science. One of my favourite subjects. It's all about ants. How they're like humans in the way they behave, and in the way they structure their society, having slaves and even keeping other insects, like we do our cattle. There are these aphids they actually milk. Ants also go to war on their enemies.

The lesson is going so quickly that when I look at my watch I see it's almost time to catch the bus home. And I realise with a sigh that for nearly an hour I haven't thought of Willem.

Right at the end, the teacher, Mr Renshaw, asks if anyone knows any other facts about ants. I glance sideways at Rosemary Pooter. She's doing the slow blink she does when she has something to say, her hand is fluttering, but not raised high enough for anyone else, except me, to see.

Celestial is sitting in an imperial sort of way, hand held up, and waving like the queen. No one else is offering anything. Most of the kids just want to go home. They're shuffling in their seats and there's a low murmur coming from most of the room.

But when Celestial mentions zombie ants, everyone stops moving and the silence is the same as when you mute a noisy commercial. Made all the more quiet for the contrast.

'There's this fungus,' she says, 'that uses the ant as part of its life cycle.' She scans the room and smiles, a twist of her lips, quick and decisive as a knife slash. 'It drops from a tree above the ants' nest and penetrates the brain of any ant inane enough to walk beneath, or get close to it, at the time of its fall.' She pauses again, surveys the room and looks at the teacher.

Mr Renshaw nods and she continues.

'Then, when the fungus has obtained full control of the ant's brain, it makes the ant climb up the tree above the nest, and causes the ant's mandibles to clamp onto a twig or leaf.' Celestial gives a light chuckle, but suppresses it. 'Next, the fungus consumes the ant from inside and bursts out to drop on, or pair up with once again, any other ant stupid enough to come within its reach.'

I'm wondering if it's all really true. I'm going to Google it when I get home. Looking at Celestial, who's now gazing with that fixed stare she does at Kaleen, I think it is. I make a note to do some other research when I get home as well.

The school bus is late picking us up again. Kaleen and Celestial are talking, huddled together in the way of shared secrets. Kiss is there too, but Cheryl, her best friend, must have got a lift home from school.

Maybe I should have walked over to the hospital, come home with Mum, but she's working shift tonight and I'm too exhausted to stay up late. I actually wish Rosemary Pooter was with me, but she lives here in town and doesn't have to catch the bus.

I close my eyes, stand back and lean against the fence. I hope Kiss won't notice me, or won't bother with me if she does. But, in the way of my lousy week, my hope goes unanswered.

Kiss sidles over, bag slung across one shoulder, mouth in the gyrations of chewing gum. Kaleen, Celestial and a few of the other kids look up and watch. Kaleen's eyes, when they meet mine, are glazed as if she doesn't even know me. Celestial's are intense and as sharp as the smile she gave when she was telling the class about the ant zombies.

'And here we have poor little Velveteen Rabbit,' Kiss says, sweeping her hand in front of me like I'm some sort of exhibit at the zoo.

Celestial takes a step forward and stares even more intently. But now it seems to be in Kiss's direction. A sort of questioning look, an eyebrow half raised and lips set, almost as if she's noticing Kiss for the first time. And liking what she sees.

'Velveteen looks so sad. Doesn't she, everybody?' Kiss says. 'Missing her little Dutch boy, Willem. He's gone back to his windmills and his clogs and another Fraulein.'

I want to yell they don't call them Frauleins in Holland, but I hold my tongue.

'Look at her. She's so way lame. Who would want to be with her?' Kiss glances over at Kaleen, who hasn't moved. She flicks her hand in Kaleen's direction. 'Even Kaleen's sick of her.'

Kaleen shifts from one foot to the other and her eyes clear a little. Her mouth opens like she's about to speak, but then she snaps it shut.

Celestial moves closer. She reminds me of a predator on the scent of its prey.

When I give no reaction, Kiss shoves me and swipes at my face. As I lift my arm to push her hand away, her fingers catch in my hair. My swearing is lost in the squeal of brakes as the bus pulls up at the school gates.

Kaleen moves towards us. Her mouth's making shapes, but nothing's coming out. Then her eyes clear completely and she begins to speak. At first her words are slow, but soon they're gathering momentum like the weekend's storm. Then her voice comes out as a shout. 'Blurry-well leave her alone, Kiss. You're nothing but a moron, no more brains than that stupid fungus.' Kaleen looks at me. Her lips whisper sorry, and she shrugs away from Celestial, who has come up behind her.

Kaleen leads me to the bus. Celestial doesn't seem to mind. When I look back, she's whispering to Kiss and Kiss is smiling and giggling and touching Celestial's arm. Celestial darts a sly glance in our direction, says something and their giggling becomes conjoined laughter. Oh shit, I think.

Kaleen sits with me on the bus in our usual place, about halfway down. She grabs my hand and I'm so relieved I don't even feel embarrassed. She keeps saying she's sorry over and over, and I keep saying she doesn't need to. It's okay.

As Celestial passes us, with Kiss following like a disciple, she's held up by a kid who has stopped in front of her to pick up a dropped bag.

I see something in the white of Celestial's eye. A tiny bloodshot crack in her mirror image. Fractured as a snake's tongue. Then a thin red line pulses beneath it like a laser and quickly the crack merges and fuses. I blink twice, it's gone, and I wonder if I've seen anything at all.

Friday 12 October – evening

I've copied some more notes from my time capsule's Journal, about the category monster types. The Journal's getting mouldy, with the warmth of spring weather, and if I don't put them in this diary now, they'll be lost forever. Of course I'd still hold them in my mind, but Kaleen says that once you've written something down and then lost it, it's very hard to remember and write it exactly the same way again, so I thought I'd better do it now.

Category Four – AKA Head in the Sand Monster. Hates conflict. Changes sides for its own benefit. But if you have to meet a monster, one of the best, relatively speaking. Often they are actual relatives, as in Dad and my brother, Danny, although they're modified versions.

Category Three – AKA Away in the Clouds Monster. Severe daydreamer, handles problems by denying them. Can say nasty things – has a knack of knowing what nasty things to say about the person that will hurt them the most. Kaleen's sister, Coral Lee, is an almost category three since she's been in love with her boyfriend, Dwayne.

Category Two – AKA Angry at the Drop of a Rat Monster. Pretty self-explanatory. Handles everything with extreme anger at the slightest provocation. Often red in the face, or has a fire-red aura.

Category One – AKA Up Your Own Arse Monster. Like our PE teacher, Hanker Wanker. Has a purple aura in jagged lines. Extremely vain. Loves itself exclusively. Lacks empathy. Enjoys hurting other people and/or animals.

NB: I've read that autism sufferers may lack empathy, but it's their sensory overload and social anxiety which make it hard for them to understand what others are feeling, not that they don't care. A Category One doesn't care at all. It knows what people are thinking/feeling and uses this to manipulate them to their own advantage.

Saturday 13 October

I haven't slept, because Kaleen and I have been talking all night. She rang me at nine. She has this phone-plan where all her calls are free after seven p.m. I can only afford recharge.

We talked about Celestial Moonstone. I told Kaleen how crazy weird Celestial looked to me, an unreflective mirror, no edges or a familiar aura. Kaleen told me what the last week had been like as Celestial's exclusive friend. Surreal was one of the words she used. It all reminded me of the zombie ants, with Celestial being the fungus and poor Kaleen the unwitting ant who'd come into its territory.

It's morning now and Kaleen has rung off to get some sleep. I still can't. Now that our friendship is okay again, my focus on Willem has redoubled my growing doubt. Why hasn't he contacted me? I'm lying here, staring at the ceiling, trying to get my mind on my day ahead (all my Saturday chores) when my iPhone buzzes a text. It's Kaleen wanting to ring again, asking if I was asleep. Before I can text back that I'm awake, my phone starts to ring. It's Kaleen of course and I answer quickly. It's only 6 a.m. and Dad and Mum and Danny are still asleep. I don't want to wake them.

Sebby gives a faint bleat from his yard, so he's heard the phone. Sebby has super hearing just like Celestial Moonstone's brother seems to have, and Celestial herself, for all I know.

'Hey, Vel, are you awake? Silly question, sorry. Listen, I was thinking about Willem.'

Me too, I think, but I let her continue, press the phone to my ear so no noise escapes except my sigh.

'You know, Rita may not be his sister,' she says quietly.

I take the phone away and hold it face down on the bed, wanting to smother her words. Then I pick it up and hiss, while trying to keep the sting of hurt from my voice. 'Shit, Kaleen, do you think I haven't already thought of that? But she's got his last name. Van Den Hoven. They have to be related.'

For a few seconds there's silence like a void, from Kaleen's side. 'People write anything on Facebook, Vel,' she says.

Later I'm cleaning my room: washing sheets, the first of my chores. I've already fed Sebby and put him out on his tether to pick at the spring grass. He's not classified as a chore, more of a pet responsibility.

I try to concentrate on what I'm doing. Try and live in the mindless moment. I mean, stripping the bed and washing sheets, how much can you find in that? But it's surprising what I do see. The warp and weft of the cotton. The way the eucalyptus 'organic' liquid washing detergent smells, sort of fresh, but with an underlying tone of something indiscernible, and the whirlpool action of the machine living up to its name. Eddying like my thoughts.

I drag out the vacuum – damn it, another innuendo. I leave it, and the cleaner, in the middle of my room, boot up my laptop and click onto Facebook.

Rita must be a Van Den Hoven. Well, she says she is on her FB page. But then, like Kaleen said…

I notice there's been no more activity from Rita or Willem since I last looked, exactly a week ago.

Like some sort of masochist, I open Willem's pic folder again and stare at the photo of his boxing trophy cabinet. Slowly, it becomes all blurry. I wipe tears from my eyes and it clears, gold and shining, overflowing with his conquests.

Sunday 14 October

Willem and I are finished. He hasn't answered any of my text messages, doesn't answer his iPhone or Skype. Hasn't emailed me.

I'm still wearing the pendant necklace, not because he gave it to me but because I really like the look of it. And it contains a bit of Spirit's mane. I'm not thinking about the blue ribbon entwined with it, the colour of Willem's eyes.

I have more to think about now. Old Ma Izzy rang me early this morning. She believes Zeus's 'time' has come. Her word. Then she asked to talk to Mum. Luckily I've already told Mum what I'll be doing, but I minimised any danger I might be facing. Mum knows little than less about horses, thinks they're big soft puppy dogs and not dangerous at all, so I'm not surprised when Mum says it's okay for me to go.

It's one of those lovely blue and white days, full of breeze and sweet scents of honeysuckle. Okay, I'm exaggerating (and going poetic again) but the weather is certainly better than it's been. I feel curiously light, sort of hollow. Almost like I'm another person. Disassociated. I hope it doesn't affect my riding. No, I won't let it.

Kaleen's coming to Old Ma Izzy's after lunch. She told me she's working on an important part of her second book, as yet unnamed. I'm betting it has something to do with zombies. She hasn't said much about it, except it's not crime fiction, like her first book *Death Does Not Innocence Make*.

Before I head off to Old Ma Izzy's, I write an email to Tarrant Moselle, Kaleen's publisher from Wanda-Willow Press: Do you have any idea when the book will go to print? And what are you intending to do about marketing?

Straight to the point. I'm sick of being civil. I'm not expecting an answer any time soon, I have a feeling Tarrant likes his weekends. He's on Facebook too, and his interests include socialising, wine-tasting, parachuting and skiing. His partner (listed as 'In a long-term relationship') Hedrick Andrew Anderson, likes much the same things and there are lots of face-to-cheek photos of their holidays together, many abounding with snow and sky and falling from great heights harnessed in tandem bliss. The pics are so professional I'm sure they have their own private photographer. Tarrant's certainly not short in the cash department, so there can't be a financial reason why he hasn't yet published Kaleen's book.

I check for spelling errors, read the email aloud and then, with fingers crossed for an answer in at least the next few weeks, press Send.

Mum's tooting me from the driveway. I rush out, hold up my hand for her to wait and move Sebby to a new patch of grass. I place his water bucket just within his reach, although whatever I do he always seems to manage to knock it over.

I slide into the passenger seat and then realise I don't have my riding boots on. Mum sighs and turns back the key. The Holden's engine shudders to a relieved silence. God, I hope it'll start again. Why couldn't Dad be interested in cars instead of sheep? He's bundled some of them off for shearing today. He has this old trailer which can only take three at a time and the leftover sheep are doing a great impression of Little Bo Peep, staring forlornly towards the road to where their 'lost' sisters have departed. They'll be extra strange when the others get back all shaved and shorn. But not for long – then it's their turn. The trailer's pulled by Dad's old Ford, circa 1970, with the same reliability as Mum's Holden.

Finally I get to Old Ma Izzy's. I pat the Holden's side as Mum waves me goodbye with a flourish, saying she'll pick me up after her shift, so she could be a little late, but before dark.

Odin comes out from behind the house to greet me, all grinning jaws and wagging tail. Several of the stabled horses neigh loudly in welcome, and some of the paddock ones gallop up to the nearest fence, snorting and stomping. It's almost like they know something important is going to happen. I take a long breath and look over at the riding yard with its six-foot wooden fences.

Zeus, tail held like a plume, is its only occupant. With sweat gleaming silver on his grey shoulders, he's doing laps, cutting corners. Suddenly he stops. Facing me like a challenge, he spins on his heels and bucks so high I close my eyes. Oh my God, can I really do this?

I feel Old Ma Izzy's hand on my shoulder. 'Take no notice of him Velvet,' she says in her quiet lilt. So soothing her voice. ''Tis his coltish ways. I had the saddle on him earlier and he was a lamb, lipping my hands for the treats. 'Tis the way of Entires.'

I know she's referring to the fact that Zeus isn't gelded. I suppose he's bound to be skittish and full of himself. All that testosterone. Like Willem. Oh God, why hadn't I let him go to bed with me? I shake my head and I can feel Old Ma Izzy looking at me.

She touches my arm and leads me over to where Zeus's gear is hanging over the fence. I've done this dozens of times before, saddled and bridled him. But today it will be different. I'll be riding him for the very first time. Anything could happen.

I need to calm myself. I breathe in deeply and look at the ground, then I follow the hoof prints to where Zeus is standing. I bridle him, talk quietly and scratch his neck. I feel his skin loosen, his head comes down to my lowered hand and his breath is warm, short puffs on my wrist. I lead him over to his saddle. Soon he's ready.

I've been sliding my weight onto his back, lying flat over the saddle, every time I've worked with him, so he hardly moves when I do it today.

Old Ma Izzy is standing on the other side of the fence. I slide off the saddle and she hands me a carrot. Zeus takes it from my fingers; his lips mouth me in that coltish fashion even after the carrot has disappeared. I rub his sweet spot over the withers, where horses soft-bite each other in mutual grooming.

But then when I pick up the reins to mount, Zeus stiffens on his forelegs, stretches away and snorts down his nose. He takes a step back and snorts again.

'Come away with you now, Velvet.' Old Ma Izzy enters the riding yard and takes the reins. She dismisses me with a half-raised hand. 'You're not ready. Not today.'

After Old Ma Izzy has unsaddled Zeus, she heads back into the house. Even Odin avoids looking at me. For many minutes I can't move. I lean on the rails, stare at my boots. See the dust forming over them like a glaze. I look over and watch as Zeus gallops out of the open gates of the riding yard to join up with his paddock mate, Mercury. They fly across the field in a blur of bay and grey until I can no longer see them through my tears. I bring my hand across my eyes and try and stem the flow. What have I done wrong, anyway?

My phone rings. I retrieve it from my backpack, see it's Kaleen. Maybe she's coming early. God, I hope not. How can I explain what's happened or, more correctly, what's not happened?

I let it ring several times before answering, then I speak before she can say a word. 'Hi, Kaleen. How's it going?' My voice sounds normal. Maybe I should try out for the school play.

'Hey, Vel, guess what? Mother and Father have decided to go on holidays early. We're flying out to Canada tonight and then going on a cruise ship. Should be awesome. How's Zeus? Have you got on him yet?'

I set my actor tone to disappointed. 'Does this mean you won't be coming to watch?'

'Yeah, sorry, Vel. I'll be away from school all next week as well. Hey, send me some pics. That's if that old phone of yours can still take them.'

I know Kaleen doesn't mean to do it, but sometimes she throws her wealth in my face. Or more accurately she rubs my nose in my poverty. Like the disparaging comment she once made about my cheap jeans. Hell, I wish Dad would get some work soon. I suppose the wool cheque will come in handy, but I bet it's already earmarked for bills. No holidays for us. Not that I could care less about that at the moment.

Two years back, just before Dad lost his job, there had been plans for a trip to England. Even got our passports. Seems so long ago now.

Kaleen doesn't appear to notice that I haven't answered. 'I gotta go, Vel,' she says, sounding breathless. 'I have to see what to pack, and Mother's taking me shopping for some more cold weather clothes. It's not spring over in Canada.'

When she hangs up, I hear Old Ma Izzy. 'Velvet,' she calls, her voice at a distance, 'the kettle has boiled and I have some of your favourite cake. Come in now.'

I take slow steps to the back door. I actually count them. Sixty-five in total.

The door opens noiselessly, but Old Ma Izzy calls out from deep inside the house. 'We're up here in the dining room today, Velvet.'

I follow the hallway to the end, come into a room, high-ceilinged with burgundy drapes to the floor and candelabra with actual candles, swinging softly in the draught from my entrance. The candle flames flicker but spring upright to life as the sway ceases. On the table, a strawberry cake with real cream (I know this from experience) sits on a silver salver, a large knife ready at its side. There are also plates of cupcakes, sausage rolls and tiny pies, all hand- and home-made. She must have been cooking all morning.

A celebration, now a commiseration. I hiccup a sob, but when I look up from the table I see Old Ma Izzy smiling kindly.

She pulls out a chair for me, facing hers. 'Sit,' she says and I do so.

I'm trying to keep the tears behind my eyes, stop them from spilling out. But soon I'm sobbing into one of the white linen napkins. It seems all I do lately is cry.

After I stop, she cuts me a huge piece of cake. 'Eat,' she says, sliding the plate in front of me.

I take a small bite but it won't go down. My throat has closed off and I feel like I'm going to choke. I take a sip of water and gasp. This is wine! I stare open-mouthed at Old Ma Izzy.

She waves her hand in dismissal. 'Ah, 'tis only just begun. New vintage. Drink.'

Sit, eat, drink. Sounds like that movie. The warmth from my stomach soothes my mind and my voice comes out clear.

'Why?' The word sits in the air between us and the wine and the cake and the goodies.

I find my hand hovering over a pie. Now, surprisingly, I feel ravenous.

Old Ma Izzy lets me finish the pastry. 'You're not yet ready. I thought you were. But you are not,' she says, her tone firm.

I wipe my fingers. 'But how do you know?'

'I don't, Velvet. But Zeus does.'

Then I remember his reaction when I picked up the reins. 'Yes,' I say, just one word again.

Old Ma Izzy nods. 'Horses tune into vibrations, Velvet. It would have been remiss of me to let you continue. I promised your mother you would come to no harm.'

Sunday 14 October – evening

I'm home, lying on my bed, staring at the ceiling again. There's this strange crack, reminds me a bit of Celestial Moonstone's eyeball one, except this is grey and much longer. I think the plaster may be coming loose. I can't stand the idea of it falling on me so I get up and move my bed across to the other side of the room. Everything looks different from here. Another perspective, our English teacher would say.

I rub my face, put my hands behind my head. Why am I not ready to ride Zeus yet? What's stopping me? The answer comes: fear of the unknown. Instantly I pin this to my feelings about Willem. The fear of the unknown.

Imaginings of him with another girl grip my mind in all their graphic techno-porn detail. Then running images of what could happen when I ride Zeus for the very first time speed up my thoughts. He could bolt, buck or even crash though a fence with me. I clench my eyelids shut. Feel my heart rate jumping like a roo.

I need to calm myself. I try a relaxation technique I read in one of Mum's self-help books. Breathe in for ten seconds, hold for ten, let out for ten. My pounding chest slows to palpitations.

I tell myself, Look at the facts.

1. Old Ma Izzy knows her stuff.

2. She believes in me.

3. Zeus, even though he is a working-stallion in waiting, has never lifted a hoof against me, or bitten me.

4. Mostly, except for this morning, he's been quiet with everything I've done to him. The leading and tying up. The mouthing. The long-rein driving. The girthing. Those many months of education mean he's more than ready for backing.

Will I stay on?

Facts again.

1. My riding's improved out of space since I've had Spirit. He's been the best schoolmaster and he's taught me so much.

2. Lots of bareback riding has given me a very 'independent seat', as Kaleen calls it.

3. One of the stock horses bucked with me last week and I barely lifted out of the saddle. Kaleen said she wished she'd been quick enough to take a pic. 'That would show Kiss and co. that you can ride.' Her exact words. So Kaleen believes in me too. And she's been riding since she was four, so she'd know.

I feel my fear draining away like a river to the sea. It's replaced with certainty. I am ready. I know I am. This is what I needed. To know myself. To believe in myself. I will do it. Sooner will be best. Tonight. Now! I am ready.

Sunday 14 October – just before midnight

Thank God the parents have finally gone to bed. Danny took a little longer, but I heard his electric toothbrush buzzing ten minutes ago so I know he's gone off too.

I'm going to drive Dad's Ford to Old Ma Izzy's. Then I'm going to ride Zeus. I've never felt so sure about anything before in my life. It's a feeling like steel, like something unbreakable inside my guts. Teenage invincibility is what our school psychologist would call it. But I know it's not that.

I creep down the hallway, hear Dad's snoring and Mum's heavy breathing. I'm not worried about Danny; he sleeps with his TV on and his door shut. For some reason I think of Hanker Wanker and almost laugh.

I scrabble around in the bowl we keep by the front door for the keys. Dad's keys have a cat's bell on the key ring, for when Dad was working, doing afternoon shift and didn't want to put on the hallway light to find them. I'm extra careful and find them easily. I'm also careful when opening the front door, it needs to be realigned, something to do with expansion. But it still makes a scraping noise.

The Ford is parked out in the paddock with the trailer attached. I've driven it before, around the paddocks, helping Dad pick up firewood. I wind down the jockey wheel, lift the coupling off the tow bar and roll the trailer back. Two of the sheep come over to investigate, followed quickly by the other four. After their ordeal today, they're keeping close together. I almost giggle at their strange appearance. Then I grimace at all the purple antiseptic spray. Dad's mate does the shearing but he's not much good at it. Poor sheep. Lots of nicks and scrapes. Still, they'll survive. They're pretty lucky really, destined to die of old age, not the knife.

I get into the driver's side, put the key into the ignition and turn it. The engine roars into life and the car lurches forward. I brake with my other foot and it seems to do a rolling shuffle dance on the spot, neither going forwards nor backwards. Shit! It's in first gear. I should have put it in neutral to start. The engine sounds even worse than it did this morning. After a splutter or two, it stops making any noise at all. Stalled. I try the key again. More nothing, except for a thin whine like a tomcat's mating call. I flick it off. Look over my shoulder at the house. A light's come on and Sebby's bleating, damn him. I slink down behind the seat.

The front door of the house screeches open. A battery-drained torch scans the car and flashes the dashboard. I scrunch further down, close my eyes. If I can't see them, maybe they won't see me. I count a hundred shallow breaths, then open my eyes wide to the darkness like I'm blind. Finally I hear the front door close in a sharp crack and Sebby shuts up at last.

I do the breathing stuff and stretch to upright in the seat. So much for driving Dad's car to Old Ma Izzy's. What now? Hysterically I feel 'The Facts' coming on again.

1. Old Ma Izzy's place is twenty ks away.

2. Oh, bugger 2. There has to be some way to get there.

Then I almost smack my head in stupidity. I have a fully functional bike and a wonderfully quiet horse waiting at Kaleen's within bike-riding range.

I sneak back inside, grab some carrots and bread from the cupboard and slink out again. Before I can give Sebby the bread, he bleats loudly and I freeze on the spot.

The window opens. Mum sticks her head out. With the light behind her, I can see her eyes squinting. She shades them with her hand, like she's looking at the sun.

'Shut up, Sebby. Some of us have to go to work tomorrow,' she yells.

The window slams shut.

Shit, I haven't even left home yet and I've nearly had two heart attacks already. I run to the shed, get on my bike and, without looking back, pedal up our driveway. My little lamp casts ghost-shadows, an owl hoots in derision, and the crickets with their incessant whine sound like Hanker Wanker's wheedling voice.

I pedal faster.

It's so strange riding at night; every movement in the bushes screams 'predator' to my brain, the part which kept humans safe, I guess, when humans were not at the top of the food chain. I shiver despite it being a warm night. I've ridden the route so often I swear my bike knows the way there without my direction.

Twenty minutes later, I'm at Kaleen's farm gates. They're locked but I know where the keys are and her tack shed ones.

The working dogs are going off their brains, sounding like demented werewolves, but the Pingellys are on their Canadian holiday, so no one's in the house to hear them. I also know that the head stockman, the one who took over from Donovan O'Reilly after he did a runner earlier this year (long story), doesn't stay in the stockman's quarters. And Kaleen's mother's new gardener, who lives in the gardener's cottage, although being gifted in the green thumb business, is profoundly deaf. That's understandable. He must be at least forty.

Kaleen's put Spirit in the stable next to Watson for company. Watson's being locked up at night and only allowed out in the 'Jenny Craig Paddock' (as sparse of feed as it sounds) for a few hours a day. It's to stop him from developing laminitis, which he's prone to in spring. Luckily I don't have that problem with Spirit.

Spirit sticks his head over the half door and takes the carrot almost as his due. He doesn't bat a forelock hair when I bridle him, lead him out and swing on board. I don't want to bother with a saddle. I need to get to Old Ma Izzy's as fast as I can.

I have my iPod. I'm listening to Lady Gaga's Bad Romance. I love her songs. I can sing along with the lyrics. I don't have to be quiet here.

I've put Spirit into what I call his cruise control mode, an easy sit canter which burns up the kilometres. I'm riding on the buckle, as they say, touching the reins, my hands as light as gossamer thread. Old Ma Izzy has taught me this. 'Good hands' are one of her musts.

Spirit stays at the one pace without falter, or adjustment on my part. We're bypassing all the jumps Kaleen and I have set up along the way. I want to get to Old Ma Izzy's place quickly and, anyway, it's far too dangerous to jump them with only the moon for light. I shiver again when I see it's full; it's been behind clouds and I hadn't noticed it before. Strange it is too, huge and blood-red and set in a shimmery golden halo.

I'm relaxed and singing, not thinking about anything except the chorus of 'Bad Romance' when, without any warning, Spirit skids to a halt. I scan the road ahead. Is there a snake crossing it? I know they hunt at night. But Spirit isn't looking at the path; his head is turned to the side. Then I see through the trees and scrub another light, flickering crazily. A lantern? Torch? Motorbike headlight?

Before I can stop him, Spirit has gone off the track into the forest and he's trotting faster and faster towards the light, like an insect to a candle flame. I shorten my reins, but he lengthens his stride until we're galloping. I have to lean across his neck to stop from being swiped off by overhanging branches. He's never done this before. My heart is going at the same rate as his hoof beats, timing out in the sand, but all I can think of is that at least we're still heading in the direction of Old Ma Izzy's.

Spirit's head is low, his neck outstretched, and the wind we're creating is taking my breath. He's not running away, it's more like he's being drawn towards something. The weird thing is the light isn't getting any closer and he seems to have forgotten I'm here. My reins are useless and I can't use my seat or my weight to slow him down, as I can't sit up. I talk softly, as I would to a baby, although I can feel through his skin that he's perfectly calm; it's me who's not. Perhaps that's the problem. Like Old Ma Izzy said, 'They know.'

Again without warning, Spirit slows and then stops. His breathing is fine. Mine is ragged and coming in gasps. I take a breath and hold it. This is not where I rode last time. I've never seen this part of the forest before.

The light has disappeared, but through the trees I see a small campfire. There's a ring of stones around it, and it's burning in sinuously red and golden flames. They almost match the moon.

I slip from Spirit's back, try to lead him, but he refuses to move. His feet are planted and his eyes, statue-like, are fixed ahead.

Near the fire are three people. Two guys and a girl. Side on, I can see her breasts thinly covered in a crossover white robe which brushes the ground. She's silently struggling with one of the guys. I'm as mesmerised as Spirit. Then my breath escapes in a rush before I can stop it. The one holding her snaps a look to where I am standing. He points. The girl sees me too. And now I see their faces. It's Celestial Moonstone and her brother, Alan. The other guy comes towards me. I recognise him as well. It's Celestial's older brother. I don't know his name, he doesn't go to our school, but I've seen him on the bus. Celestial breaks free and dashes off. She runs zigzag between bushes and trees, like a gazelle escaping wolves. The two brothers, without calling out or looking in my direction, tear off after her.

My breath is coming in short gasps. Perspiration is rising on my forehead and sweat is trickling down the small of my back. I stand for many minutes staring straight into the fire. I feel welded to the spot, like I've grown roots as deep as the trees which surround us.

The fire burns low. Spirit paws the ground, turns his head homewards and begins to walk off, but I check him back. Something primordial stirs within me and I have an urge to run into the clearing and circle the fire, follow those little pebbles around and around. Never ending. Perpetual, like time. Goose pimples rise on my arms and the hairs on the nape of my neck prickle like tiny electric shocks.

When I close my eyes, I see Alan Moonstone, his face staring at me, his finger pointing. Could he see me clearly with the firelight behind his back, or was he almost blind to my place in the darkness, the same way Mum was when she'd looked out of the window at home?

I could certainly see him, and what I saw shocked me. It wasn't there before. I'm sure I would have noticed it. Last week he even helped me and Rosemary Pooter with our poetry project. But tonight Alan Moonstone had the unmistakable wavering lines and boxed edges of a Category Two Monster. And rage seemed to be feeding his aura, increasing like my pulse rate, and leaping in fiery red streams from his body like solar flares from the sun.

Monday 15 October – 2 a.m.

I've finally got to Old Ma Izzy's. I'm determined not to let the forest encounter affect me. Spirit is fine and he can have a rest while I ride Zeus.

The moon's half covered but still making enough light for us to see. No dogs stir at Old Ma Izzy's; they're all in the house, sleeping on her bed.

I won't be able to ride in the fenced-off riding yard. There's another horse in there. It's one of the broodmares and her time has almost come too, but not like Zeus's – she's going to foal. She's wearing a foaling device which will alert Old Ma Izzy when she goes into labour. I hope that's not tonight.

With a flick of my hair, I shake off this problem of where I'm going to ride, but then bite my lip when I realise that even though I know where the keys to the tack shed are, I can't get them. They're in the house and all the doors are locked. Oh, why hadn't I ridden Spirit here with his saddle on? I can't get Zeus's bridle either.

The broodmare whickers out, long and barely audible. I walk Spirit over and she noses him though the rails. They'll be fine together. I lead him into the yard, slip off his bridle and hang it over my shoulder. At least I have that to put on Zeus.

I climb through the railed gates and begin the trek across the paddock to where Zeus lives with his mate, Mercury. I get to the top of the hill and there, at the bottom beneath a cluster of willows, I see them standing nose to nose, heads down. In a synchronistic movement, they look up as I descend the slope towards them.

I hold out a carrot, first to Mercury and then to Zeus when he pushes his muzzle into my hand. Like dozens of times before, in all the lessons we've had together, I slip the bridle onto him. Then I carefully make adjustments to the cheek straps, lengthening them. Zeus is a much bigger horse than Spirit. At least sixteen hands. He's built like a draught horse, but has clean legs, without a draught horse's 'feathers', and a long black mane and tail.

There's no way I can get on him. And this first ride needs to be done without scramble or rush, nothing to tie it to a bad experience. Spirit is used to my awkward way of mounting bareback. Zeus being bigger will make it even harder for me to get on smoothly.

I look around for a fallen log to use as a mounting block, but no such luck. Leading Zeus, with Mercury following, I begin the steep climb up the hill back to the riding yard. Maybe I can still ride in there with Spirit and the broodmare. Use the rails to help me mount.

As we approach the riding yard, the mare rushes up to the fence, teeth bared and ears flat. Spirit looks up from the pile of hay he's been eating and holds his head to one side, like a quizzical dog.

It's because Zeus and Mercury are colts that the mare feels unsafe. I can't ride in there tonight.

The moon snuggles behind the clouds and a blanket of darkness covers the farm except for the security light at the back of Old Ma Izzy's house, which casts a glow over her backyard.

I smile to myself. I can ride in there. Adjoining the paddocks, it's securely fenced off with wire and roses and big enough to canter and trot around. I lead Zeus though the gate and Mercury sticks his head over it. I see both Spirit and the broodmare doing the same through the high rails of the riding yard. I have an audience. At least they can't laugh if I fall off.

Zeus crops the already short grass and seems unconcerned. It's funny but I feel perfectly okay too. Once again I scan around for something to help me get on. There's absolutely nothing here I can use either. The fence wouldn't hold my weight and anyway it's too low.

I sit on the lawn, let Zeus continue to graze. I will ride him tonight.

Then I remember some old footage I'd seen, of a horse whisperer back in the days when they weren't even known as that. He managed to work an unhandled colt in a small but high-fenced yard. First he rode into the yard on a obviously quiet horse. When he got close enough, he simply slid over onto the colt's back. A sort of transfer.

I could do that. Spirit and Zeus had spent time in the paddock together when we came here to look after the place while Old Ma Izzy was in hospital for an operation. They'd got on well then, not even a pecking order dispute.

The broodmare whickers out again as if encouraging me to get on with it. But how can I, with no saddle and only one bridle?

I look at her and then I know what I'm going to do. I take Zeus's reins and loop them over his neck, as I would if I was about to mount. I tie them in a loose knot over his withers, so they don't hang down. Then I go into the riding yard, take off the mare's halter and tie some binder twine onto it for reins. After I slip the mare's halter onto Spirit, I lead him out and then into the house backyard and do my scrabble up thing. Zeus comes over and they greet each other by touching noses. No squealing. Good.

I ride Spirit alongside Zeus and take up Zeus's reins, unlooping the knot. Spirit stands perfectly still, as if he knows what I'm about to do.

I bring my right leg back as if I'm about to dismount, and then, while still on board, I lean over to Zeus and slide my weight, belly down, onto his bare back. For many moments I stay like this, slung across his back, before I bring my right leg over his side.

I stay forward, my upper body flat along his neck. He snorts and I freeze, but it's that sort of low, long snort which means he's relaxed. Good.

I sit up slowly. He brings his head up, jumps forward and raises his back in a sort of hump. I shorten my reins and talk to him. 'It's okay, Zeus. Look, there's your mate, Mercury.' I babble some other inane stuff and make soothing sounds while I scratch his withers.

Spirit takes a few steps ahead of us and looks over his shoulder.

I'm thinking, You clever boy, Spirit.

I loosen my reins, still keeping in touch with Zeus's nose (this is a bitless bridle) and lean forward, like encouragement. He takes a stiff step towards Spirit and even though Spirit has no one aboard, he walks off as slowly as if he's carrying a little kid. We follow him round the yard. Zeus's back hollows to normal and when he puts his head down to snatch a small mouthful of grass, I let him.

Finally it hits me. I'm riding Zeus. I'm actually on his back. Where no man (or woman) has gone before. I reckon this must be how Armstrong felt when he walked on the moon. I'm bubbling inside and tingling all over. If I can do this, I can do anything! And then it happens.

Zeus stops and refuses to go another step.

Spirit comes up alongside like a nursemaid. He nudges Zeus's neck with his nose. I gently squeeze my legs and even use the words I did when long reining. Nothing. Zeus's feet are as firmly planted as Spirit's were when we were at the fire in the forest.

It's now I have this eerie feeling of being watched. I scan around. I've been quiet, and Old Ma Izzy's bedroom is at the front of the house where the bay window looks out over her paddocks. She couldn't hear me from where I am, at the back of the house.

I think of the photos sitting in her window ledge, facing outwards. Pics of all of those horses she's loved and lost over so many years. I wonder how many Old Ma Izzy had ridden for their first time? She'd know what to do. All I know is that this first ride is so crucial. For Zeus and for me.

I have to take control. No, that doesn't sound right, but I need to do something. I realise that what's really been happening is I've been taken for a ride, not riding. Sitting up here while Zeus just follows Spirit around. Now that he doesn't want to follow any more, he's stopped. A sort of defiance. Or confusion?

What I need to be is Zeus's leader. And I need him to understand what I want him to do. He already trusts me; I've been working with him for months, keeping the lessons short and fun, but no-nonsense.

He's never refused me like this from the ground. Does he even know I'm up here? I stretch down and rub his shoulders, then up his neck, turn his nose towards me, let him see me. I put my hand back over his rump, and rub and scratch him there. Another sweet spot. I feel him loosen again. I turn the rein, give a stronger leg aid. He holds his head to one side, and still refuses to move, although he does lean over in that direction. I alternate reins, try to unbalance him a little, make him take a step. He just shifts his weight from leg to leg. I shorten the nearside rein, hoping he'll walk around, but he still doesn't follow through.

Spirit looks at us, sighs and ambles away, over to the gate. He and Mercury squeal out at each other like mares. Zeus's ears spring forward and he starts to move towards them, but I check him. This time he does obey me. I've spent a lot of time on stopping in our training. 'Very important to put brakes on them,' as Old Ma Izzy says. I used squeeze back and release and he'd halted almost as automatically as Spirit would have. But when I give the signal to go forwards, Zeus still refuses.

I need to get him moving. I try backing him up. I only ask for a few steps. This he does easily without any problems.

Spirit and Mercury are standing quietly together and staring at us, as if they can't see the big deal. Zeus snorts and begins to move in their direction again. I'm not sure if horses get jealous, but I do know they don't like being left out. This time, I let Zeus walk towards the gate and when he gets into stride I slow him back, a half halt, turn him round and squeeze my legs. It works. I make definite signals, firm, not harsh. But then, in the middle of a figure eight, once again he stops and refuses to move. I back him up a couple of steps.

Abruptly he bolts forward. He's trying to get to Spirit and Mercury. His head is down and he's bucking. Not high, thank God, and he's keeping it in a straight line. Easier to sit. I lean back, my legs forward, like they do in rodeos, keep the bottom of my spine aligned with his (I can barely feel it really, he's in as good condition as Spirit). I get his head up. It's all over quickly and when I turn and trot him away from his mates, I know I have him. Not that I'd ever lost him, he wasn't seriously trying to get me off.

I feel exhilaration rising like a gale. I bring him around, trot across the yard, open the gate and gently elbow the other two horses out of the way. Zeus and I canter out into the freedom of the paddock. We're flying! And just for this moment I feel nothing will ever be as hard, or as easy, again in my life.

Monday 15 October – 6.30 a.m.

I've made it home safely. I'm so lucky, not only with how awesome it went with Zeus but, as I'm coming in, the landline rings and drowns out any noise I'm making trying to get the front door open. It's stuck even worse than last night.

I remember to put Dad's car keys back in the bowl and manage to get into my pyjamas and slip into bed just before Mum opens my door.

'Are you still asleep, Velvet?' she says in a loud voice which ensures I wouldn't be even if I was. 'Old Ma Izzy – I mean, Mrs Islington-Prior – just rang. She wants you to go over to her place this morning.'

Shit, I think; maybe she did see me. I grunt in reply.

Mum continues, like she hasn't noticed. 'If you hurry up, I can drive you there on my way to work. Mrs Islington-Prior said she'll drop you off at school in time.'

I rush to get my clothes back on. They're still warm and surprisingly not too dirty, although I have distinctive horseback marks over the backside and inner legs of my jeans. I'll wear another pair. I can take my school uniform to Old Ma Izzy's. Shower and change there.

On the drive over, I'm exempt from answering Mum, because my mouth is full of my lunchtime sandwiches. I haven't had time to eat breakfast and Mum's given me five dollars to buy a pasty or something for lunch. If I wasn't so nervous about what Old Ma Izzy is going to say to me, I'd reckon this is heading out to be one brilliant day.

Mum's smiling funny as we pull up in the driveway. I look over to where her smile is shining and I see it. A tiny foal. OMG! The broodmare might have even foaled as I was riding Spirit back to Kaleen's. The foal, a little filly, is galloping and bucking around the horse yard, 'borne' on a beautiful spring day and to such a wonderful owner.

There's Old Ma Izzy sitting on a milk crate in the middle of the riding yard. She's smiling too. She holds up a glass of wine in one hand and waves with the other.

I look at Mum, see the shared smiles and realise Mum already knew about the foal. Must have been told to keep it secret until we got here.

This is a great day. Now what would make it a perfect day would be if I didn't have to go to school.

I *don't* have to go to school! Old Ma Izzy's had trouble starting her truck, so she can't take me. And although she hasn't said anything to me, or told me off, I'm sure she knows what I did overnight. It's just the way she keeps looking at me. Also she keeps asking me if I might need a nap.

The foal is so adorable. She's grey like Zeus, but Old Ma Izzy said they can start off grey and turn into another colour sometimes. Her sire is chestnut like Old Ma Izzy's riding mare, Freya.

I'm sitting on the old lounge chair (the one that belongs to Paladin, Old Ma Izzy's miniature horse) with the footrest up, and I feel sleepy. I really thought I wasn't tired, but now I can't stop yawning.

I close my eyes. There's Alan Moonstone again, finger pointing, like a kadaitcha man pointing the bone, and the other brother hulking towards me. What the hell were they doing with their sister? Should I have gone to get help? But Mum always says what families do is their own business. I lean back and relax.

When I look at the clock, it's nearly eleven-thirty. I must have fallen asleep. I sit up, glance around the room. Through the window, I can see Old Ma Izzy outside. Probably feeding up or doing other horse or farm-related stuff. God, I wish I could swap places with her. Be here all the time.

She comes inside carrying a basket overflowing with home-grown vegetables. 'Had a good sleep, Velvet?' she says, eyebrows a little raised and a knowing smile turning up the corners of her mouth. 'I've got the truck going again. I can take you to school now, if you wish.'

Going to school is my last wish, but we have English lit after lunch and mine and Rosemary Pooter's combined poetry project is due today.

On the way to school, the truck doesn't miss a beat. I wonder what was wrong with it. It's always sounded heaps quieter than our two cars. But then most cars do.

Old Ma Izzy stops at the corner store. Run by Mick the Greek, it's one of those stores which sells everything for a price rising in percentage of distance to the nearest city. Generic things like pies, pasties and cakes are the regular price, though.

As I go in, the chime above the door rings like a cowbell. Actually I think it is a cowbell. Another customer, who's rummaging in the potato crisp stand, flicks a frown at me. I try not to gasp. It's Celestial Moonstone, without her brothers. She seems fine.

As I walk up to the counter, Mick the Greek, carrying a wooden box of apples, emerges from the storeroom.

'Which of you ladies is next?' he says, placing the box behind him on a wide shelf.

A 'Willem memory' pang grips my throat when he says 'Ladies', but I swallow it and say 'I am' at exactly the same time that Celestial, who is still at the crisps stand, shouts, 'Me.'

I'm struck speechless. She's nowhere near the counter, and by the look of it hasn't even decided what she's buying. Mick folds his arms and I see Celestial doing the same. Their eyes meet but Mick is the first to lower his.

'That one is special,' he says, indicating the packet of crisps Celestial is now holding. 'Just one dollar fifty.'

Celestial creases her eyebrows.

'Bew-di-ful day,' Mick says, fingers opening fan like. 'Only one dollar for you, this morning.' He holds out his hand like a proposal.

As Celestial goes to give Mick a fifty-dollar note, the cowbell rings again. Old Ma Izzy sweeps across the shop and by walking in front of her blocks Celestial from paying. She turns round and their eyes lock. This time it's Celestial who's the first to look away.

I snatch a pre-packed salad roll from the little shop fridge, put the correct money into Mick the Greek's still outstretched hand and get out of there.

Back in the truck, I'm quiet. Old Ma Izzy looks pale and I hope she's okay. Not getting ill again. Or 'poorly', as Kaleen calls it. That's what they say in the UK. Kaleen's parents are from England, the same as Old Ma Izzy. I think that's why Kaleen doesn't swear, having such posh parents.

'Take care you don't get too close to that girl in the shop, Velvet. In all ways,' Old Ma Izzy says, speaking at last. She rubs white knuckles across her forehead, then sits up straight like she's almost doing a rethink. 'Ah, though, perhaps she'll…'

Ten minutes later, as I'm climbing the stairs into school, I'm wondering if Old Ma Izzy was going to say, 'Perhaps she'll come good?' Or maybe, 'Perhaps she'll get worse?' I'm making a bet on the latter. And what of her brothers? I should avoid them too. Although Alan was so helpful with our poetry project.

I'm wondering if I should tell Old Ma Izzy what I know about the Moonstone family. Not that I know much. And if I say about Alan being a Category Two, Angry at the Drop of a Rat Monster, it would mean telling her about my ability. I'm not quite ready to do that.

After lunch, we all hang up our projects. We've done them on large posters, six A4 sheets joined together, to put up around the classroom in time for parents' night, tomorrow.

On the top of mine and Rosemary Pooter's we've written the heading 'Dickinson versus Byron', with photocopied pictures of their heads. Last week I asked Alan Moonstone – he'd seemed perfectly okay then, no monster aura – to draw little arms attached to the heads, with boxing-gloved hands held up in the proper stance. They look amazing.

Under each poet's name we've listed their poems and what we liked about them. Also our reasons why our favourite poet should win 'The Bout', as I'd called it. I was still thinking so much about Willem when I'd come up with the boxing theme.

At the bottom of the poster, in a paragraph for each poet, was the 'Knockout Blow'. I thought I'd nailed it. My argument would easily down Rosemary Pooter's. Hers was a bit flowery, like Byron's poetry.

As I unfold the poster, those words, Knockout Blow, in huge red letters, catch my mind. What if that's what's happened to Willem? He's been punched in the head in one of his boxing matches and has amnesia. You hear of things like that. But then why hasn't Rita let me know, or answered my FB messages? I try and slip the thought away, but it keeps sliding back.

Rosemary Pooter is almost smiling, which I've learned is her 'intensely happy' mode. She's nodding at the poster and making strange little animal-like noises in the back of her throat. Weird. Instantly I feel all sorts of mean. She can't help it, and unlike Kaleen, whose mind is often away with her latest book when we work on something together, RP has been really focused. She's the one who found the pictures and supplied the neat coloured pen work. And, if I was to be honest (and how can I be anything else with the facts staring at me in print on paper?), she's done heaps more research and writing than me. I still think my closing argument is better, though. Just to stretch the boxing metaphor a little further, RP would be 'down for the count'. Not that we're being judged against each other; it's a joint venture. 'Working together promotes harmony' is our class motto. I wonder what Clarissa 'Kiss' Rothchile's class motto would be? 'Everyone for themselves,' if she had any say in it. She's in 9GF, we're in 9AB. That's something I'm thankful for – the only time our classes mix is in PE.

It's bad luck that Celestial Moonstone's in the same class as me, though.

I saw her and Kiss together at lunch break. It's funny, but now they seem to move in unison, like conjoined twins, and Kiss has developed an even more unnatural-looking aura, sort of double-glazed if that makes any sense. Often it morphs into the colour of an overcooked fake tan. I can't look at it for long.

After we put up our posters, we walk around the room, looking at everyone else's. I'm mildly gratified that no one has come up with the boxing idea. Celestial and Kaleen's (I wish Kaleen was here to see it hanging up) is pretty good, but I'm sure it's mostly because of Kaleen's input.

They have their poets on stage like modern day ones in 'open mic' competitions. Celestial's poet is Rilke, known for his 'metaphors and contradictions', and it doesn't surprise me that her favourite poem of his is 'Impermanence'. Kaleen's poet is Noel Coward – he just squeaks in as nineteenth century; he was born in 1899. I swallow hard when I read the poem she's chosen is 'I am No Good at Love'.

All the writing on Celestial and Kaleen's poster is by hand and gothic-looking. Old Ma Izzy has a poem written in calligraphy like this, about Norse gods.

Sometimes I wish I was religious. I could pray to a god to let me know what the hell is going on. Especially with Willem. I've thought of him three times today (or is it four?) and I'd been so sure I'd got him out of my head. I've been in denial. And I've been busy, backing my first horse. I haven't told anyone about that yet. Not even emailed or texted Kaleen. I really want to tell someone what I've done.

Later, while sharing afternoon recess – I'd bought some lollies (Kaleen would call them sweets like they do in England) – I tell Rosemary Pooter about it.

She doesn't seem fazed. 'So haven't you ever done that before?' she says, chewing on a jube with her mouth open. 'Not even for the Melbourne Cup?'

For a second I can't speak. I know Rosemary Pooter can be a bit dozy sometimes, but this is crazy. Then I realise what I've said.

'No, not backing a horse like in a horse race. Riding it. Getting on its back for the first time.'

Rosemary Pooter's face goes as blank as an empty page. Then, for someone who knows nothing about horses, she fills it in with surprising insight. 'Isn't that really like, dangerous?' She opens her eyes larger than I've ever seen before. She actually has lovely ones. Bright blue and clear. Almost the same colour as Willem's eyes. Damn it.

She grabs my arm. 'Oh, I'd love to do that, Vel,' she says, her voice crackling. 'Not ride a horse for the first time. But just ride a horse. I didn't know you did.'

I marvel how she missed Kaleen's YouTube video of me jumping Spirit, and Kiss telling everyone about it, making fun of how I'd grabbed hold of the saddle. It had thousands of hits after that. I feel my cheeks burning.

I look at RP, think how small her life probably is. She lives in town, in a home unit, with her mother. Her dad was killed in Iraq when she was seven.

She's gazing at me with a look like hero worship. She still has hold of my hand. I wonder if this is how the gods must feel. They must get so sick of answering, or at least hearing, all those prayers to them, though. And are there still followers of the olden-day gods, like Poseidon and Athena? Or have they become as redundant as the flat earth theory? Then I remember there are people who still believe in that too.

'I could take you with me this weekend, RP. I have my own horse, you know. He's called Spirit and he's amazingly quiet.'

Rosemary Pooter's face glows. Her aura becomes as pink as a newborn. 'Oh, could I, Vel? You are sooo lucky. What colour is he? Was he the one you've just ridden for the first time?'

I tell her he's a Cremello gelding. Cream, with blue eyes and a white mane and tail. And how, when he has his fine summer coat, you can see a faint white blaze trailing down his nose. Then I remember her other question.

'No, I rode a colt called Zeus. One of Old Ma Izzy's.' Everyone knew Old Ma Izzy or at least had heard of her.

'What's the difference, Vel, between a colt and a gelding?' Rosemary Pooter asks.

At that moment, Kiss and Celestial walk by. I shake RP's hand loose.

Before I can answer, Kiss starts laughing. Celestial grins. I've only heard Celestial laugh once and that was shortly after she paired up with Kiss. Then she sounded like an emu, which makes a low, drainpipe-clearing sort of noise.

'One has his balls cut off, you dumb bitch,' Kiss says. She nudges

Celestial, who says nothing but stares at me with a squinted expression, like she's trying to pick me out as the main suspect from a line-up of crims.

I suck up a breath. Did she see me in the forest?

On the bus trip home, I tuck the image of Willem behind thoughts of Kaleen. I hope she'll be back in time for our trip to Adelaide to see the Agatha Christie play *The Mousetrap*. We were going to stay overnight with Kaleen's Aunty Margie. But I guess Kaleen hasn't any say into when they get home. That would be up to her parents' tour plans. And one little play doesn't add up to much when faced with the multiple assets of beautiful Canada. She's probably forgotten all about it.

My stomach sinks when I realise how alone I am. Will I ever hear from Willem again? Will it ever get easier? I haven't heard from Kaleen since Saturday, but that's understandable with jet lag and everything.

I'm having problems getting online. I've rebooted my computer twice, but it's still stalling. I think the server must be updating. Wish I could do that with my life: update and change it.

Finally, I get online and click my gmail open. My hand freezes on the mouse. I press my pendant against my chest and through it I can feel the palpable beating of my heart. There, between a dozen emails, I see two Facebook ones: a generic 'join my cause' from a friend I can't remember, and the other from Rita Van Den Hoven.

I read the subject line and breathe out in a rush. It's just the usual Rita Van Den Hoven has confirmed you're friends on Facebook! I'm not sure how I feel about that. I'm beginning to see what Mum would call a 'Dear John' letter (that's what break-up or piss-off letters were called back in her day) coming up. Except this would be a 'Dear Velvet' letter. And not from Willem, but from the girl who calls herself a Van Den Hoven. I mean, even if it is her real name (and I'm seriously having doubts), maybe they're cousins? There are no incest laws against cousins getting it off. I think of the famous Elvis movie *Kissing Cousins*. Mum has the DVD. Latest version. 'Digitally enhanced'. Always conjures up images of fingers behaving badly when I read that.

I close my eyes and for a microsecond, I see Willem and Rita doing things together with lips and hands. I almost gag. I'm about to switch off my laptop when I notice a name pulsing at the bottom of the page. Rita's online.

I pop up the box. It seems to be in another language, then I realise it's not, it's just misspelled English. I'm surprised at this. I know from Willem that most Dutch kids study English at school. I feel my mouth turn inwards. Maybe she's a slow learner.

Ned 2 spek 2 yoo. hapned lots – *fiets*. Can yoo Skype? Ritaromper15

I try answering, but Rita has already gone. I log onto Skype and type in her Skype name. I have to wait until she 'accepts' me (how ironic) before we can talk.

Staring at the screen, I tap my fingers on the mouse pad then I close my eyes and re-decipher her FB message in my mind. I know 'ned 2 spek 2 yoo' means 'need to speak to you', and 'hapned' would be 'happened', but what the hell does *fiets* mean? It twangs a familiarity button at the back of my brain, but I can't switch it on.

Another ten minutes go by. Nothing. Perhaps she's got cold feet? No 'Dear Velvet' disclosure tonight. I feel more frustrated than relieved. I slip off Skype and onto Google. I look up the exact time differences between Australia and the Netherlands. It confirms what I thought. We're nine hours ahead, which means as it's nearly 6 p.m. here, it would be almost 9 a.m. in Holland. She's probably gone off to school. Needs to with such bad English. I tell myself off. I know how hard it is to learn another language. I only get C minus in French on a good day.

Tuesday 16 October

It's afternoon and so far today's been totally weird. First, and this is the strangest thing – although thinking about it, it isn't really – the police, led in by our headmaster, Mr Deangriss, interrupted our morning PE lesson and arrested, yes, ARRESTED, Hanker Wanker. They didn't handcuff him, but it looked serious. They wore the same expressions that creased the faces of those other detectives when they'd interviewed Kaleen's father over the murder of Chocka and Jim. And here's another crazy thing: as Hanker Wanker was being ushered out, Celestial Moonstone, with Kiss in tow, actually moved forward and brushed against him. At that moment I could barely look at any of them. The over-tanned wavering shape of Kiss's Category Three aura, and Hanker Wanker's vile purple-edged distortions of a Category One, mixed with Celestial Moonstone's mirrored shimmer, all congealed into one melting pot of disgustingness. Gross!

Of course no one's telling us what Hanker Wanker's done.

The female student teacher, who was at PE last time, was absent today so Mr Deangriss took over the lesson, but he didn't say anything except to organise us into pairs to play volleyball again.

Anyway, the next weird thing was at morning recess. Rosemary Pooter gave me a frog cake. This is another South Australian exclusive, like the special YoYo biscuits Kaleen and I took on our quest to Adelaide.

Frog cakes are what they sound like: a cake made to look like a frog. They're about as big as a fist, jam sponge filled with mock cream and covered with a layer of coloured icing. The sort of indestructible icing you find on wedding and fruit cakes. My favourite frog is the green one, which is what RP had given me. Don't know how she knew.

She had the pink one. Frog cakes have dark beady eyes and their little mouths are open, showing the cream within. This amphibian artistry comes at a high price, though. I rarely had one myself, I couldn't afford it, and Kaleen thought them too sickly sweet, in appearance and taste, to ever buy us one.

The thing is I'd never, ever seen RP with a bought lunch, or as much as a packet of crisps. Her clothes were always last century's, and her shoes less functional than mine. (Which is saying something, seeing I often get Danny's worn-me-downs.)

Rosemary Pooter had presented the frog cake to me like the queen bestowing a knighthood. I thought of the godlike feeling I got from the adoring look she'd given me yesterday. It kinda feels good. I've always felt a little shabby in Kaleen's presence. But then, like Kaleen says, she can't help being rich.

'Mama wants to meet you soon, Vel, to talk about me going riding,' RP said, as we wiped our faces with paper towels.

Mama? I thought. That's a bit babyish. Although, from what RP has told me, Mrs Pooter is very, and I mean very, protective of her. Kind of understandable in the light of her losing her husband like she did. I may have a more difficult time convincing 'Mama' that horses are as safe as puppies. Anyway, I've agreed to go back to Rosemary Pooter's place, after school. I rang Mum to pick me up from there when she finishes work at the hospital this evening. I'm glad I'm doing this for RP; it'll get my mind off what Rita is probably about to tell me. She still hasn't 'accepted' me on Skype, but maybe she will have by the time I get home.

I watch the bus disappear with Kiss and co., exhale my relief in a puff, and turn my back on it. I follow Rosemary Pooter down the road to her place. She only lives a few blocks from school – it must be handy if you sleep in late.

RP often comes in early and works on the school's computers (she's that good she even designed the school's website). I don't think her own computer's up to much; I don't even know if she has one. I've had emails from her but they've always had the school's email address.

RP's place turns out to be very small, not even a home unit like I'd thought, but really a flat. It's joined to four others and hers is the last one on the end. Out the front of the other flats are pots of petunias and one has a standard white rose in a square of dirt, where some of the pavement has been removed. All, except RP's, have their doors freshly painted and lacy curtains at the windows.

Rosemary Pooter hunches her shoulders, looks over one of them at me, and shrugs. It's a funny movement, but I'm getting used to her ways. She lifts up what appears to be a large plastic slug (shedding grey skin paint) from near a threaded doormat and retrieves a key. Not a good hiding place, I think. Anyone would look there. I'm also surprised her mother hasn't let her in. Maybe she's out shopping.

The door doesn't stick like ours does at home, and it seems solid, but that's where any cosmetic improvement over my place ends. As we enter, I try and avert my eyes from the wooden floorboards, where the stain polish is faded to the same colour as the doorstop slug. Vertical blinds, at surprisingly clean windows, hang crookedly, slats either missing or alternating between open and shut. Instantly I see why security is not a priority. The place is so poorly furnished that any robber with even a sliver of heart, however cold, would probably end up by leaving a donation.

The TV, old before remote control days, sits on a squatting table of the same vintage and the couch sags under a snot-green candlewick spread, not unlike my granny's. On the other side of the room there's a tiny kitchenette in original 1950s style with a melamine table and two chairs, their legs freckled in rust. A radio perches on the breakfast bar; it looks mock-retro until I get close enough and see it's real. (I do a rethink: bakelite radio…now that would be worth stealing.) The two doors coming off the main room are both closed, but there's a distinctive hum, like a swarm of bees, from behind the door nearest to us.

RP is frozen mid-step. She stands staring, like she doesn't want to make a noise and wake anybody up. Her shoulders hunch again, but she's not looking at me this time.

A voice lifts above the hum. It's shrill and screech-worthy. 'Rose…marie. Come to Mama, right this instant!'

RP staggers forward and ploughs into the room. I follow haltingly, like I'm attached to her by an elastic band.

As I enter her mother's bedroom, my head goes down and my hand instinctively clamps over my nose and mouth. In a nanosecond I'm transported by smell nostalgia, back to when Rosemary Pooter and I were about seven years old. It was morning recess, we were on the oval, and Kiss had centre stage of half the Year Twos.

'You smell like wet the bed, Pooter Pants,' she'd screamed at Rosemary Pooter. Even at that age, Kiss was great at being a bitch, but pretty poor at grammar.

All the other kids joined in, pinching their noses shut, and chanting, 'Wet the bed, wet the bed, Pooter smells like wet the bed', as if it was some sort of exotic, obnoxious fragrance.

Rosemary literally went to ground, hunched in a ball on the grass, like she was trying to make herself smaller than she already was. And she's always been a tiny kid. I didn't join in, but I didn't stand up for her either.

I swallow my guilt now and tell myself back then I was too young to know any better.

When I look up, I see a wall-to-wall bed and, covering it like an inflated human bedspread, is what must be Rosemary Pooter's mother. On her enormous bulging lap teeters a laptop, and in the hand not occupied with its grease-glistening keyboard is a half eaten, but still humongous, cream bun. Empty packets of crisps and oil-patterned pizza boxes are scattered across the room. Even as we enter, she keeps up a steady flow of tapping on the buzzing computer. She doesn't notice me.

'Mama, I've brought Vel…' Rosemary pauses. Her eyes look downwards, almost closed. Her hands clasp, opening and shutting like a fish's mouth, behind her back.

RP's mother flips us a look. Then, still staring at the screen, she slams down the cream bun. I watch mesmerised as its innards splatter, instantly melting into the colour of the sheets.

Her empty fist punches the bed, punctuating her following words, 'What…have you done…with the…frogs? There…were four…this morning. You greedy little…slut!' With the last punch, a glob of cream sticking to her hand flicks loose, flies across the room and smacks Rosemary in the forehead.

RP stands still as stone and doesn't move to wipe it off.

I take step a backwards, but it's too late, Rosemary Pooter's mother has seen me.

Her hand becomes a point, fingers so fat it appears to be a mitt. Her voice lowers to a menacing whisper. 'You, out.'

I start to leave, but stop. RP sees me hesitating and shakes her head emphatically. Urges me to go on. I take another step, but then I turn round. This time I'm going to say something.

'Mrs Pooter. It's my fault. I told Rosemary how much I love frog cakes and…'

'And? And? Who. The. Hell. Are. You?' Mrs Pooter's eyes narrow, almost disappearing into rolls of flesh.

I tell her my name, look her in the eyes, what's left of them. Then I lose my nerve. Rosemary slides towards the door. She gets there just before I do.

A musical tune, like those you hear from poker machines in the pub, rings out from the laptop. I feel drawn to look back.

Mrs Pooter shrieks and I'm about to dive out of the room when I see her expression change. Her face widens even further, this time into a grin, and her hand comes up in a beckoning motion. Now it seems like Rosemary Pooter is on an elastic band, or more likely an emotional umbilical cord. She springs forward in one fluid movement, as if she's rehearsed it a thousand times, and is at her mother's side in an instant. She stares intently at the screen.

'You bloody little ripper!' Mrs Pooter screeches.

I can see she's not referring to her daughter. Her fist lifts up the air and for a single, sickening second I think of Willem and his boxing victory pics.

Without meeting our eyes, her hand curves, beckons us closer. I obey, although not as fast as Rosemary, and soon I'm staring at her computer too. There are fireworks going off in splashing colours, and although she's turned down the sound, I can hear faint popping noises like champagne bottles being uncorked. The words Seven Hundred Dollars streak across the screen in intervals of about five seconds; their gold lettering reflects in Mrs Pooter's eyes and off her nasty little yellow teeth.

Later, over a cup of tea that RP makes us, Mrs Pooter finally turns away from her laptop and scans me like a page from the web. 'Velvet Brown,' she says, her lip curling, like a bad Elvis impression. 'What an interesting name.'

At six o'clock, when Mum picks me up, I reach over and, before she can start the car, give her one long hug and a kiss on her cheek.

'What have I done to deserve that?' Mum asks.

But I don't answer and she doesn't press for one.

Back home in my room, sitting on my bed, I can still hardly believe what happened at Rosemary Pooter's place.

Nothing like someone else's shitty life to put your own into perspective, though. Poor RP. But she'd seemed unfazed. Even at her mother's extra strange behaviour after winning all that money. I guess it'd be bound to make a difference to how you're feeling, but RP's mother did a complete turnaround that was unnerving by its contrast. She'd even given us some of the pizza she had left over. From her lunch, she said, although I suspect her day is one long lunch, or one long breakfast.

I'm trying to be understanding about it all. I mean, the poor woman has lost her husband (even though it was seven years ago) and I couldn't detect anything monsterish (except her size) about her. Although her aura, which was pale puce, kept ebbing and flowing like dirty foam on a beach after a storm.

The good news is RP's allowed to come riding with me. It turns out her mother grew up on a farm and had a pony, a well behaved one, thank God, so there was no need for me to play down any danger. Anyway, Spirit is as safe as a puppy. And I'll use Kaleen's indoor riding arena, so we don't have any distractions from the stock horses, or from anything else.

Mum calls me into the kitchen for dinner. Yay, fritz and eggs on toast. Fritz (now, why am I thinking of that *fiets* word that Rita wrote in her email?) is another South Australian icon. Not sold in any other Australian state or territory. They have strasburg and bologna and other precooked spicy sausage, sort of similar, but not the same, though devon comes close. You can have slices of fritz fried, or cold. I like it fried and crispy, with tomato sauce. Mum always apologises for what she calls a scrappy meal (because she had to work late) but I love it. And, in light of my crazy day, it's something so normal it helps me chill out.

The TV's going. Danny's got it on the music channel. Taylor Swift's song and video clip 'We Are Never, Ever Getting Back Together' comes up, reminding me of some unfinished business I have to do tonight.

After helping with the dishes, and on the pretence of massive homework with strict instructions not to be disturbed, I go to my room, switch on my laptop and log onto Skype.

Rita has 'accepted' me but she's not online. Working back the hours, I figure it's about eleven o'clock in the morning in Holland, so she's probably at school. Maybe she comes home for lunch.

I minimise Skype and look up zombie ants. Everything Celestial Moonstone has told us about them is true.

I find a page titled National Geographic News and read about the recent discovery of a fungus, as yet unnamed, that's keeping the zombie ant fungus in check.

So there's a fungus which attacks the fungus that's attacking the ants! Wow. Can't wait to tell Kaleen and Rosemary Pooter. Feeling a small twist at RP's inclusion in my mind, I realise I'm actually good friends with her too, now. I don't know exactly why, but I really like her.

In the next blink, my computer goes offline. Surely it's not updating again? It comes back on long enough to flash a message telling me that Protectalot, my antivirus software, has been switched off and my computer is in danger. Yeah, I think, pursing my lips: in danger of being smashed up against the wall. When am I ever going to get to speak to Rita? She may be on Skype now, for all I know. I stare at the swirling blue waves and cloud-scudded sky of my screen saver, and grit my teeth.

Wednesday 17 October

It's early morning and Danny is complaining about the main computer, so it still must be offline. I can hear him whining to Dad about how crap this computer is and how we should get a new one. Dad's having a dummy spit, telling him if he wants a new computer he'll have to buy it himself. Danny says he might just do that, thereby ensuring the last word. Dad would never argue with anyone else offering to buy stuff for the house. And since Danny has held down his latest job, he may just keep his threat. I hope so.

I had nightmares about Rita last night and now I feel like I did when riding Zeus for the first time. I just want to get it over with.

Rosemary Pooter is almost late for school, turning up at the same time as the bus. She looks as dishevelled as her clothes. She rolls her eyes towards home in a 'Don't ask' look as we climb the steps into our first class for the day, English lit.

We have our marks for the poetry projects. Ours has an A minus, and Celestial Moonstone and Kaleen have scored an A plus, which is fair enough, really. Strangely enough, RP seems devastated. At recess she sits on the bench under the cedar trees, knees up cupping her chin. (I wonder how Kaleen will feel about Rosemary Pooter sharing our favourite spot.) She tells me Mama will be pissed off. What's new? I think.

But I lower my voice to serious. 'What will she say?'

'Mama always expects me to get the best marks in the class.' RP chews a strand of hair which has escaped one of her plaits. 'Anything less…' She closes her eyes and her words trail to nothing.

I lean over and touch her arm, but she doesn't move. 'That's okay then, RP,' I say, pitching my tone to high. 'You can say we got top of the class. I can lie for you. Anyway an A minus is a great score.'

And, my mind purrs silently, Mrs Pooter will never find out. It's
not like she'll come into school and see. I mean, can she even walk? I
feel all kinds of terrible for thinking this. It would be awful to be so…
large. Inwardly I pat myself on my back at my political correctness, and
then pull myself up again for my self-righteousness. I sigh defeat and
look at RP. She's staring at me like I've gone mad, or like I've suggested
stealing the crown jewels or something. It's then I know what I like
about her. Her honesty.

Although honesty can be taken too far sometimes. Then it slants
into tactlessness. Dad and Danny, mild Category Four Monsters, are
good at that. Like if you ask them, 'Do these jeans make my bum look
big?' they're apt to answer, 'No, the jeans don't, but your bum does.'
For a category which hates conflict, they certainly make a lot of it for
themselves.

I try again. 'Could you just not tell her about it at all, then?'

'Lying by omission,' Rosemary Pooter murmurs.

I take a deep breath. 'Okay,' I say exhaling slowly. 'What if I come
home with you again tonight? I'm getting a ride with Mum anyway
and she won't mind waiting while I go and see your mama.' Inwardly
my brain is dashing itself on the inside of my skull, screaming for me
to stop.

Rosemary glances at me, eyes hooded, but she brings down her legs.
'Maybe,' she says, her tone softly doubtful. 'Maybe,' she continues, her
voice rising. 'If we just come in and say how much we got, like it's a
good thing.'

'It is a good thing, RP. It's a great thing. An A minus is a wonderful
thing!' I'm hoping my enthusiasm will be catching.

I mean it too. It's not every day I get such a top grade. My mum
will be rapt. But I don't say that to RP.

It all turns out well. Better than we could have expected. It's helped
by the fact that Mrs Pooter has had some more wins today. Two
thousand dollars, to be exact. Although God knows how much she's
lost winning that amount. Dad says gambling's a mug's game. The only

ones who win are those running it. Normally I'd agree, but Dad doesn't know about Rosemary Pooter. She's worked out a 'system'. She tried to explain it to me at lunchtime, but I think I need much more than an hour to get my head around it. I've never been good with numbers. Or computer calculations.

RP would be the first to say her system isn't foolproof, though. It's only estimates, and based on chance, but maximising it. Lately it was paying off for her mama, literally. Anyway, how it's all turned out is RP is coming home with me, and Mum's dropping us off at Kaleen's. I'm going to give RP her first riding lesson and she's happier than a paddock full of ponies.

Wednesday 17 October – late afternoon

Spirit and Rosemary Pooter adore each other. If I didn't like RP so much, I could be jealous. Even with no bridle on, Spirit's been following her round, and after he'd been saddled I swear he bent his left knee so it was easier for her to mount. And RP is a natural. She's lovely and relaxed and doesn't have the habit, like a lot of learner riders do, of hanging onto the reins to keep her balance. Whenever she feels unsure, she grabs hold of the saddle instead.

Most of this lesson, I lead her around and even take her for a jog. Too early yet to bother with learning to rise to the trot. I'll do that in the round yard. Spirit goes to voice commands, so I can stop him or speed him up at any time. And if I stand in the middle of the yard, I can see how RP's going, and call out instructions.

I feel quite proud of how much I've learned from Kaleen and how much I remember. But I also realise how much I don't know. Like why do we have to mount a horse from the left? (Although Old Ma Izzy makes us get up from both sides in the Training.) And why is a curry comb called a 'comb' when it looks more like a rubber brush?

The hour before Mum picks us up goes as swift as a wasp. I recheck my watch – can't believe it's six o'clock already.

RP is almost turned inside out with joy. I was so right about her small life. She keeps saying how this is the best thing she has ever, ever done and the most fun too. And, more embarrassingly, she keeps hugging me and asking if there's anything she can do for me in return.

As we're getting into the car, she says it again. 'Vel, if there's anything I can do for you, just ask.'

I'm about to graciously refuse for the umpteenth time when the thunderbolt of my stupidity hits me. I'm almost breathless with my answer. 'Actually there is something, RP. Could you take a look at our main computer? I've been having trouble getting online.'

Rosemary Pooter squirms happily in her seat, her face lighting up like a torch. 'Of course I can, Vel. I'll take it with me when I go.' Then, just as quickly, her face clouds over like my screen saver. 'Did I really do good today?' she asks, her voice husky. 'I'm usually so clumsy. But it really did feel great. And Spirit is such a dream horse. You are so, so lucky.'

Before I can answer in the affirmative, I'm transported to a different perspective. I become Kaleen, listening to me. How many times had I said that to her? Am I doing okay? and You are so lucky. I listen to Spirit whickering out to me, glance over at Mum, who's patiently driven her old bomb of a car here to pick us up, and I think, Perhaps I am. Then I remember Willem, and the feeling fizzes away as quickly as mist on a summer morning.

Thursday 18 October

It's a student-free day today. Mum's working morning shift at the hospital, so she's dropping me off at Rosemary Pooter's place at seven. RP told me it's fine for me to come that early as she's already up at six, doing her 'Mama duties', as she calls them.

I had trouble getting up in time. Kaleen and I were texting each other throughout the night. Kaleen's first text was at 1 a.m. – she'd forgotten about the time difference, and she'd been out of range until then. She was over the clouds to find out she'd got an A plus in the poetry project until she remembered that meant Celestial Moonstone had got an A plus too. Kaleen's having an awesome holiday, been skiing and everything. They're touring through Europe next.

I get to RP's a couple of minutes before seven, in time to see her emptying her mother's commode. I'd never even heard of a commode before. It's a chair with an adult-sized potty in it. Rosemary's mother can't go to the regular toilet. The room's too small.

RP has draped clean toilet paper over the potty, but as she carries it to the bathroom some of the paper lifts off and my nose shrivels up like a salted snail. Surely something died? Maybe RP has chopped her mother up, and is disposing of her in little bits? I look sideways at RP, but she seems fine, no mother-killing monster morphing. People can do that, morph into a monster type, but it's usually only temporary.

I tell her I can't follow her to the toilet, but I'll wait in the main room.

'It's not that bad,' Rosemary calls out, her voice echoing. 'And Mama only does Number Twos twice a day. Mostly it's just wee. But she has trouble with her aim so that's why...'

Number Twos: God, I haven't heard that reference since I was a toddler. I shudder as I think of what Rosemary was going to say next. No doubt involving spillage of urine and stained carpet, although it would explain the smell in her mother's bedroom.

I wrestle up words in a desperate attempt to change the subject. 'Have…you…had a chance to look at our computer…yet?' I hear a toilet flush and wait until Rosemary returns before I repeat my question.

'Yes, I did actually,' she answers. 'Last night, as soon as your mum dropped me off. But I didn't have time to check it out properly. I have to be in bed by nine-thirty. Hang on a sec.' RP takes the now clean potty back into her mother's room and shuts the door behind her.

It's some minutes before she comes back into the main room. She's carrying a basin of grey, frothy water and has a towel draped over her arm, like a waiter. I follow her and watch as she pours the contents of the basin into the laundry trough.

'Mama's bed bath,' she says, with an apology in her voice as she refills the basin with clean warm water. 'Don't worry, I'll be finished soon.'

I pick up a magazine on the kitchen table and scoot through its pages. Someone has completed the cryptic and hard crosswords and the extra hard sudoku as well. All filled in with pen, and no scribbles or corrections in any of them. I recognise the writing from our poetry project. It's Rosemary's.

When I hear her emptying out the basin again, I look up. Soon she scurries into the kitchen, puts on the kettle and gets out three mugs. One of them, as large as a jug, shouts in red print, THE WORLD'S BEST MOTHER. I scrunch up inside at what our lit teacher would call the irony, or maybe the hypocrisy.

After RP takes a side of beef and a jumbo family-sized chocolate cake into her mother with the tea, she finally sits down. (I'm lying about the side of beef.)

She sips her tea and looks at me under half-closed lids. 'I'm not sure if I can get your computer going, Vel. I think you've been hacked.'

When I don't answer straight away, she adds, 'In fact, I'm sure you've been hacked. BigPond's probably turned off your account. You need to ring them and let them know about it.'

'How? I mean, why? Is it anything I've done?' I tell her about the last site I was on, National Geographic, and what I'd read.

'National Geographic? No, that wouldn't do it,' she says. 'That's safe.' She takes a long drink, glances over at the closed door of her mother's room, stiffens like she's hearing something and then relaxes. 'Interesting about the zombie fungus's fungus, Vel,' she says, 'Nature's balance. Incredible really.' Her eyes take a faraway look. Their 'Willem Blue' pierces my heart, but flashes up an idea.

'RP, could I look something up on your computer? I really need to get in touch with someone.'

RP's cup stops midway to her mouth, her face drops like a spaniel's. She puts down her tea. 'Oh, Velvet, I'm sorry. I can't. I mean we only have one computer here and it's Mama's.'

She doesn't need to say any more. It's then I tell RP about Willem and all that's happened. Halfway through, Mama interrupts us and RP scoots off to make a phone call for a takeaway. I listen as she makes the order. Enough pizza to feed our entire school. But I wonder if we'll even get a slice. I guess it depends on how well RP's system is working.

When she sits down again, I ask if she has to do everything for her mother.

'Oh, no, Vel,' she says, her eyes brightening a little. 'Mama has the district nurse, Jenny, come in every second day to shower her. And she has Meals On Wheels five days a week. Sometimes when Mama has them, I don't have to cook for her.'

I read into this that most days (even Meals On Wheels ones) RP still has to cook for herself and for her mother.

She seems to scan my thoughts. 'I usually don't like takeaway and you'd be surprised, but Mama likes vegetables too, and fruit.'

God, is there no end to the self-centredness and gluttony of this woman? Not only eating the Meals On Wheels meals but, even then, making her daughter cook more food for her as well. And what about all the other junk food her mother eats in between?

It turns out we do get a slice of pizza each for lunch, but it doesn't make me remorseful for my thoughts. Mrs Pooter is only in the full flush of generousness from several more wins.

Maybe RP should patent her system.

On the way home, I tell Mum about the hacking. I've strapped the computer into a safety belt in the back seat. I don't want to be near it; I feel like it's been invaded. I'm hoping to hell no one has found anything I've put on my laptop. I'd already deleted (and emptied the trash) the ISM (I See Monsters) files, the ones I'd printed out and pasted into my time capsule journal, and all my entries in this diary are by hand. But I've heard of really top hackers being able to access everything, even stuff that's been deleted. I make a note to ask Rosemary Pooter about it tomorrow.

As I unstrap the computer, Mum seems to notice my expression, because she takes the computer from me. 'Just get the other bits, will you, Velvet.' She indicates the keyboard and screen. 'And cheer up,' she says, shifting the weight of the computer to under her arm, and walking ahead. 'I'm sure it'll be fine. I always thought a computer only got hacked into if you weren't too careful who you gave your details to. But I know you're too sensible for that.'

Instantly I think of Rita Van Den Hoven and feel dread rushing up my body like frost.

Sunday 21 October

When Danny rang up our internet provider on Thursday evening, he was told they thought we were the hackers and that's why we'd been taken offline. Apparently lots of dodgy emails (hidden in spam) had been filtered through our account and forwarded from our email address. BigPond told Danny it's often what happens when you're hacked, but they had to err on the side of caution. They were understanding, though, and reconnected us, so it turned out okay.

On Friday, Danny took our computer to Computer Encounters in Adelaide, to see if they could do anything, but he ended up bringing it back along with a brand-new one. Dad was happy, until he realised that now Danny held the virtual reins he probably wouldn't get a look in, even during the day when Danny was at work. Knowing Danny, he'll have an impenetrable, incomprehensible (to anyone else) and therefore ironclad, password.

My laptop works on wireless, and I mostly go online in the evening (when Danny's usually online) so it won't affect me too much. But I have another problem. Yesterday morning when I switched on my laptop, it didn't boot up, no swirling screen saver, nothing, only the same blank dark screen. I rang RP and got her mother, eek, but she seemed to be in her winning mood and put Rosemary on straight away, like she'd been standing next to her bed, which she probably was. RP sounded happy too, and said she'd take a look tomorrow (today) because she'd just asked if she could come over to my place and Mama had said yes! I should have remembered then that Mum was working today ('Double time on Sundays and we need the money, Velvet') and wouldn't be able to pick her up. Dad's car is still not going. I think what I did to it, the night of Zeus's debut ride, finally finished it off.

I make the phone call. It's ten o'clock, so RP should have completed most of her mama duties by now.

RP answers on the third ring. I get in fast and tell her about Mum not being available to give her a lift here, but her voice still holds to happy.

'No problems, Vel. Mama's paying for a taxi.' She drops into a whisper. 'Everything, you know, is going really…good.'

I know exactly what she means. The system is still kicking along and Mrs Pooter is hitting it big time.

The taxi sidles up at our place at lunchtime. Rosemary Pooter hugs me like she hasn't seen me for a year and then brings out some crisps and two more frogs. Chocolate-covered ones this time. Wow, Mrs Pooter must have struck the jackpot. I cringe at my inner sceptic. Wonder what's happening to me.

The next surprise is that RP has brought her pyjamas. She can stay the night. Awesome. And it turns out she's never had fritz before, not fried or otherwise. I go about setting that straight and soon she's sitting at the table scoffing a big plate of the best. Five thick slices. Crispy on the outside and soft in the middle.

After we finish, I lean back, hands behind my head. Then a thought sits me upright. 'RP, What about your mama duties?'

RP picks up a crumb of frog, puts it in her mouth and sighs contentedly. 'Oh, that. No problem, Vel. Jenny, the district nurse, comes on Monday morning. And I'll go home from school for lunch tomorrow, and catch up on anything else.'

We're going riding again. I'm letting Rosemary Pooter borrow my bike so we can get to Kaleen's. I've got out Danny's old bike. All it needed was the tyres pumped up and the chain oiled. It hasn't been that long since Danny rode it; he lost his licence for six months last year, for drink-driving and had to ride it then.

RP hasn't ridden a bike since she was seven, not long before her dad died.

She seems matter of fact when she tells me this. 'I've had a bike, Vel, but I didn't want to ride it after Dada was killed. Then I grew out of it. He helped me learn to ride. Ran along beside me, and held onto the back of the bike while I pedalled like crazy, you know, and didn't tell me when he'd let go.'

RP has a few wobbly moments, but I guess it's true what they say about riding a bike. You never forget.

She shoots along, ahead of me. Actually, Danny's bike is a bastard of a thing. I don't like boy's bikes anyway. Hate the crossbar and his bike's too big for me too.

I draw up alongside. 'It's four kilometres to Kaleen's. We'll be there in about fifteen minutes. You're doing great by the way.'

RP grins. 'Yes, I'm sort of pleased with myself.' Her tone drops to confidential. 'You know, Vel, after riding Spirit I feel like I can do anything. Strange really.'

Not really, I think, remembering how when I'd first ridden Spirit, he'd made me feel like a better rider than I knew I was.

'He's a magic horse,' I say, pulling over to miss a pothole.

'Really?'

I glance at RP to see if she's joking, but her face is serious, although it could be from concentrating on staying upright. She does that sometimes, takes silly things literally, which is probably why some kids think she's weird. But maybe she's right this time.

I come alongside again. 'Do you miss him? Your dad?'

A few minutes pass before RP answers. A flock of pink and white galahs screech a raucous tune overhead in monosyllables. And a roo, with her peeping joey passenger, stops grazing and bounds off, disappearing silently into the forest.

'No, not really. Well, I do, but it was seven years ago now. I felt awful, though, the other day, when I had to get out his picture to remind myself what he looked like.'

'Doesn't your mother have a photo of him up in the flat?'

RP shakes her head, and swerves. She starts to zigzag like a tacking yacht, but then straightens her handlebars and regains control.

The last vestige of sympathy for RP's mother dies in me like a flattened firefly. She may have lost a husband, but Rosemary's lost a father. Surely Mrs Pooter should be keeping his memory alive, for her daughter's sake.

We're nearing Kaleen's and I can see the big farm gates about two hundred yards away, but I feel I need to know. 'How come there's no pics in the flat?' I ask.

'There was an argument over something. I don't know what. I think Mama has never forgiven him.' RP turns her head away and sighs.

The riding lesson goes even better than the last one. We spend three hours this time, and in the end it's only RP getting sore legs that makes us stop. In fact, pedalling home is out of the question, so we have to walk the bikes along.

I'm not sure why I start to tell Rosemary Pooter about my ability, but I do. I've never told anyone else, only Kaleen, but it feels right. I really trust RP. Even though it's been such a short time, I'm heaps close to her, and she's told me so much about her own life. Never holding anything back. Also I have a burning need to tell someone (I'm sure I'll self-combust if I don't) about Celestial Moonstone and I can't do that without explaining everything.

When I finish, Rosemary's eyes are clear and open as they meet mine, and I know she believes me. About seeing monster shapes and auras, and all about Celestial Moonstone and her brothers' sinister meeting in the forest.

'So, Vel, did you ever find out what Celestial was doing at the fire? Or what her brothers were up to?'

'No, I haven't. Well, I can't really ask her, or them, can I?'

'Sounds like a ritual of some sort to me, Vel.'

At that moment the galahs return, circling directly overhead. The flock seems to have trebled in size and for the rest of the way home we can't even hear ourselves for the screeching.

We get back to my place at five-thirty. As we enter, Mum (not long home from work) gets up from an armchair, stretches, yawns and asks if RP needs a lift.

'Thanks, Mrs Brown, but if it's okay with you, can I stay the night? I'll cook dinner if you like.'

Mum looks pleasantly shocked and, as she slumps down into the chair, smilingly agrees to both suggestions.

RP shows me how to cook spaghetti bol, Dad and Danny's favourite. 'It was Dada's favourite too,' she says, her voice wavering, as she divides up the garlic bread.

After dinner, I lead Sebby back to his yard, give him some hay and pellets and refresh his water. RP leans over the fence and scratches his back. Sebby dips down and closes his eyes.

'Thanks so much for today, Vel,' she says. 'I had a wonderful time again. I was scared riding the bike, but it all turned out great.'

I glance over at the bike shed and see our bikes propped against each other like lovers. Danny's bike doesn't have a stand. It's funny, but all day I've had this niggling feeling, like I should be remembering something – something about bikes and fritz and *fiets*.

Rosemary Pooter has fixed my computer. I feel like singing it like a mantra. She is truly amazing.

When I tell her this, she just shrugs and goes pink in the face. 'It's nothing, Vel,' she says. 'You just had it on sleep mode and I woke it up.'

She chuckles at her own joke, but I'm mortified. How did I do that? What a bloody idiot I am.

She looks at me funny and adds, 'Don't worry, it's easy enough to do. You should see the stupid things Mama does sometimes with her computer.'

I shrivel even more at being referenced along with her mama.

Again RP picks up the vibe. Goes a deeper pink. 'Everyone does silly things with computers, Vel.' Then her voice takes on a slightly frantic tone. 'I've done heaps of stup…id…' She breaks off helplessly, I look at her earnest face and start to giggle.

I soft punch her shoulder. 'Don't worry about it, RP. I know I'm a bit of a technophobe. I'm really grateful. Honest.'

The first thing I do is log onto Skype. Rosemary sits at the back of my room with one of Mum's magazines. She's not flicking through, but actually reading that stuff. She's funny, but sort of 'out there' too. A contradiction in terms, our lit teacher would say.

Of course Rita isn't online. And I can't put it down to her being at school, seeing it would be mid-Sunday morning in Holland.

I go into Facebook, check out her page again. I notice she hasn't many friends ('Not surprising,' my nasty voice says, before I slap it down), mostly relatives. But looking back at old posts (there are still no new ones) I see she only joined FB six months ago. I sigh loudly and RP looks up, finger on the page of what she was reading.

'No luck, then, Vel? But it's daytime over there, isn't it? She's probably gone out.'

Yes, I think, out with Willem. Oh god, is there no bloody end to this pain? It isn't getting better. I feel like I've swallowed a nest full of bull ants and they're all biting me simultaneously, sending their poison to my brain. Fogging my reasoning and turning me insane. Oh no, I'm rhyming. How lame! I slump over in my chair and put my head on my desk.

RP comes over and gently rubs my back. 'How about I make us a nice cuppa?' she says, sounding like my gran, 'I'll ask your mum and dad, and Danny, if they want one too.'

She's gone from the room before I have time to say 'Yes.'

Monday 22 October

When I come in for breakfast (RP is showering), the table seems unusually harmonious. Mum (she has today off) is all smiles, Dad's paper is flickering and Danny is up to his nose in the latest breakfast cereal, a dirty-brown bird grit concoction. The cereal packet has headlines of health, larger than the newspaper's. I don't believe either of them.

'What a nice girl that Rosemary Pooter is, Velvet,' Mum says, with the emphasis on 'nice'.

Dad drops his paper to give a momentary nod of agreement.

Even Danny does a thumbs up with the hand not ladling the spoon to his mouth. 'Did you know,' he says, his teeth skittering along the bird grit, 'that RP's father was a top cyclist? Rode in the Adelaide Cup or something.'

Rosemary must've talked to Danny last night when she took him his tea. Athletic prowess always impresses him. Probably because his athletic endeavours only go as far as the bedroom. (Although I'm not meant to know anything about that. Or the RSI in his hand – just kidding.)

'Tour Down Under,' I say listlessly. I'm not sharing everyone's happy morning. Rita still wasn't online.

'Whaaat?' Danny intones, like a drunk. He finishes his mouthful in a gulp. 'Oh, I knew that,' he says. 'Tour Down Under, yeah.'

Danny and Dad are armchair riders, but only when it comes to far distant races, such as the Tour de France. Closer to home like Adelaide, where the Tour Down Under is held, something to do with cultural cringe kicks in. And they tune out.

I know about the Tour Down Under because of Willem; he'd hoped to get here next year and watch it with me. Bikes are huge in Holland, not in size, but in quantity, everybody rides them. And the place is so bike friendly they even have their own bike stop lights and bike ferries.

When Kaleen and I camped at Adelaide on our quest, Brandon and Willem had brought us our tent, and other gear, on their heavy-duty bikes. We'd only seen them on their racing bikes before then. Brandon had loaned Willem one of his. They're both mad keen racing cyclists and Brandon is as wealthy as Kaleen, and just as generous. As I think of this, another image, the one which has been creeping behind my mind comes up in pictures and words. My stomach has the bull ant feeling again. And they're biting hard. I know now what I've been trying to remember. The thing about Fritz and *fiets*, I tie it to Rita's message, rounding out the sense of it, swallow a breath and hope to God I'm wrong.

Just then RP rushes into the kitchen, damp hair flailing in wet wisps and red spots forming on both her cheeks. 'Quick, Vel,' she gasps, like she's run an Olympic marathon. 'Rita's come online.'

I close the bedroom door behind me and adjust my cam. The little pic of me pops up in a square at the top of the screen. I look terrible, but I feel worse. I click the green telephone. Rita comes on almost before it finishes its first ring. She looks washed out too. She has swollen red eyes and I can see where tears have tracked make-up down her face.

'I'm sorry Velvet, for only...de Facebook...de message. I speak English better den I can...write it.'

Her voice is trippingly slow and heavily accented, but I can understand her. Willem speaks English so well, but being an exchange student and staying in Australia, naturally gave him the edge.

I feel tears pushing up. I think I'm right about my fears. The thing is, the Dutch language is very similar to English, but not in the way you'd expect. Lots of their words, although they sound the same, often have different meanings. It's great for association learning, like 'been' means 'leg' in Dutch, so when Willem told me that, I imagined a picture of a string 'bean' in the shape of a leg. Easy to remember. When I'd asked him how to say 'bike' in Dutch and he'd replied *fiets* (pronounced 'fitz'), naturally I paired it up with fritz. I imagined riding a bike eating a fritz sandwich. Why I couldn't remember it until a minute ago, I don't know. Maybe I hadn't wanted to. 'Hapned lots – *fiets*.' Now it makes perfect sense.

Rita and I talk for what seems like hours, until I wish it had all been as simple as a cheating love affair. Anything but this.

Mum yells out that I'll need to hurry or I'll miss the bus. I wouldn't care, but I have to think of RP.

I can't talk at all on the way to school. I should have stayed home. I feel cold all over and sort of away somewhere, but not here. Rosemary doesn't bug me to tell her what's happened. I think my face says it all.

I sit alone at lunchtime. RP has gone home for lunch to catch up on all her mama duties. The only good thing that's happened today is that Kiss is not at school.

At afternoon recess, I feel like I'm ready to talk. Rosemary Pooter puts her arm around me.

I take a gulp of air and begin. 'Willem's had a terrible accident on his bike, RP. Not his racing one. It happened when he was going to the shops. A guy on holidays, from the UK, was riding a moped but was on the wrong side of the bike path, and came around the corner straight into Willem. The guy was okay, he had his helmet on, but Willem didn't. It's not compulsory to wear helmets in Holland, like it is here,' I add quickly, before RP can ask why he hadn't.

I take a deep breath, feel like it's someone else who's talking. 'Rita told me the doctors put Willem into a medically induced coma. The day she got in contact with me on Facebook was the day they were going to bring him out of it. But he relapsed. That's why she didn't come back online for so long.' I choke on my tears and hiccup a cough. 'Since then they've had to operate on him twice.'

'That's what Dada had. Two operations.' RP's voice is as small as the pet name for her father.

I glance up and see she's crying too. We hug each other, then she pulls away and holds me at arm's length. Looks me in the face.

'It will be fine, Vel. Don't worry. Doctors can do so much now.'

I gulp out words between swallowed tears. 'But…I was thinking… all…those bloody awful things…about him. Like he was cheating with Rita… I was so…wrong. And she really is his sister. She's been too upset to talk to anyone, until now.'

Rosemary Pooter strokes my hair, I lean up against her strong little body and, with her next words, feel its strength ebb into mine.

'Willem's a fighter – remember that, Vel. He's never lost a bout. And he won't give up. He has you to come back to now.'

When we go into our next lesson, our science teacher, Mr Renshaw, takes one look at us and sends us off to the school nurse. She gives us each a glass of water and leaves us alone in the sickroom.

After we finish our drinks, RP leans towards me. 'Here's something I learned today, Vel,' she says, behind a half-closed hand. 'You're so right about Hanker Wanker. There's a rumour circulating that he tried it on with the female student teacher. You know, the heavy word, and from what's been tweeted, the heavy hand too.'

'Of the law,' I add, sniffing.

'Hey?' says Rosemary Pooter, her eyes squinting. Then the light goes on. 'Oh, I get it. The heavy hand of the law.'

And despite everything we start laughing, until the school nurse comes in and tells us to quieten down or get back to our class.

Tuesday 23 October

I haven't gone to school today. I can't face anything beyond the walls of my bedroom, and I'm waiting for Rita to come on Skype and give me an update on Willem.

I shuffle through some pics Kaleen took of me and Willem (with her camera) before he left to go back to the Netherlands. (My iPhone, a worn-me-down of the electronic kind from Danny, is crap at taking photos.) Kaleen made double prints as a sort of going away gift for Willem, so he and I could both have identical ones. I have to hold them to one side to stop my tears from dripping onto them, and causing water damage. OMG, we look so happy, sort of misty-eyed and rosy-cheeked. They say being in love makes you extra-healthy and, looking at these, I believe it.

I gulp a sob. Oh, if we could only go back to then. I can't grasp what's happening now, the unreality of it.

I've checked out 'medically induced coma' on Google, but all that's done is made me more paranoid. I do understand why doctors do it, but it still seems unclear about the prognosis in the case of head traumas, as they call them. And if the fluid around the brain increases too much, it can cause irreparable brain injury. From what Rita's told me, that's what the two operations were for. To relieve the pressure.

I can't help rearing scenarios: Willem unable to walk or talk, or ride his bike, or even worse…Willem not making it…

I wipe my eyes, shake my mind of my doubts and take one of the pictures aside. Our favourite one. It's of us at our lunchtime getaway from school, Caz's Café. I'm glowing and Willem's smiling that broad sexy smile I recall so well in all my good dreams.

I remove the current photo I have on my desk, a slightly blurry one I took of Willem with my phone, and replace it with the pic of us together. I position the frame to where I can see it from every angle. I want to focus my energy on Willem, all those positive vibes.

Once again, I think of Old Ma Izzy's pics of her horses and what she'd told Kaleen and me about the Australian Aboriginals. How they believe the shade (or soul) is connected to photos in some sacred way. They won't look at pictures of anyone who's died. I think of my great grandmother. There's no photos of her.

The day before Willem was to return to Holland, he'd come back to my place (I was still grounded because of the TAOB – To Adelaide Or Bust – quest). No one else was home. Dad had gone off with Danny to the pub. Mum was working shift. God, it seems miles ago now.

I lie back on my bed, wrap my pillow in my arms, close my eyes and feel the memory rising like a hot spring. Willem and I had almost gone too far – his words. They were coupled with too young and my rebuffs as clear as air, though not as honest: I'm nearly fifteen, I'm old enough.

I'm closer to that now, less than ten weeks away. Not that fifteen will cut it. If I lived in one of those easy-going states in the US where they allow sex early, it'd be fine, but here in South Australia the age of consent is seventeen. Willem's age. Would he wait that long? He said he would.

I stretch out on my bed where it almost happened, arch my back and rub my pillow in gentle circular movements, like curry combing a horse. Sigh at the recall of Willem's hands. And then my own hands, cupping and stroking, the soft over hard, the steel in silk of himself, as he pressed up against me.

He told me he loved me that evening, and now I believe him.

In a warm rush like Old Ma Izzy's wine, I'm reborn again to the thought of this. New wine she had called it and in a way it's new love too, but now made even stronger for the underlay of the old.

Wednesday 24 October – morning

Mum said we can give Rosemary our dud computer. RP reckons she can sort it out, and even if she can't, she said it'll be great just for word processing.

I've got the computer with me, bloody heavy thing. My school bag's on my back, so I have my hands free, but it's a hell of a struggle getting onto the bus. Mum said she could have dropped the computer off after work tomorrow, but RP can't wait. She already has an old screen and keyboard, so I didn't have to take those. Not that I could have, really.

If Kaleen was on the bus, she would have helped me, but God knows when she'll be getting home. They're in Egypt at the moment, so it's even bigger than a European holiday, more like a world trip. I do miss her.

She Skyped me the other night, about twelve. It was lucky Danny was still online and I'd been surfing the net. I did manage to tell her about Willem, but she was on a tight schedule (a cruise down the river Nile) and had to go before I could fully explain about Rosemary Pooter and her mum and the System and even how RP and I are becoming good friends. Certainly I haven't told Kaleen about revealing my monster-seeing ability to RP. I'm not sure how she'll take it. Our friendship or the disclosure.

RP and I have talked heaps about it – the monster stuff, that is – and I've even printed out the pages for her, explaining the category types. And how I see auras around both monsters and normal people. But how the monsters' auras have distorted shapes and stronger colours.

'So, Vel, do all people have auras, then? I have heard about auras before, you know,' Rosemary says, as we eat our lunch.

I see she's bought her lunch today, a salad roll, A Mick The Greek's Special. They're the best. It reminds me of what happened at his shop that morning with Celestial, how she seemed to wield some sort of control over Mick. But not over Old Ma Izzy, although I could tell even she was rattled.

'Pretty much. Most people do have auras,' I answer, after finishing a mouthful of sandwich. Cold fritz today; nowhere near as good as fried.

RP wraps up the other half of her salad roll. She swings around on the bench. 'How about me?'

I stare at her. Where is her aura? But then I see it, aqua blue, wispy and sad. I gasp. Why hadn't I noticed it before?

She sucks in a breath too. 'What is it, Vel? What do you see? I'm not a monster, am I? Please tell me I'm not.'

I explode into laughter with the silliness of this question. Just like Old Ma Izzy, Rosemary Pooter is as far removed from a monster as anyone could possibly be. Which is what I tell her. Her face clears like a bathroom mirror after you switch the exhaust fan on.

Wednesday 24 October – evening

I've heard from Rita again. A text message. She Skyped me yesterday and I gave her my mobile number, so now she can contact me anytime. The message is an abbreviation of what she told me online. No improvement. I've also heard from Kaleen. She's mortifiably sorry, but there's no way she can get back for the Agatha Christie play. I'd forgotten all about it, but even if I had remembered I would've known she couldn't go. It's on Friday night, so her family would have to be heading back now for her to make it home in time.

Because the tickets were an early birthday present, they're at Kaleen's place. I have to go there to pick them up. Kaleen's sister, Coral Lee, and her dozy boyfriend, Dwayne, came back last weekend – their finances couldn't stretch to the world tour bit – so they'll be home to let me in.

I'm not going to the play. I don't think RP would want to go either; she has enough drama at home. Like, on Monday night her mother fell over in her walk-in robe and got stuck. Rosemary rang an ambulance and they ended up ringing the fire brigade. They had to use the jaws of life – you know, those huge hydraulic tools they use to cut people free from bad car wrecks – to get Mrs Pooter out. RP just shudders when I ask for more details, so I've stopped questioning her. On a lighter note, she's got our old computer running like a dream. She told me what she's done, things involving extra rams and stuff. I blanked over when she really got into it, but I'm still very impressed.

I'm selling the Agatha Christie tickets on eBay. I've put them up, and got a bid, only about a quarter of what I paid, but there are still twenty-four hours to go before it closes. I'll stay on the bus to Kaleen's after school tomorrow, and get the tickets from her place then. I've already stipulated that whoever wins the bid will have to pick them up. There won't be time to post them.

Thursday 25 October

This morning I woke to no new bids, and the one I do have hasn't made the reserve, so if there aren't any more, I've lost my money. What usually happens with eBay, though, is people don't bid until the last few seconds. It's a ploy to beat the clock and any rivals. But time is running out – tomorrow's the final showing of *The Mousetrap*. My tickets will be worthless after that. I drop my reserve to way under half-price; anything is better than nothing.

Sometimes I feel I'm living in a parallel universe: Kaleen world tripping; me, best friends with the least cool kid in school, Rosemary Pooter; and the most unbelievable thing, my sweet Willem so close to…not being here any more… (I can't say the 'D' word.) I bite my lip. I'm not going to think like that. Things are still hopeful. He'll improve soon and the doctor will bring him out of his coma and this will all be a terrible nightmare, one to be forgotten.

Another unreality is the transformation of Spider Johnson, the bus clown. Every day he's become more and more subdued, and I'm positive Celestial Moonstone has something to do with it. I guess it's a case of bad people sometimes doing good. Anyway, it's great. Spider's become so quiet on the bus I've been able to catch up on homework. For our next assignment in English lit, we're reading *Jonathan Livingston Seagull*. I've read it tons of times before, but it's one of those classics you can read over and over and still discover something new, or perhaps a different way of looking at it. I'm trying to put into words what I see in it (that's the assignment). Some say it's biblical, but I don't agree. Spiritual, yes, and a great premise for living. Strive for what you believe and don't give up, even when everyone else (and sometimes even yourself) has doubts in what you are doing. I write this down, push back in my seat on the bus and again open the first page of the book.

The day glides by without anything unusual occurring. Maybe the Universe has run low on 'weird' for a little while. Hey, I'm not complaining.

After school, I stay on the bus and get off at Kaleen's. When I collect the tickets and give Spirit his treat, I'm going to walk home, that's if Coral Lee or Dwayne don't give me a lift. It's about four ks, but I welcome the thought of being on my own. Time and space to think.

Coral Lee answers the door. She's wearing red lipstick the colour of bad sunburn and the exact hue of her cheeks. Her hair is swept back with a silver clip and piled high on her head, although most of it's escaped, or is trying to.

She lets me in with a grunt and then, curving a half-dismissive wave, she glides off in the direction of Kaleen's room. I know I've caught her and Dwayne in the middle of something when I see Dwayne sprawled out on the sofa, his jeans half-mast. He's wearing the same colour lipstick in smudged kisses along his neck and trailing down his white waxed stomach. I swallow heavily and avert my eyes.

The rest of the room, which spills into the dining area, looks as untidy as Mrs Pooter's bedroom, but it's sort of upmarket messy: sushi boxes, used plastic chopsticks, and empty bottles of red wine in full litter.

When she returns, Coral Lee glares at me and thrusts the envelope with the tickets into my hand. She starts to usher me to the door, but I don't need any encouragement. As I'm leaving, she gives me a little shove, but then grabs my T-shirt and pulls me back.

'Hang on a tic, Velvet,' she says, glancing over at Dwayne, who's staring at her with a puppy-eyed look of longing. 'I'm just going to ask Velvet if she knows anything about the stolen horse,' she throws back at him in a hiss.

I step inside the doorway. My eyebrows lift, I can feel them creasing my forehead. Stolen horse? That could only be Ganymede, the former head stockman Donovan's horse. Oh shit. I try and will my face to normal, my quizzical look to bored.

When I leave, I give Spirit his carrot treat, and a sugar-free Polo mint to Watson, who's still on a diet. I scan a long view over the paddocks that contain the stock horses. No sign of Ganymede, thank God. He must be behind the trees. Whoever had been enquiring would have been sure to ask about a horse with a distinctive white blaze like a question mark. And then if Ganymede – Ganny, as Kaleen and I call him – had been nearby, it would have been an easy thing for Coral Lee to spot him and report back, 'Yes. Yes he is here.'

I walk home, head down, eyes sweeping the path ahead of me like one of those gold detectors. I don't know what I think I might find. Certainly not answers. But I have to do something about Ganymede. We have to do something and, because of the tyranny of distance, that we is no longer Kaleen and me, but me and Rosemary Pooter. I sigh loudly and an echidna, about to enter the path ahead of me, shuffles backwards and begins burying himself in fallen bark. Soon he's disappeared. Lucky thing. Wish I could do that.

I inhale deeply. Just when I was thinking the day was wacky-free, it does this to me. A blast from the past.

When I get back to my place, RP's online. She hasn't got Skype (no mic or cam) but I quickly join up with her on FB and we message each other. It's garbled with overlapped questions as we type ahead of, or behind, each message. I hate having conversations like this. I ask if she can get on the landline. It's very important, I add, misspelling important as impotent, and cursing as soon as I've sent it.

Sure enough, RP answers. Impotent?

Anyway, I think, gritting my teeth, it's exactly how I feel. Powerless, especially with Willem. Is being in love worth all this crap? Immediately I feel guilty. The bull ants are biting inside me again.

I'm pleased when I hear the phone ringing in the kitchen. I race to answer, but it's only one of those telemarketers trying to get us to change our phone service provider. He keeps on going, even when I tell him we already subscribe to the one he's trying to sell us. In the end I slam the phone down and start back for my room. I'm stopped mid-hallway as the phone rings again. This time it's Rosemary.

'Impotent? Who's impotent?' RP's voice sounds distant, much further away than the twenty or so kilometres between us.

I take the phone into my room. 'I meant important,' I say, and before RP can answer, 'Actually it's more than important, RP. A life depends on us and what we do next.'

I hear her swallow. 'Go on, Vel.' She sounds firm, determined even.

I tell her about Donovan O'Reilly, the Pingellys' former head stockman, his affair with Mrs Pingelly and how Kaleen's parents nearly broke up over it. Also, how he was a suspect in the Chocka and Jim murders, and how he did a runner. First riding off somewhere on Cody, and then getting out of the country.

'I don't understand,' Rosemary says. 'Why did he do that?'

There was lots of publicity about the homicides, and because it was a local case, everyone knew how the trial had gone and who was found guilty.

I shrug, move the phone to my right ear. 'Who can tell? Scared of Mr Pingelly? Or maybe Donovan didn't want to draw any more attention to Ganymede.'

RP had seen Ganymede at our last riding lesson, when I'd taken her and Spirit into the round yard. She'd asked why he'd been left behind, in a paddock on his own, when all the other stock horses were out herding the cattle. I'd told her no one had been able to ride Ganny since Donovan had left.

'Oh, Ganny, yes,' RP says now. 'I really like that horse. He's gorgeous. I love his blaze.'

'Yeah, it's hereditary. From his sire, Tareek Hazzan. Most of his foals have got it.'

'Tareek Hazzan? Sounds Arabic.'

'That's because it is. Ganymede's an Arab. They can be wonderful horses, but very sensitive. And he was badly treated by his last owner.'

There's a pause before RP asks, 'Who? Donovan?'

I'm quick to answer. 'No, Donovan never owned him. He belonged to a stud farm in Western Australia, Donovan's last place before working for the Pingellys.'

There's an even longer pause before RP stutters, 'N-now…I'm…more…confused. You told me Donovan brought Ganymede with him to the Pingellys.'

I wait a few more moments. Let Rosemary gather the evidence.

She picks it up quickly. 'Oh,' she says, 'Donovan stole him.'

Before I can agree (although I would've used the word kidnapped or maybe horsenapped), Mum calls out that dinner's ready and can I bring back the phone. She has to ring work and see if the roster's been changed. She's asked for this weekend off.

I get up from my bed. 'I have to go, RP. I'll ring you later.'

Now it's Rosemary's turn to answer quickly. 'Don't do that, Vel. Mama hates phone calls after eight. She has her long nap then. Before she starts her all-night vigil, with…you know.'

Hell, Mrs Pooter really has got the gambling bug bad. I hang up after I tell RP I'll talk more about Ganymede tomorrow, at school. There's a bit to work out. What to do with him for a start. He can't stay at Kaleen's. The people looking for him are bound to turn up there sooner or later. I mean, they only have to get in contact with Mr and Mrs Pingelly to find out more details and realise they're on the right track.

Kaleen's father may not be sure about which horse they mean. He doesn't have a whole lot to do with running the farm, or any of the horses, which is why he has a head stockman. Most of his time is spent at his car parts factory. But what I didn't have time to tell RP is that Donovan O'Reilly is an alias. These people are looking for a Reilly O'Donovan. Which is who he really is. Clever of Donovan, I mean Reilly, swapping his names around like that. It's probably why it's taken so long to hunt him down, and even now they wouldn't be sure. But Mr Pingelly is bound to put it together and he'd do it as happily as a boxer delivers a knockout blow. He has a huge unfinished score to settle, not only with Donovan sleeping with his wife, but Donovan setting up a false trail to try and pin the murders onto him. Come to think of it, the police might still be after Donovan for that as well. Perverting the course of justice. Not that I'm worried about Donovan, I mean Reilly. I'm far more concerned for Ganymede. In fact, they don't have to find Reilly, just know for sure that he worked for the Pingellys. Then they'll come looking. And find Ganny.

Remembering what Reilly told me and Kaleen about the stud farm's treatment of their horses, especially Ganymede, I can't bear the thought of Ganny going back to that cruel place.

Among other atrocities, one of the things the trainer did was put electrical currents through the jump poles, so Ganny would be zapped if he didn't jump high enough and clear them. And they weren't mild shocks either, Reilly told us; they left burn marks. He showed Kaleen and me the thin lines of white flecked grey on Ganny's hindquarters, where the hair hadn't fully grown back.

Apparently, when Reilly complained to the RSPCA, the stud farm fired him. And he was never able to prove anything conclusive to the RSPCA (there was some sort of cover-up) so as far as we know the stud owners are just as brutal as their staff. Whatever else he was, it was nothing short of heroic what Dono… Reilly did, horsenapping Ganymede. If I can help it, I'm never letting Ganny go back there. Ever.

I've sold the tickets! I got a dollar over my reserve price, but if I put this with the money I have from working for Old Ma Izzy, there'll be enough for Spirit's upkeep until mid-next year. Kaleen's only charging me a flat agistment rate. I mean, she didn't want to charge me anything, but I insisted. I also need to put some money aside for a replacement present, even though she'll still be in Europe. Her birthday's coming up soon, on the second of November.

I know what I'm going to do with Ganny, so that's one worry less. Although, when I was thinking about that, I wasn't thinking about

Willem – well, not as much. A case of one worry overcasting another, hiding it behind the shadow of angst (poetry mode again).

I'm feeling so tired. I haven't slept properly since I found out about Willem. I know I'm not going to sleep well tonight, either, so I keep trawling the net, looking for more medical answers about Willem's condition, trying to find some sort of certainty where I know none exists. Luckily, once again, Danny is still online, or maybe he's left his computer on, so I haven't been cut off yet and it's already 1 a.m.

Kaleen comes on Skype and immediately I see how happy she is, bubbling even. She's trying to hide it, I know, in deference to what I'm going through, but the corners of her mouth keep lifting.

'Oh, Vel,' she says, adjusting her cam so she has eye contact. 'Mother and Father are getting married. Tomorrow.'

This jolts me fully awake. 'What? But aren't they already married?' I'd often seen (even this afternoon, in fact) the ornate, framed hand-painted portrait of much younger Kaleen-parentals in full wedded whiteness, hanging in their dining room.

'Oops, sorry, Vel. I meant remarried. You know, renewing their vows. This trip was really a second honeymoon. Father's surprise for Mother.'

Once again I feel confused. 'Shouldn't that come after the re-wedding?'

Kaleen laughs and I turn down the sound. 'Sheez, Vel, You're getting as pedantic as Rosemary Pooter. Anyway, we're doing the river cruises of Europe.'

I see her pick up a map and unfold it.

'You know, the Seine, the Nile, the Rhine, all of those. And before you go all literal on me again, yes, I know the Nile isn't in Europe. It's in Egypt. It was awesome. The Valley of the Kings especially. Way cool.'

God, she sounds like a geography lesson. I feel too flat, too exhausted to be jealous or even envious. But then a thought strikes me in the chest like an arrow. Soon Kaleen will be nearer to Willem than me. The Rhine is in Germany and Germany borders with the Netherlands.

Friday 26 October

I woke this morning to a moment of terror. My name was being called and it sounded like Celestial Moonstone's voice. When I half lifted my lids, my heart pounded. Two long black-shrouded figures, one several inches shorter than the other, were standing on the far side of my bed. In another blink, they became my dressing gown and my open closet door. I've put it all down to sleep deprivation, like jet lag. Just night wear from tiredness. My room was semi-dark, it was early dawn and the shadows of my dreams must have still been dancing in my mind.

Last night, when I told Kaleen about the Ganymede problem, she suggested hiding Ganny at Old Ma Izzy's, which is what I'd first thought of doing too. I'll be working for Old Ma Izzy tomorrow, so I'll ask her then. I'm hoping RP will be able to stay tonight and can come with me.

I've just got back home from waiting for the bus. God knows what's happened to it. I couldn't wait any longer. I sweltered in our tiny tin bus shelter for over an hour. But it didn't turn up.

In Spider Johnson's clown days (now gone), it wasn't unusual for the bus to be two hours past the pick-up time. One of the bus drivers had the policy of stop-the-bloody-bus, in an effort to sit out Spider Johnson's antics. Secretly, I think Spider got off on the power of making the bus late for school. But since Mr Moonstone took over, the bus has been on time, apart from the odd morning or two.

I get on my laptop (Danny's gone to work, so he's left his computer on), check my emails. There are three from RP, one from her computer, sent last night, and two from the school's computer, sent earlier this morning. She must be updating their website.

Rosypoot14 to BrownVelvet sent: 10.09 p.m. Thursday 25th

Hey Vel, I've been thinking. Why don't we take Ganymede to Old Ma Izzy's place? Talk tomorrow, RP.

Integracollege to Brownvelvet sent: 9 a.m. Friday 26th

How come you're not at school? Are you okay? RP.

Integracollege to Brownvelvet sent: 9.22 a.m. Friday 26th

Scrap that last email. Just found out the bus has broken down. Hope you're not stranded on it somewhere. See you when you get here, RP.

ps I have frogs.

That was sent nearly an hour ago. I sit back in my chair, puff air through loose lips. Well, at least I know now why the bus didn't get to my stop. It broke down before it could.

I send an email to Rosemary telling her I won't be at school today. I also tell her I wish she had an iPhone, so I could ring her.

In less than five minutes, I have a reply.

Integracollege to Brownvelvet sent: 10.26 a.m. Friday 26th

Sorry about no iPhone. I'll be home at lunch, I can ring on the landline then. RP

ps does this mean I have to eat both the frogs?

Before I can reply another email pops up.

Integracollege to Brownvelvet sent: 10.29 a.m. Friday 26th

Only joking about the frogs. I wouldn't be that greedy. RP.

I give a chuckle. RP does have a funny side, but she doesn't show it very often. Nothing much to laugh at in her life, I guess, unless you're into extreme black humour.

I collapse on my bed, half close my eyes, feel the room swinging around me like I'm on a carousel. I shut my eyes tightly and the sensation disappears. I see an ocean of blue, concentrate on that and will it to green and then to red. A colour meditation. I'm so exhausted I'm semi-drifting to sleep. A picture forms, clear and concise like a deep pond on a still day. Willem is with me and we're having a conversation.

It's one I remember so well. I hadn't laughed so much for so long, even being grounded at the time hadn't mattered.

'Tell me, Velvet, more of de English language. Seeing I have been telling you de Dutch words for different tings.'

I smiled at his accent and he smiled with me.

'Bloody T-aitches,' he said, as he tried to bring his tongue into position behind his teeth, like I'd shown him to do. Then he laughed, scooped me into his arms and kissed me long and hard.

When he released me, I asked him what he wanted to know.

'Something I read about, Velvet – de Second World War. What is propaganda?' Before I could answer seriously, his face lit up like a candle. 'So, im-propaganda, is dis being a wayward goose?' he said.

I doubled up with laughter. And then when he asked about propagate, I knew for sure he was having me on.

'A gate propped up?' I offered.

His eyes sparked, 'Im-propagate,' he said, 'a gate having no fences.'

I wake to my phone skittering along my desk powered by the buzz of a new text message. Willem? I snatch up hope even in the face of improbability. The feeling escalates a tingle all the way down to my toenails.

But it's only a message from school. The bus will be picking me up in ten minutes. Crap. I skid from my bed and grab my bag. The shed bus stop is a kilometre from our gate; our gate is about three hundred metres from our house. I do the maths. I'm going to have to run. Fast.

I get there just as the bus is coming around the bend. A haze of heat lifts from its dark painted roof and I can see the large dent of a recent impact on its fender. Probably a roo. Poor thing.

I'm the only one on the bus. So it's Mr Moonstone and me. I find out the other kids were picked up by their parents after it hit an emu. I was wrong about the species, but right about the roadkill. I only make it to the front seat before the bus takes off again. That's when I ask Mr Moonstone what happened and he tells me how this group of emus crossed in front of him from nowhere. He managed to miss them all, but then this straggler came and…he moved his hand off the steering wheel in a dismissive gesture. The radiator was smashed and it took two hours for another one to be brought from Adelaide.

I keep looking at him. At one point our eyes meet briefly in the rear-vision mirror before his move back to the road. He seems fine. Absolutely nothing monsterish, and his aura is non-committal. Brown, but soft, with pinkish edges. Maybe it's only his kids who are…what? I really have no idea. I turn away and look down my legs to the dusty floor of the bus, notice my shoes, and feel mildly shocked when I see they're mismatched. I sigh loudly. At least they're both black.

We get to school at lunch hour, so I don't have that embarrassing moment of entering the classroom with everyone going quiet as they look at me. Rosemary Pooter has already gone home, and is probably trying to ring my landline as I think, I don't have enough credit on my phone. I get my allowance tomorrow, although the way things are going on the home money front I'm not even sure about that.

I leave my bag in my locker, take my lunch and fast leg it to RP's. I'm glad it's so close. I knock softly and after waiting about five minutes I'm almost about to knock again when Rosemary opens the door. She has a slap mark on her right cheek and she's carrying a tissue. When she sees me there, her eyes open wide and her hand dashes to the mark, like it's magnetised. Her palm only covers half of it.

'Bus turned up,' I say, as I enter.

I notice a plate with one frog cake sitting there on the table, another frog peeping out candidly from a white paper bag. Seems sort of cruel to eat them. Had she taken these without asking? Again? Is that why Mrs Pooter hit her?

RP sees my look. 'That's yours,' she whispers, indicating the peeping one. 'It's okay. Honestly. Mama said we could have them.' She clears her throat. 'I felt so awful when I stole the other two. I'll never do that again.'

Stole? Once again, I wouldn't have stuck that word to it.

I point at her cheek. 'What happened?'

RP shakes her head and I know better than to keep asking.

After I eat my sandwiches (fritz again) and my frog, RP leads me into her bedroom. On a small table, she's set up our old computer. It's humming smoothly along, and I'm amazed at how fast it brings up the pages. It never did that for me.

'Look, Vel, I've found that Arabian stud farm. I typed in Ganymede's sire's name and came up with this.'

'Arabian Antiquity Arabs,' I read. 'The world's oldest and best bloodlines.'

It's a beautiful website, as glossy and shiny as their horses. They have five stallions standing at stud, with the fees ranging from high to humungous. Tareek Hazzan's is the latter.

RP touches the screen. 'What does LFG stand for?'

'Live foal guaranteed. It means if your mare doesn't get pregnant you can bring her back to the stallion until she does. Or if she slips the foal early, you get a free service.'

'Does service mean… You know?' RP's face flushes. It reminds me of Coral Lee's lipstick.

I giggle. 'Best job in the world, being a stallion.'

Back at school with English lit up next, I start to relax, until I see we have a relief teacher. Damn it, no quiet lesson today. No chance to write any more about Jonathan L Seagull. When we have a relief, the other kids always take liberties and go feral, especially if it's one of those teachers fresh out of college and wet behind the knees when it comes to any sort of class control. I'm right, too; the teacher can't even hear herself talk. I bury my face in my book and try and block out the noise. Then I feel a tap on my shoulder.

'Velvet? Velvet Brown?' the teacher says, tracing a line in the printout she's holding and looking almost apologetic for interrupting.

'Yes, that's me,' I say. I don't know her name. I couldn't hear it when she introduced herself.

'It says here you're down for remedial reading. You have to report to Mr Franco's, room 12.'

For a moment I can't answer. It must be a mistake. It has to be. I've never had problems with reading, or English. Different if it'd been maths.

The teacher has already turned away before I stutter out my protest. She shakes her head, she can't hear me. I shrug defeat, pick up my books and head out. Anyway it's bound to be quieter in room 12. I can explain the misunderstanding to Mr Franco and then maybe I can get some work done.

As I enter remedial reading, all the students look up and scan me from head to foot, like I'm an alien. A lot of the kids look like Ralph from *The Simpsons*.

Mr Franco won't listen. He shows me the computer printout and my name, dragging his finger along it so I read it with him. I realise I'm drawing the words out, like a learner reader, Vel…vet…Brrr…own, thus confirming his assumption. Oh, crap.

'Check my assignments for English lit,' I say feebly, before I slump into an empty chair nearest the back.

Halfway through the lesson, minutes before it's my turn to read aloud *The Hungry Caterpillar*, Mr Franco dismisses me. (He must have checked my records.) No apology, nothing.

When I get back to my class, the din has redoubled. There are even sounds like breaking glass, although I know one of the boys can fart like that.

I'm definitely not going back in there. I flop down on the time-out bench, outside the door, and manage to scribble a few more notes before the siren goes for afternoon recess.

'What happened to you, Vel?' RP asks, when we're sitting at our spot under the trees. 'How come the teacher made you leave? You weren't doing anything wrong.'

I explain it to her.

She nods, her head bobbing. 'I think it's got something to do with the school's computer system, Vel. That's what I was working on this morning. It's been having glitches. Nothing catastrophic, but things like what happened to you today. Like yesterday one of the new student teachers had trouble with the class layout. You know how they get a seat and name pairing chart printout, so they don't have to learn all the kid's names straight away?' She pauses for breath, then continues without waiting for affirmation. 'Well, it was all mixed up. Pretty embarrassing for the poor teacher, especially when she started calling the girls by boys' names.'

I look up sharply and see she's grinning. Another RP joke?

I grin back at her. 'Speaking of systems, RP, how's yours going? How's your mama? Do you think she'll let you stay overnight at my place?'

Rosemary Pooter's grin fades like *Alice in Wonderland*'s Cheshire cat. She shakes her head, chin dipping. 'No way. Sorry, Vel.' She creases forward, touches her cheek.

I don't think she knows she doing it. It's still an angry red. We sit in silence, watch two groups of guys kicking a footy across the oval to each other. They're screaming 'Over here. Over here,' along with their names. Funny what some of them are called. No wonder the teacher was confused. Maybe Rosemary Pooter wasn't joking. It's hard to tell with her. Although I'm just glad it cheered her up a bit.

After school, I catch up with Rosemary, but only for the time it takes to say 'See you next week' and 'I'll ring you', before the bus comes to carry me home.

Saturday 27 October

I wake to an anticipation which seems to have put the bull ants in second place. What my stomach contains now I have no idea. I don't even feel hungry like I normally do in the morning. I've slept well enough though, but it was one of those sleeps where it feels like you've died, it was so deep. God, is it like that for Willem? I clench my hands and open my eyes. No shrouded shapes this morning, thank goodness, and I'm determined to keep 'positive and strong', like they say in Mum's self-help books.

Rita Skyped me again last night and we chatted for hours. She's much better at speaking English than writing it. There's still no change with Willem, but he's stable. So I'm sticking my hope to that. She's going to try and sneak her iPad into ICU and take some pics to send me. I'm not sure if she should do that. For one thing, they have reasons for not allowing electronic devices (other than medical ones) into those places, and also I really want to remember Willem how I last saw him. Smiling and well and waving me goodbye. I choke back tears. Maybe just one pic.

Over breakfast, Mum breaks the news about my pocket money. There isn't going to be any. Not this week and maybe not next week either. She's taking her car in for repairs this morning and has no idea how much it's going to cost. Danny has offered to bring her back and take her in again when it's been fixed. He's been wonderful lately. Now I look at him, his aura has way improved and his monster shadow has all but faded. I skim a glance over at Dad, but no such luck. Still a Category Four.

I flash Danny my simpering sister eyes. 'Could you drop me off at Old Ma Izzy's?' I say, my lip at half-pout.

He tosses me a mock shock look in return. 'What am I?' he says. 'A bloody taxi? It'll cost you,' he adds, with what I know he calls his boyish leer.

I smile, sigh and withdraw my previous thoughts about him improving. Still, petrol is pretty expensive. Anyway, I can afford it. I have the ticket money and my last wages from Old Ma Izzy, and she'll pay me for this weekend as well.

I'm looking forward to riding Zeus again. I've talked to Old Ma Izzy on the landline and she's been riding him every day, so he's bound to have improved a lot. She's been wonderful too, helped me so much with her amazing insight and ways of coping, when I first told her about Willem's accident. She was the one who taught me how to 'colour meditate'. I think of the lovely mind-picture conversation recall I'd had earlier of Willem. I'm not sure what I'd do without Old Ma Izzy. She's been my rock.

I haven't told Mum anything, not even how much in love Willem and I are. OMG, I almost wrote 'were'. Mum knows nothing about Willem crashing his bike, or the coma, or Rita Van Den Hoven. Zilch. It's not that I don't like confiding in Mum, it's just that she has enough to worry about lately. Dad still out of work, a broken-down car and bills mounting up. I heard her whispering to Dad the other night when I went past their bedroom door on the way to the toilet, about how the land and house rates were due next month. 'And Christmas coming up soon too,' I'd heard her say, when I came past again on my way back, her voice catching like the front door.

Saturday 27 October – evening

I don't believe it. Old Ma Izzy said no, she can't have Ganymede at her place.

I'm pacing my room in disbelief, or shock or something. I was so certain it would be okay for her to hide him in one of her many paddocks. I'm sure it's nothing I've done. After Danny dropped me off this morning, I got straight into mucking out the stables and even worked until noon on the riding yard. I actually got fifteen wheelbarrows of manure from there. Then I rode Zeus, a quick ride, no more than twenty minutes. Old Ma Izzy's told me young horses lose concentration fast, so the shorter the better. He went brilliantly too, no problems.

I was dying to tell her about Ganymede, but she was off fixing a broken post and rail fence, which a tree had fallen on overnight, and could only wave to me from afar. When she finally came back and called me in, I was like an overripe melon in hundred-degree heat, fit to explode. She made me drink some water and then settled back in her chair, letting me do all the talking, and only lifting her eyebrows from time to time or nodding. More than once she frowned deeply, especially when I told her about Ganymede's last owners and how he, and many of the other horses, had been treated. She even gasped when I told her about the electric shocks.

I was so convinced she was going to help, but when I told her what I wanted to do, bring Ganny to her place, she said, 'No.' And it was a definite, flat, take-no-argument-to-the-contrary type of 'no'. Over my lifetime I've had lots of those from Dad and Danny, and to a lesser degree, Mum, so I recognised the futility of trying to convince Old Ma Izzy to change her mind.

I couldn't talk after that; my throat had closed up somehow. I went out to the tack shed and oiled some saddles and bridles and then, before I knew it, the day had shot away and Mum was there to pick me up in her freshly fixed car. Old Ma Izzy didn't even come out to say goodbye, just called out 'Farewell' to us through her office window. She'd been inside, working on her computer all afternoon.

I have to go back to her place tomorrow. I promised I'd work for the whole weekend and I have to pick up my pay. Wish I'd thought of asking for what she owed me for today. Then I wouldn't have to go back.

I thump my bed with tight fists, but it does nothing for my frustration and shock. Why am I so surprised, I wonder. All bloody adults are the same. But now what the hell am I supposed to do about the Ganny problem?

Sunday 28 October

Not such a deep sleep last night. I glance over my bed, notice the top sheet has gone adrift and is tangled around my legs. Tossing and turning didn't come into it; more like storming and ranting. And, like the morning after a storm, I feel drained and washed out.

I haven't thought of a single thing I can do with Ganny. I'm also feeling mighty pissed off with Kaleen and although I know that's irrational, I can't help it. Why couldn't she be home? I've tried texting her to ask when she'll be back, but no answer. She's probably riding a camel to the pyramids. I can't ring RP on the landline yet; she'll be busy at least until lunchtime with her extra Sunday (to make up for the one she missed – even though she'd done catch up work last Monday) Mama duties. No day off for her.

Mum's offered to take me to Old Ma Izzy's. She doesn't want any petrol money. It's a sort of trade-off because she can't pay me my allowance.

I whiz around, putting sheets into the washing machine and vacuuming my room, even under my bed. I couldn't do my weekly chores yesterday morning, as Danny and Mum had to leave really early and I had to go with them if I wanted my lift to Old Ma Izzy's. The repairs cost a fortune and the mechanics found more things wrong with the car than Mum had first thought. Well, more than she knew about anyway. She's booked it into the garage again for next Saturday.

As I work, I come up with an idea. Not a good one, but it's worth a try. I'm going to plead long and strong to Old Ma Izzy. I may even squeeze out a few tears – always works on Mum. It will be easy to cry too, not much of a squeeze really. I'm virtually on the point of tears most days lately. I think of Ganymede, and his terrible scars, not only the visible ones. Then I glance over at the pic of me and Willem and feel the tears welling again already.

Mum drops me off at ten o'clock. It's a late start for me on a Sunday, and I'm surprised to see Old Ma Izzy's truck missing. She doesn't go to church, but maybe she's off picking up some horse feed or something. I know we're getting low on Founder Guard, the stuff we give the horses to help them from developing laminitis.

When I get to the back door, I notice an open notepad of the paper kind on the outside table. It's a letter to me. I pull up a chair and begin to read.

Dear Velvet,

I have to be afar awhile. I've seen Reuben. He'll be feeding up and looking after everything while I'm gone. I have no time to tell him of all things, but he knows we need more Founder Guard, which he'll purchase through the week. Could you fill in the details of feeds and et ceteras in this notepad, and leave it out for him, on the table.

I believe Zeus is ready for a longer ride. About an hour should suit him fine.

Many thanks,
Old Ma Izzy.

I read it through twice. My hand is shaking so much I have to put the notepad down and grab my hand with my other one, like someone who's got Parkinson's.

My mind is throbbing. I try to bring up the colours, but only strobe lights come, as jagged as the shapes of a Category One.

What's happened to this woman I know? Or obviously don't know. There's not even a mention about Ganny, or what I should do, where I should take him. Surely she doesn't think it's right for him to go back to his owners. It's so out of character for her to be this uncaring. I just can't believe it.

Reuben is Old Ma Izzy's closest neighbour, in distance and in kind. He has stallions too, Arabs and Quarter horses. Not in the same league bloodline wise as Arabian Antiquity Arabs, but still gorgeous boys.

Perhaps Old Ma Izzy is trying to tell me something with this line:

'I have no time to tell him of all things.' Does she mean for me to tell him, not only about the farm's running routine, but to ask him for help? Help with the Ganny problem?

My eyes scan across nature's palette of verdant pastures, grey gum trees and the cloud-clotted sky and my breath exhales with the calming of wonder. When I look down, I see my hands are no longer shaking.

After I've written down all the notes on the type of feed, and quantities, for the horses and the dogs (and the one cat), I saddle Zeus and lead him into the riding yard. For almost an hour I concentrate fiercely on figure eights, half-halts and backing up. In the end, I have him going from a standing position straight into a controlled canter. He's such a fast learner.

I'm so 'in the moment' (as Mum's self-help books also say) I only sink back to reality and the unsolved Ganny problem, after I've unsaddled Zeus and he's off free running again with Mercury.

When Mum picks me up, I get her to stop at the half-gallon-tin letter box that's at Old Ma Izzy's front gate. I'm hoping she's left my pay in there, but when I open the flap all I see is the resident daddy-long-legs spider curling up against the light and retreating backward as quickly as my hopes.

After dinner, beans on toast, and fruit for dessert, I ring Rosemary on the landline. I give her a brief run down on what's happened, try to keep the emotion out of my voice.

But she jumps headlong into the full flush of hers. 'I thought you said Old Ma Izzy was nice? Did you tell her about the electric shocks, the burns?' Her voice goes up like a scale with each word. Then she's almost screaming. 'Oh my God, Vel, Ganny was being tortured. Those cruel bastards. I can't understand why the RSPCA didn't find anything.'

I try to calm her down with soft words, but she won't be stopped.

'We have to get him out of there, Vel. We have to. Before they come for him.' She's crying now, sobbing into the phone like a child. 'I know what it's like,' she gulps between sobs.

I feel a chill rush down my body like a cold shower on a winter morning. I realise I've never seen any bit of RP's bare skin. Except for face and hands. Even on the hottest day, she's always wearing long-sleeved tops, or her old jacket. And she's never in shorts or swimming clothes. Could she have things she doesn't want me to see? Hidden scars?

I speak over her protests. 'Calm down, Rosemary. It'll all be okay, don't worry.' When she still continues, I play a card, one I hate to use, but for this shocked moment, I can't think of any other way to get her quiet. 'You don't want your mama to hear you, do you?' I say firmly.

The silence is instant. It's like I'd pushed the hang-up button.

When she finally speaks, her voice is thinner than a whisper. 'What if you take Ganny to your place? You could put him out with the sheep. It's a big paddock.'

I clear my throat. My heart is thumping and goose pimples prickle my skin like thorns. I want to scream at Rosemary, yell at her, 'What about you? What the hell is happening to you? You're equally important as Ganymede, more so. Ganny isn't in any immediate danger. You count. Your life counts and it's the only one you'll ever have.'

But instead, surprised at my own calmness, I answer, 'Dad won't have horses here. And the paddock's pretty bare. We've been hand feeding.' I hear a scraping sound like someone has slipped to the floor. 'RP, are you all right? Are you still there? You can always talk to me anytime, you know that don't you?'

'I know that, Vel.' She pauses.

I hear breathing and then, surprisingly, what sounds like a faint chuckle.

'Don't mind me,' she says, her voice quivering. 'I giggled because I was nodding. For a second, I forgot you can't see me.'

In more ways than one, I think.

I'm lying in bed, thinking back over the day, all the words spoken, written and unsaid. I think of Old Ma Izzy's letter to me. My eyes flick open. I sit upright. She signed herself Old Ma Izzy! She knows what we all call her and she doesn't mind! I lie back slowly, pull up my fresh, clean sheet around my chin, and put my judgement on hold.

Monday 29 October – evening

I couldn't write earlier, I've been too upset. This morning, not long before I had to catch the bus to school, Rita came on Skype. She was crying so much I found it even harder than usual to understand what she was saying. But I got the gist of it. Willem has got worse. Much worse and there has to be another operation.

I couldn't concentrate all day at school and RP was absent, so I didn't even have her to talk to. I went to her place at lunchtime but no one was home, or answering the door. So, I'm worried about her too, now. And I have a confession, about something I wouldn't have thought I'd do, although desperate times call for desperate measures. That's what Kaleen always says when her good-guy characters step a bit outside their integrity. What happened is, after school I stayed on the bus and got out at Kaleen's. I was going to talk to Coral Lee to find out if those people had rung back about Ganny. No one came when I knocked on the door, but it was open and I went in. (Kaleen always does this at my place – enters without being asked to – and she doesn't even knock.) I called out 'Coral Lee' and even tried a few 'Dwaynes' as well, keeping a question mark in my voice like I'd only just stepped inside.

In the hallway I saw the landline message bank flashing. Two lights. Two messages. I thought, What if one of those is from the investigators looking for Ganymede? Before I could stop myself, I'd switched it on.

As far as my recall goes, this is what the first message said, 'Hello, Kaleen? It's your Aunty Margie here. Look, I've lost those dates when you were supposed to come and stay overnight for the Agatha Christie play. I know it was in October some time. Really looking forward to catching up with you, and meeting your friend, Velvet. What a fab name that is. Anyway, give me a call back, my little mate. Love Ya.'

I smiled when I heard that. Kaleen's told me about her Aunty Margie. She was her father's sister, brought up in Australia when his parents divorced. Totally different from the rest of the Pingellys. Kaleen always calls Aunty Margie her 'rad aunt'. Rad, short for radical. And hearing her now for the first time, I had to agree, she seemed way cool. She was the aunty Kaleen had gone to stay with for several weeks after Kaleen's horse Holmsey was killed.

The second message was a cut-off sigh, probably a telemarketer after he realised he'd got the answering machine. It was then the full gravity of what I'd done hit me. What the hell was I thinking?

I ran out and almost crashed into Coral Lee and Dwayne coming around the corner of the house, wrapped around each other, and nearly as blind as I was to anyone else's presence.

I click onto my emails, see RP sent me one at 2.20 p.m. I open it, glance at the time, and dash to our landline. I get there a moment before it starts ringing.

'Oh, good, Vel. You got my email then? Seven o'clock's the only time I could ring.' She sounds breathless, like she's been doing the running.

I bring her up on the latest, try to keep the tears from my voice, but fail. After she hugs me with sympathetic words, I tell her about my telephone eavesdropping. I thought she might be shocked but her tone has a shrug in it.

'So, Vel, did you manage to ask Coral Lee? You know, about Ganny?'

'I did actually, and they've heard nothing, so that's good news.' I feel my heart rate drop when I realise this is true. It is good.

The trouble with me is when something frightening happens I tend to think the rest of my life will somehow fall into bad, but it never goes that way.

I tell RP I have to hang up, that I'm waiting for Rita to come on Skype to let me know how Willem's operation has gone.

When I get off the phone, I have a stabbing moment of reproach.

I hadn't asked Rosemary why she'd rung, or even why she hadn't been at school today. Damn it, I can't ring after eight, because of her mama's nap time, and it's fast approaching that now. I feel too drained to beat myself up further. She'll be at school tomorrow. We'll talk then.

Tuesday 30 October

This morning, Rita emails me the photo I was simultaneously dreading and hoping for. I print it out. It's of Willem, taken last night after he'd been brought back from surgery. He's attached to all these machines, one to breathe for him, a heart monitor, like you see in hospital dramas, and others I'm not sure of. Willem's as pale as the sheet that covers him and his eyes are closed. Rita's email said the operation was successful, but it was very bad. Her words.

I don't want to think what she means, but I know anyway. The next few days will be the critical factor. OMG, I want to go to him so badly, hold him, tell him I love him. I'm sure if I could just be there, he'd get better.

Mum finds me crying and asks what's wrong and do I want to miss the bus. It'll be here in ten. All I can do is show her the pic of Willem.

She takes it from me. 'Oh dear, that doesn't look good,' she says, handing it back. 'Who is he?'

Anger reaches my tongue and I almost scream, 'Willem! Don't you remember? You did meet him.' But I stop myself. What's the point? I could try and explain about me and Willem being in love, but nobody takes you seriously at fourteen…nearly fifteen. I know it's real, though, and deep as anyone's. Age doesn't come into it.

And what Mum has said makes me feel even worse. She knows when things don't look good. Working at the hospital, she's around sick people all the time and recognises the signs.

I have to run for the bus again and I nearly miss it. I wanted to really, but I'm also worried about RP. And there's nothing I can do at home.

During the trip to school, Kaleen sends me some pics. These are happy snaps of an impossibly blue river, the Danube. And photos of her parents, definitely in love all over again, to the backdrop of an equally blue sky. There's a message from Kaleen as well: 'Set off from Hungary yesterday, Vel, travelling through Budapest – will be in Germany in two days.'

Germany, a dart's throw from Holland. Maybe I could trade places with Kaleen, sort of teleport myself into her and she into me, and then I could go and see Willem. OMG, I'm jealous again, I can't help it. Why do we have to be so poor? If we were rich, I could convince Mum to take me there. Or I could go there by myself. Under-age travellers can travel abroad without an adult; you just need an adult's permission. It's bullshit about age anyway. In the nineteenth century, women were often married at fourteen. And had children. I do a double take, remembering what I recently read about the mortality rate of women in childbirth back then. Maybe the age law isn't so silly.

Or I could go there by myself. That line re-enters my head, but I squash it. Now who's being silly?

RP comes to school at lunchtime with her right arm in a sling. Pink plaster is visible through the loosely woven linen and her face looks nearly as pale as Willem's. We're heading back into class when she turns up, so I have no time to ask her how she did it.

At recess she tells me she fell off the sofa yesterday morning. 'So stupid of me, Vel, I was leaning over to get the remote and I overbalanced.'

It sounds so plausible I'm almost convinced. But while she's saying it she plucks at a blade of grass growing up against the bench. Avoids meeting my eyes.

I bet her mama has something to do with it. But I can't be sure and there's no way to make Rosemary Pooter tell me.

I show her the pic of Willem and she stares at it for a long time. When her eyes do meet mine, we're sharing tears again. I seem to have an endless supply lately and, looking at RP's eyes, I reckon they've been red for a few days at least.

'Vel,' she says quietly. 'I'm so sorry about Willem.' She hands me back the photo. Then she clears her throat. 'I know you probably don't want to talk about this now, Vel. But what are we going to do about Ganny? He's still a problem, isn't he?'

I'd forgotten all about him, and for a second I say nothing. She's right. Even though the investigators haven't been in contact, they could still turn up any day. Or at the very least, phone Mr and Mrs Pingelly and discover too much. And I can't keep asking Coral Lee if anything's been happening. She's going to get awfully suspicious if I do.

I blow my nose. 'I hadn't thought of it, RP. I've been too busy worrying about Willem. But you're right. We need to do something. And soon.'

We sit in silence, which stretches through the rest of recess. After school, it's the same thing. Then the bus comes and I have to go before we can work anything out. This is bloody ridiculous. I need to get control of my life.

When I get home I do the list thing.

The Ganny Problem

1. Do nothing and hope they don't come looking.

2. Hide his blaze – with boot polish or dye, like Reilly did.

3. Ask Old Ma Izzy's neighbour, Reuben, for help.

4. Bring him here and parentals be damned.

I like the last one. I'm still cross with Mum from this morning. And Dad – I've been angry with him long before this.

I send the list to Rosemary Pooter, ask which one she'd choose, and wait for a reply. After dinner of beans on toast again (gee, we are broke, bloody car), there are three emails waiting for me.

Rosypoot14 to BrownVelvet sent: 6.30 Tuesday 30 October
    Not sure. Which one do you like?
    ps I thought your dad wouldn't have horses at your place? RP.

Rosypoot14 to BrownVelvet sent: 6.31 Tuesday 30 October
    Oh, I get it – 'parentals be damned!' You'd do it in spite of them. RP.

Gee, I think, how did she type the email so quickly with a broken right arm? Then I remember Rosemary Pooter is left-handed.

Rosypoot14 to BrownVelvet sent: 6.40 Tuesday 30 October

I guess you're not at your computer, Vel. I've made a discovery on your old one. I found all those emails which had been hacked and forwarded, and would affect the recipients' computers if they opened the attachments. (Which of course I haven't.) They were in spam. And originally from – get this! – Celestial Moonstone! Don't ask me how I know, if you're not up to hearing a long explanation, which I know you love. (Sorry – my attempt at a joke. I know you hate that. Long explanations, that is.) Anyway, all I'll say is, it's to do with domain names and my access to the school's computers, which I'm pretty sure Celestial Moonstone's hacked into, too. That's why you were sent to remedial reading. She did it. It also explains all those other hiccups as well, computer-wise. And here's another shocker, though not surprising: I think Hanker Wanker's involved in it as well. I'm going to Mr Deangriss as soon as I have enough evidence.

Hope you read these emails, soon. Catch you on FB. RP.

I'm sure Rosemary's right about Hanker Wanker being involved. I remember how Celestial purposely brushed against him (it was so obvious) as he was being led out by the detectives. Maybe she slipped him a note or something.

I'm about to log onto Facebook when Mum comes in after a quick double knock. 'This came in the post for you today.' She holds out a small package, the shape of a book.

I take it from her, mutter 'Thanks' without looking up.

'Oh and Velvet, I'm really sorry about this morning, darling. I know who it was in the photo now. I remember. It was Willem, wasn't it? He was that lad who cycled here to see you sometimes, wasn't he? That exchange student staying at Brandon Quinn's place?'

When I only shrug she keeps trying. 'Came from Holland? Really polite, lovely accent?'

I look up, see Mum's expression, a mixture of confusion and contrition. Now I feel awful. How could I have expected her to recognise Willem, especially from that terrible photo of him in ICU? I get up and give her a hug. Tell her it's okay. I've forgiven her. She gives me a long hug in return, like I'm about to depart on an impossible journey.

After she's gone, I slump back in my chair and close my eyes. Another picture of Willem emerges as bright as any summer day. Us outside, under the ghost gum trees, Sebby at our feet. We've just given him the crusts from our picnic sandwiches. A breeze tickles up the back of my neck and I can feel Willem's hands on my shoulders as he gently straightens me towards him. Then he wipes some crumbs from my mouth and covers it with his. Soft but demanding. I feel my hands lifting up in real time, out towards the unknown. Oh God, Willem, will I ever see you again? Will I ever get to hold you like that again?

I open my eyes to the muted glow of my computer. I switch on my bedside light and unwrap the package Mum has given me. It's from Old Ma Izzy, a cheque with my pay (twice what I expected) and a book. A new diary. There's a blue post-it note stuck to the front cover: 'Thought you might be needing this. OMI.' (There's that reference to her nickname again. In an acronym!) I'm not sure if she means the new diary or the money. Although she'd be right on both counts.

This diary is nearly full, I've written in it so much lately. And I can always do with money. It's the same type of diary as this, too. It doesn't have individual dates, so you can write as many pages as you need for each entry. The front cover is a landscape print by Hans Heysen. Ghost gum trees, wearing distinctive spectral bark and olive-grey leaves, filter the hazy light from the baking Australian sun. It's so familiar, the only thing missing is Sebby.

I check out the empty wrapper. The postmark is dated Monday 29th Oct 9.25 a.m. Ceduna PO is stamped above it, in a half curve of red ink.

I look Ceduna up on Google maps – it's over seven hundred ks west of here. That's a long way from home. Old Ma Izzy must have driven all day Sunday to have sent it Monday morning. She must be in a hurry. I can't imagine what for. Or what was up to make her leave with no explanation to anyone.

I log onto FB and Rosemary. We message each other back and forth like ping-pong. I ask her if she thinks Kiss is involved with the hacking. She doesn't know for certain. All she can come up with is probabilities. I talk about Willem. RP talks about her mama and the district nurse. And her broken arm. I talk about Willem again.

Before she goes, I tell her something else I just thought of. Something we could do about the Ganymede problem. She doesn't write anything more, but sends rows and rows of smiley faces.

Tomorrow's the day we roll my plan onto wheels, and it looks like RP's definitely on board.

After I've logged off, I make one phone call, have a heart to heart with Mum over a cup of hot chocolate (no marshmallows) and then slip into bed, perchance not to dream. Sorry, Shakespeare.

Wednesday 31 October

Kaleen texts me through the night, early morning to be exact. She can't seem to get her head around the time differences. She doesn't mind that I'd listened to the phone messages at her place. Says she'd do the same thing in my position. Then she tells me she's going to text her Aunty Margie and let her know what's happened. I text back, 'Don't expect her to answer, it's 2.20 a.m. over here.'

After Kaleen goes, I can't sleep. It's so hard to stay positive when faced with things which seem unsolvable. I turn on my bedside light, read *Jonathan Livingston Seagull*, wish for my own terminal velocity in problem solving, and fall asleep for what seems like only minutes before the alarm's ringing for me to get up again.

Over breakfast, Mum pats my arm and smiles at me as she passes by with more toast for Danny. Dad is dressed to the max today. Tie, suit, the works. He's got an interview in town at the same place Danny's employed, Canny Cars and Supplies. Run by a Scotsman, Mr McManus, so the pay's not high. But he's a great boss to work for, Danny tells Dad through a mouthful of toast. 'Always telling jokes and stories. Cool as.' Back in Scotland, Mr McManus was into the caber toss and all things Scottish, like bagpipes and thistles and such, so I can just imagine.

Dad doesn't look too keen. He's hardly touched his toast. But with Dad out of the house, it works way brill for me, with what I've planned. And because Danny's giving Dad a lift in (Dad's car's still not fixed) Dad will have to wait until Danny finishes work for a ride home. So he'll be gone all day.

I pack my bag with my lunch and, at the right time, rush off for the tin bus shelter. When I get there, I hide behind it and wait until the bus passes. I check my watch: still twenty minutes to go before the house is clear. Mum's working double shifts to make up for her weekend off, so she'll leave even before Dad and Danny.

Kaleen and I painted the bus shelter two years ago in some leftover black and white paint. It was Kaleen's idea to go with a piebald design. She was reading Stephen King's *Lisey's Story* at the time. Brilliant book (I read it after she'd finished) full of unforgettable stuff like the Long Piebald Boy, which was her inspiration for the shelter shed. The bus drivers like it too – it's hard to miss.

I trace my fingers around the large black patches, see the paint flaking off and make a mental note that we need to fix it up soon. I'm deliberately trying to live in the moment (another suggestion in Mum's self-help books). And it works until I think of Willem. I glance at my watch, breathe deeply and slowly through my nose and start to walk home.

When I get back home, Mum's and Danny's cars are gone, so I find the spare house key in its hidden spot and go inside. Luckily Danny's left the modem on again, so I'm able to boot up, log onto FB and send Rosemary Pooter the 'all clear' message. She's hiding in her house until she hears from me. Mama Pooter stays in her own bedroom all day, and always has the door shut, so it will have been easy. But I need to get RP out of there. The district nurse, Jenny, comes at ten. She's coming every day now, since Rosemary has a broken arm and can't do any Mama duties.

After RP acknowledges my message, I ring a taxi to bring her to my place. I get the same driver who brought her before, so he knows the way.

While I'm waiting, I find my old riding boots. They're too small for me but should fit Rosemary fine, may even be a bit big, but double socks will fix that. I fill four bottles of water and put them in the freezer to get really cold, and find some sugar cubes and a half packet of Polo mints at the back of the cupboard. Mum's run out of carrots.

RP dashes around to me after she gets out of the taxi and I'm paying the driver. (I'm using some of my Spirit fund.)

'Careful of your arm,' I say, putting mine out to steady her.

'Nothing wrong with my legs,' RP says, smiling, as we enter the house.

The coolness hits us like air conditioning. Our farmhouse has thick walls.

I grab a large bottle of sunscreen from Danny's room. Not sure why he had it – he rarely goes outside.

'Slap this on any bare places. It's going to be bloody hot today.'

Rosemary takes the bottle from me, puts it on the counter and pumps some of it into her free hand. She rubs it over the only bare places she has – her face and neck and the back of her hands. 'Thanks so much, Vel, for paying for the taxi. I'll pay you back.'

'No need,' I say, wondering how she'd be able to pay me back if I'd wanted her to. I've never seen her with any money of her own. Then I think of RP's system and grin, maybe she could've. If she could get any of it from her mama, that is.

I rub the sunscreen over my arms and up and around my neck. 'By the way, RP, how is the system going?'

Rosemary inhales sharply. 'Not good, Vel. Well, it hasn't for the last few days. But it seems to be kicking on track this morning. When I was hiding in the kitchen, I could hear Mama cheering.'

I hand RP the riding boots. Her face lights up in a huge smile. They fit her well and with our backpacks full of bottles of water and sandwiches, we head off to Kaleen's.

I've put a cushion on my bike-carrier. I'm giving Rosemary a lift there. It's a bit hard starting the bike off but she doesn't weigh much, so once we're rolling it's a breeze.

RP holds me around the waist with her good arm. 'How did it go when you called Brandon last night, Vel? Did he say he'd help?'

'Sure did. And with follow-up stuff too.'

I feel her relax. Her grip loosens. I pedal harder. We have a long day ahead, and time, as Kaleen would say in her crime writing, is of the essence. Never really understood what the hell that means. Perhaps there's not much time and it's important.

When we get to Kaleen's, I'm relieved to see the stockmen and the other stock horses, Topper and Cody, are off somewhere. I think they're drafting the calves from the cows today. Ganny has been left behind, as usual. I give him a sugar cube over the fence.

RP scratches him on his poll, the forelocked lump between his ears. 'How come they can't use Ganny, Vel?' she says quietly. 'I mean, I know you said he won't let them ride him, but what does he actually do wrong?'

'The one time I saw them trying to saddle him up, RP,' I say, 'he was spinning around and rearing. Mainly they can't get near him, you know. To catch him even.' I give Ganny another sugar cube and, as he stretches out to take it, I lean over, rub him on the shoulder and slip a long piece of binder twine around his neck. 'The stockmen don't like mucking around with treats or anything. They have work to do, and hate any of this sort of nonsense.'

'So they'd rather not catch him, then?' Rosemary asks, shaking her head in disbelief.

'Old Ma Izzy believes in it, though, RP. Giving horses treats, especially in the training. And not just yummy stuff, but letting them have a rest or rubbing them on their sweet spots. That's a treat for them too.' I climb through the fence and scratch Ganny on the withers.

'He likes it here as well,' RP says, rubbing him on his poll again. She pauses. 'Anyway,' she says, 'it's no wonder he's so touchy, with what he's been through.'

I can see from here that her eyes are filling up. I push out my businesslike voice. 'Let's get this show on the road. I'll give you a lesson on riding with one hand. It's called neck-reining and Spirit's a master at it.'

The next hour is spent riding in the undercover arena. RP is even better than the last time. Her balance is rock solid and Spirit's taking even more care with her. It's as if he knows she has a broken arm. I'm riding Ganymede. He's fine too, a bit stiff, but he soon relaxes. All of the Polo mints and sugar cubes are gone by the time we've finished.

'Gee, Vel, if the stockmen could see Ganny now, they'd be way shocked,' Rosemary says, looking at me, with a touch of hero worship in her eyes.

It does feel awesome. But I can't take any of the credit really. Before Reilly did a runner, he'd done tons of work with Ganny. He understood his sensitive ways. And I have ridden Ganny before, to Old Ma Izzy's, when we first got Spirit. It was when no one knew who Spirit belonged to. Funny, she let him stay there. But I suppose he wasn't a fugitive, like Ganymede. A stolen horse. Although I call it saved.

Ganymede's probably not his real name. Reilly changed his own name, so he would've been sure to change Ganny's as well.

I leave a note for the stockmen, informing them that Kaleen has asked us to move Ganny to another paddock. And it is the truth, but not where they think he'll be. The Pingellys' farm is huge and there are heaps of paddocks. Kaleen's parents don't believe in overstocking, so lots of the paddocks are empty for most of the year. Not that we're taking Ganny to any of those.

Once we're actually on the road, RP is full of questions. 'So, tell me again, Vel, what's this place like? And how far exactly? And how will we look after Ganny once he's there?'

I answer the last question first. 'Brandon will check on him. That's what I wanted to tell you. He passes by there every day on his bike training route.'

RP looks up, eyebrows raised. 'So what's it like? How far is it?'

'Not far really. It's the old abandoned farmhouse and paddock where Kaleen and I hid out when we were being chased by that four-wheel drive I told you about.' I gather up my reins as a truck comes rattling past, but Ganny ignores the vehicle and trots on. 'We went back there last month. Found a shorter route. Had to cut through some farm properties, though. Not that anyone minded.'

Rosemary pushes Spirit into a canter and I give the leg aid for Ganny to canter as well.

I come up alongside them. 'Should take us about two hours. If we keep up a good pace.'

When we get off the main road, most of the laneways have gum trees shading them and the first farm we cross through has water, so we give the horses a drink. I feel the water temperature in the trough. It's not too cold, so the horses shouldn't get colic. We dismount, have a long drink from our water bottles and, even though we're miles from anywhere (no houses in sight), we still go behind some bushes to have a pee.

I get out our sandwiches.

RP lies back on the grass, her slinged arm across her chest. 'I love this so much, Vel. Who'd have thought I'd be out here riding like this? And with such a great friend.'

She looks at me with open eyes. Those blue, blue eyes, like Willem's. I sigh and turn my head away.

'Oh, Vel, what is it? What's wrong? What have I done? I'm riding okay, aren't I?'

I tell her of course she is and then explain how her eyes remind me of Willem's and how I so want to go to him that it's burning me up. Killing me inside.

'Why don't you, then? Go to him,' she says softly. 'Do you have your passport?'

I nod. But can't speak. Oh God, if only I could go. See my Willem again.

'Did you know I have a passport too, Vel? We used to visit Dada in Israel when he got leave. We weren't always poor.'

'That's the thing, RP. Money. Or lack of it. And anyway, Mum would never let me go by myself, even if I did have the airfare.'

After we finish our lunch, we remount and set off once more. It's such a lovely ride. The horses are fine, more than keen to canter when we ask, and not at all fazed by the heat.

We reach the old farm after one o'clock. Brandon's there already. Waiting. He's leaning up against the gate, the one without fences. I think of Willem, his play on words about im-propagate, and I smile. Brandon has his hands behind his head, and his bike, the heavy-duty one, is on its stand beside him.

'You skipped school too, then?' I say, bringing Ganny up to where the fence should be.

'Nah, not really, more like a day off. Finished all the exams. Well, we Year Twelves have. Off to Schoolies in two weeks. Victor Harbor. Not far to go.' He laughs and we laugh with him.

He scans his arm in a wide arc. 'This place is pretty run-down.' He points at the gate.

I can see either side of it, trailing along in the dirt, the powdered rusted barbed wire like a ragged line of dried blood, of what's left of the fence. 'It's better in there,' I say. 'There's a proper paddock closer to the farmhouse.'

'Yeah, I've looked. I'm not impressed, though. I've fixed the fences a bit.'

I shrug. 'It was the only place I could think of. And no one will find Ganny here.'

Brandon's voice drops to serious. 'How's Willem? Have you heard anything more?'

When I rang Brandon last night, I'd given him an update on Willem. Brandon was devastated and I felt terrible. I should have let him know a week ago. He and Willem had been great mates.

I shake my head. 'No change,' I say, my voice cracking. 'Still on the critical list.'

Brandon grimaces and rubs his eyes with the back of his hand.

I introduce Rosemary to Brandon. He tells RP that he's seen her around, at school. She blushes almost to the colour of her plaster and looks down at her free hand holding the reins. I see Brandon colouring up a bit too. Maybe the heat?

He strides over to help Rosemary off Spirit's back. She lets him, even though she's had no trouble dismounting with only one arm before. Then Brandon touches her cast, asks her how she did it. She tells him the same thing she told me. Leaning over to get the TV remote and overbalanced. Broke her fall with her arm. Another of her little jokes. Although she doesn't smile when she says it. It rings wrong about how she said she did it, but I can't figure out the tune.

And adding weirdness to oddness, today there's something I've never seen before in Brandon. It's like he's adrift. Sort of undone. Out of his comfort zone. He's nothing like when we were camping on TAOB. Then he was the classic Aussie bloke, full on bravado and balls. I recall the suggestion he made to me about his sleeping bag, how he'd warmed it for me and Willem, and feel my face heating up.

'Hey, Velvet. How's that mad friend of yours, Kaleen Pingelly, going? Miss her on the show circuit. It makes it easier for me to win, but.'

Now there's the old Brandon I remember. I tell him about Kaleen on her wonderful European river cruises. Then I mention how Rosemary has only been riding for a few weeks.

'Gee, you wouldn't know it. Bloody good seat.'

I swear I see a look of admiration glazing his eyes. Or is it something else? And Rosemary Pooter is staring at him, hanging on his every word. OMG, I think I need to talk to RP on our way home. We're going to double up on Spirit. RP doesn't weigh much. In fact, she's probably only about forty kilograms – wet.

We lead the horses over the non-fence, through the other gate, around the farmhouse and into the paddock. Brandon's done a top job straining the fence wires and he's even put some new hinges on the gate. It swings open easily when we enter. He's also fixed the trough and filled it, and several old buckets, with water.

'How does he go on his own now?' Brandon asks, as we remove Ganny's saddle.

'Fine,' I say. 'He's been moved to another paddock and he's been by himself all the time, so he's got used to it. Well, he tolerates it. Not like the stock horses, Topper and Cody. You can't take them out of each other's sight.' Brandon nods knowingly. 'Yeah, it's just I remember how Ganny was at my place, when you and Kaleen were doing – what did you both call it? – TAOB?'

RP speaks so softly I almost don't hear her. 'What's TAOB?'

'To Adelaide Or Bust,' Brandon and I say simultaneously.

'I don't like the bust bit,' Rosemary says, twisting her nose.

At that moment I can't help noticing Brandon's micro-second glance at RP's chest.

What RP lacks in height and weight, she makes up for in form. Her bust goes way beyond the training bra stage. It's well and truly accomplished. Even with her arm and sling in front of it.

I slant a frown in Brandon's direction. Maybe I should have a word with him. He is seventeen, after all, and should know better. OMG, I'm starting to sound like my mum. Eek!

There's enough grass to last Ganny for at least a month, and Brandon says he'll bring some supplement feed tomorrow.

'I have my driver's licence now, just need the car.' Brandon says with his famous heart-stopping grin.

It doesn't work on me. Willem's smile is miles better. Then I see it's directed at Rosemary and, by the look on her face, I may have to perform CPR very soon. Anyway, I reason, RP deserves some happiness. God knows she's had little of it, with her horrific Mama duties and how Mrs Pooter treats her. I look at RP's broken arm and again I wonder.

Brandon straps the wire-strainers onto his bike-carrier with a bungy line, then he stops, takes it off, turns around and places a hand on RP's shoulder. 'Hey, Rosemary, how about I give you a lift home on my bike?' He points to the wire-strainers. 'I can leave these until tomorrow when I bring the extra feed for Ganny.'

My mouth drops, but before I can protest, Rosemary has said yes!

I know I shouldn't worry really. Brandon's a good guy. But he's still a bloke and up until now, RP's led a pretty sheltered, although hard, life. I watch as Brandon spins her away, see RP holding on, over-tightly it seems to me, with her good arm around his waist. What the hell, she deserves a bit of happiness. I think of Rosemary Pooter's horrendous, selfish Mama and her awful flat. All that decrepit furniture. A vision springs to my mind of her main living room, her ancient 1950s kitchen, old sofa and matching TV. Immediately I think of what Rosemary's told us of how she broke her arm. I draw in a breath, shudder and feel cold again, and not because of the sudden cool change which has whipped up from the west. Those old TVs never had remote controls. Remote controls weren't invented back then.

After I've brushed the dried sweat off both the horses, I saddle Spirit, say 'Seeya' to Ganymede, and start off for home. I only look back once, but Ganny isn't bothered about us leaving, he's up to his knees, and the back of his teeth, in long green grass. I'm not worried about him foundering. Arabs are not so prone to it, thank goodness. All the same, just to be careful, I make a note to take some Founder Guard to school tomorrow, and give it to Brandon to mix with the supplement feed.

We make good time. The trotting jogs my mind back, down an old almost forgotten trail, although it was only earlier this year. Me riding Ganymede to Old Ma Izzy's. Kaleen atop Watson, blissfully unaware at the time that Ganny had been stolen – saved – and equally unaware how uneducated he was back then. Like Old Ma Izzy would say, greener than moss on a billion-year corpse. Actually, she really says copse, which is a sort of thicket or small wood. But Kaleen and I like our corpse version vision. Much more gratifying.

I hear Old Ma Izzy's voice. Those words she said to me about Ganymede the first day we arrived at her place: 'Take him gentle, this boy. He'll mean you no harm, but that doesn't mean it will not be harm he's taking you to.'

I smile and then feel my forehead creasing. The first bit I understand. Old Ma Izzy must have known even back then that Ganny had been abused. But what did the 'but that doesn't mean it will not be harm he's taking you to' mean? Maybe that I should be extra careful what I do regarding Ganny? I back-jog my mind over today. Everything seems so smooth, but when I get to what I did this morning, I fill my lungs and shout, 'Oh, crap, no! How could I have been so bloody stupid!' I squeeze so sharply with my legs that Spirit is soon galloping into the cooling breeze and we're skimming the kilometres to Kaleen's, as if we were airborne.

When we get there, I fling myself off Spirit's back and leave him on the spot, his reins dangling and him standing in mild amusement by the look on his long face. I dash over to where I thought I'd tied the note about Ganny to the fence, for the stockmen to see. For a breath-stopping flash, I can't see it. I can hear the stockmen approaching, too, whips cracking and dogs barking. The wind carries the deep lowing of the cattle still bemoaning the loss of their calves.

I find the note, snort out relief and crumple it into my pocket just as the herd, flanked by the two stockmen, riding Cody and Topper, comes into view.

I don't want anything to tack Ganny's disappearance to me. Chances are no one will miss him for ages. He's often out of sight behind the trees, but to make sure, I decide to do one extra thing. A sort of insurance to distance myself from any suspicion. The stockmen will be ages in the stockyards so, unnoticed, I slip into the tack shed, find the pliers and wire-cutters, the same ones Kaleen and I used on TAOB, and roughly bend and break some wires at the side of Ganny's paddock. It won't be easily seen, unless someone comes looking. Hopefully, if they do realise he's missing, it will make them think he broke out on his own.

I unsaddle and rub down Spirit once again, let him loose in his paddock with Watson, who's off his diet now, and soon I'm pedalling for home. Fear-driven energy moves my legs faster than anything fitness could do.

Tonight we're having cornflakes for dinner. Mum, face held in a look of abject apology, has promised us a roast tomorrow with all the trimmings, to make up for it. That's when she gets paid. There's a banana and some fallen apples for dessert. So the dinner almost manages the five food groups, except for protein. (And taste.)

When I log onto my emails, I find one from Rita. Although it's not from Rita, only from her email address. For a sec, I think, Oh, hell no, maybe Celestial has done her hacking thing. As I start to read, I begin to wish she had.

I finish reading, fall to the floor, curl in a ball, my arms clasping my knees. I rock and sob and chant. I can't believe it! I won't believe it. I won't believe it. Oh, bloody hell! No! No! No! NO! NO!

And this is all I'll have left of Willem? I stare at my computer through sheets of tears. This formal, cold, cold, bloody email? I'll never get to see him again, my Willem, my first and only love, not even one more time.

I pull all the bedclothes from my bed, sweep all my books from my shelf and throw my clown doll, the one Kaleen gave me, across the room. He hits the wall and lands in a heap of legs and arms, his head twisted, eyes at an angle. Mouth almost a leer. Some bloody useless friend Kaleen's been. Not here, but at this moment slinging down the river Rhine in Germany, a stone's step from Holland, sightseeing, having such 'a wonderful time' while my Willem is lying so close, so close, so close and dying, dying! There I've said it: the D word. DYING.

I'm on the floor again and Mum's come in and Dad's come in and Mum's holding me and Danny's whispering, 'What's wrong with Sis? What's wrong with Sis?' over and over and over until Dad takes him out and I'm left only with Mum.

Both of us on the floor now and me rocking back and forth, in her arms, crying and sobbing like I'd done when I was only five years old and had broken my ankle from falling out of the apple tree.

Email from RitaVHoven to BrownVelvet

Dear Velvet,

I'm Rita's English teacher, Hans Bennick, a friend of the family. I am writing this on behalf of Rita Van Den Hoven.

As you know, Willem is very ill and since the last operation he has been on the critical list. It is my sad duty to inform you that this Saturday at ten a.m., our time, due to the negative outcome of CT scans and extensive testing, Willem's life support machine will be turned off. After much soul searching, this is the family's decision and although I know how fond you are of Willem no correspondence will be entered into. Rita is too distraught to contact you personally, which is why she asked me to send you this email. I send my sincerest condolences and believe me I wish I had better news to give you.

Yours sincerely,

Hans Bennick.

31 October – late evening

Mum's gone off to bed after giving me one of her sleeping pills and a warm drink of milk. The house is silent and I'm feeling more drained than tired. Closing my eyes against the world, I bring the colours up, the blue first. It's not reluctant to come this time; must be the sleeping tablet. Now I feel a calm which goes beyond any drug.

I know what I'm going to do. I make a list in my mind. I can't afford to write this down where anyone could find it. I go over the list several times, the 'for' and 'against', and see the possibility of it. A few things will need working out, but I can do it.

And now, letting the warmth of my plans blanket my fears, I feel myself drifting off to sleep, the colours merging like a children's kaleidoscope.

It's as if I've just shut my eyes when something sits me upright in bed. I strain my hearing. Nothing but the outside sounds, merinos soft-baaing, a mopoke mopoking. Then a loud noise, a distinctive bleat from Sebby. Only Sebby. Probably calling to the sheep. That's what's woken me.

I sink back on my pillow, close my eyes. The room starts spinning. I shut my eyes tighter and pull the sheet up to my chin.

'Vel…vet,' my name, two-syllabled, like a broken hiss.

I sit up once more. I hear it again.

'Velv…et.'

I look at my cupboard, remembering the apparitions of the other morning. I turn my head towards the sound. It's coming from outside my window. Now I recognise whose voice it is. Rosemary Pooter's!

My legs are so wobbly when I get up that I have to grab the bedhead to stop myself from falling over. Bloody sleeping tablet. The floor bobs up in the moonlight towards my vision, up and down, like it's on a spring.

I close my eyes again and loud whisper back, 'Coming. Hang on a tick.'

I take a clearing breath, hold it for a second and force my eyelids to open. Everything has stopped moving. I've finally found my balance. Carefully sliding up the window, I see RP white-faced and dusty, smelling of perspiration and something else undecipherable, which wrinkles my nose. I open the window wider and, with my help, she clambers in.

'Oh, Rosemary,' I say, grabbing hold of her before she falls. 'What the hell are you doing here? Did Brandon bring you?'

I look at the dishevelled state of her clothes and imagine the worst. Has Brandon raped her? Oh, my God. The sleeve on her good arm has been ripped off and even in the pale moonlight I can see the blotches of bruising. Big finger marks. But way too big to be Brandon's.

I lead RP over to my bed and she sits down carefully, like it won't hold her weight. I give her a drink from my glass. Mum's put a jug of water on my bedside table like they do in hospitals. Rosemary sips it slowly and puts up her hand, tentatively, as if she's about to hail a cab. She swallows. Tells me she walked all the way here.

'What?' I almost shriek.

She covers my mouth, before it stretches too loud.

'Rosemary, that's over twenty kilometres!' I look at my clock. 'It's 2 a.m. You must've been walking all night.'

RP doesn't answer, but falls back onto my bed. Her sling slips away and I see writing on her plaster. Neat, black felt pen in manly script.

She becomes animated. 'I'm not going back home, Vel. No way. I'm bloody sick of her. The filthy fat, disgusting cow! I'd rather not have a mother.' RP's tone is straight and firm. No wavering lines.

I ask again what happened.

'Last night was it, Vel. I couldn't take any more. So I'm running away.' She takes another sip of water. 'I have run away. I don't care if I do get put into care. Anywhere is better than living with her.'

I'm speechless. But when RP asks if it's okay to stay the night, I whisper, 'Of course.'

I pull back the covers and she climbs into my bed and curls up. I slide in beside her, and RP begins to talk, to tell me her life, the one she's kept hidden for so long until now. Her voice stutters at first but finds clarity with trust. She's probably remembering how I've told her my innermost secrets.

Rosemary Pooter's life is far worse than anything I could ever imagine. No wonder she associates so strongly with Ganymede. Most of it is nothing short of torture. Cigarette burns are the least of it. Barbaric is the only word I can think of. Mama Pooter should be prosecuted. Strung up even.

Then I ask RP the question I already know the answer to, but not the details. 'How did you break your arm?'

'I didn't do it, Vel. Mama did.' There's a brief silence before she continues. 'It happened on Monday morning, after I emptied her commode. While I was washing her. I usually keep well out of her way when she's in the Mood, but she does this thing where I don't know that she's cross. She pretends she's not. That's what she does with everyone else, but all the time. Pretends to be so nice. And they buy it. They don't know her. And she's careful. Really careful not to be herself in front of others. Like the district nurse, Jenny.'

'She did it in front of me.' I stop and shiver. Recalling how she'd spoken to me. 'Didn't hold back when I was there.'

'That's because she regards you as a kid. Just like me. She's always telling me no one will ever believe me if I do tell anyone on her. Because I'm only a stupid, ignorant kid.'

I'm having the bull ants feeling inside my stomach again but this time they're on the warpath. God, I want to get hold of that woman and wring her bloody neck. Although my fingers wouldn't fit around it.

'If you're supposed to be so stupid, Rosemary, what about the system you made for her? That's nothing short of brilliant. She'd have to admit that.'

'The system's been part of the problem, Vel. When you asked about it yesterday morning, I played it down. Said it wasn't going too good. Actually, it's much worse than not too good. It's gone disastrously. Mama lost thousands over the weekend. Most of her winnings and then all of her pension. But I didn't know how bad it was until she got hold of me.'

'When you were washing her?'

'Yeah, she grabbed me as I was sponging her chest. Started screaming in my face how bloody hopeless my system was. How bloody hopeless and useless I was. How I thought I was so damn smart. And did I realise how much money I'd cost her? I tried to get away but she grabbed both my arms, stood up and spun me around. She's pulled one of my arms out before. You know, dislocated it.' RP begins to sob, silently like hiccups.

I pour some more water for her. She takes it and drinks it down in big long gulps. I wait, and after several minutes she starts talking.

'Then Mama lunged forward and deliberately fell on me.'

I can't help myself. Before I can stop the words, they jump from my mouth. 'Oh, my God, Rosemary, it's a wonder you weren't flattened.' I swallow back hysterical laughter. The sort you get when your emotions are stretched.

Rosemary sniffs. 'Luckily I managed to get out of her way and free one of my arms. This one.' She holds up her good arm. 'The other one wasn't so lucky.'

'What happened then?'

'She threw me across the room and then she climbed back into bed like nothing had happened.'

I'm stunned but, curiously, not surprised. Rosemary is shuddering again with those strange silent sobs. I'm betting she gets told off if she ever cries aloud.

I turn over, hold her in my arms, feeling for the first time how really thin she is, and wait for her to finish.

'Jenny, the district nurse, came shortly after. Found me on the sofa holding my arm and crying. I told her what I told you and Brandon, about the remote control thing. And she took me to the hospital.' RP shrugs. 'It could have been worse. I guess it could have been both my arms. Bit hard to explain then.'

I gasp inwardly. I can't believe how she's taking it so casually. It's as if she feels so worthless that what happens to her, however terrible, doesn't count for anything.

I ask the obvious. 'Rosemary, why didn't you say how your arm was broken? Tell someone, the doctor even?'

'Oh, Vel. Why would they believe me? Mama's bedridden, she can hardly walk. And you don't know how charming and lovely she is to other people.'

I hadn't seen that side of her. I'm feeling the exhaustion creeping back.

RP continues, her voice rising. 'Our family doctor, Dr Willits, put the plaster on and you know what he said?'

I shake my head.

'He said, "Rosemary, I hope you're being good for that wonderful mother of yours." And after he finished he frowned and sighed. "Try and keep out of trouble now. Your poor mother has been through enough. You're very accident prone." And then, Vel, because I must have looked shocked, he rubbed my good shoulder and added, "Don't worry, Rosemary. Lots of left-handed people are a bit clumsy." See what I'm up against, Vel?'

RP does have a point, but I can't stop. 'Why don't you tell someone who doesn't know Mama?'

Rosemary draws a deep breath. 'Mama said if I tell anyone, they'll take me away and I'll end up in a home for delinquent youth.'

I feel like bashing the wall, I'm so angry. I want to get hold of this woman, this Mama, and punch her to pulp. She should be in prison and that's what I tell RP. Then I ask her what happened tonight. Why she ran away? Why now?

RP's tone changes. 'I had such a brilliant, awesome day yesterday.

Until I got home. That lovely ride on Spirit. Rescuing Ganny. Meeting Brandon.' RP sighs, but it's not a sad sigh. 'Switch on your light, Vel. I want to show you what he wrote on my cast.'

I turn on my bedside light and RP thrusts her plastered arm at me. I hold it under the beam and read, 'I've known you a short while, hey girl, love your smile! Will see where it ends or begins, but let's start this together as friends. Brandon.' His mobile number was written underneath.

'He was great, Vel. Got me home on time and didn't even seem shocked to see where I lived. I was so happy and then Mama had to spoil it.'

'Did she find out you hadn't been at school?'

'No, not that. I rang up the school before you sent the taxi. I'm good at Mama's voice. It was the system again that set her off.'

I pause. 'But you said she was cheering yesterday morning.'

'Yes, Vel, but a day is a long time. Especially when you're gambling. You can lose a fortune in seconds. She had a big win in the morning, I was right about that, but began to lose steadily again, all afternoon. By the time I got home, she'd lost nearly all of it.'

'Why didn't you keep away from her?' I look at RP's ripped sleeve. She follows my gaze. 'Oh, this? No, I did this climbing through your fence. The front gate's locked. I didn't know where you kept your key.'

I chuckle softly. 'Dad's scared of rustlers getting his precious merino sheep. I'll show you where the key is tomorrow.'

RP closes her eyes, like she's reviewing the scene. 'Mama saw Brandon dropping me off on his bike. She ranted about me being a slut and a slag, and then got up and started sort of chasing me around.'

The image is too much, I laugh aloud. 'Surely you can outpace her?'

RP laughs too, and then we go quiet, hope we haven't woken anyone.

'Of course. Mama can barely walk,' RP says. 'But when she couldn't catch me and I wouldn't stop, she got so furious she threw her commode potty at me. It was full. Just missed my head. Splattered my leg.'

So that's what I could smell. Totally gross. 'Number twos,' I say, using RP's terminology.

'She wanted me to clean it up, Vel. Said if I didn't, she'd tell Jenny when she comes in the morning, that I made the mess. Threw the potty. Jenny thinks the world of Mama, she'd believe her over me.' RP stretches back in the bed. 'I tried to clean it up, but I kept dry retching and I couldn't. And you know what she said then?'

I shake my head again.

'She asked if I was pregnant. And then she screamed the most vile things about Brandon and me and what she thinks we did. I just couldn't stand it any longer. I had to get out.'

'Does she know you've gone?'

This time RP shakes her head. 'I don't think so. She was back in bed before I left.'

I tell RP about my plans, but not how ill Willem is. I don't want to lay that on her yet; she's been through enough tonight.

Just like the Ganymede plan, RP is totally on board and says she will help me in any way she can. And I tell her I'll hide her out for as long as it takes.

Watching Rosemary sleep, I start to wonder about myself. This ability of mine. What bloody use is it anyway? Why hadn't I seen Mrs Pooter as the absolute monster she is? Category One doesn't come into it. And there I have my answer! She's beyond my categories. Comes into a league all of her own. Psychopathic Sadist. (Maybe that's why I can't decipher Celestial. Perhaps she's more dangerous than I thought, too.) I mean, over the years I've realised that Category One Monsters are probably psychopaths (and evil lurks there – often suppressed) but I've learned not all psychopaths are intentionally cruel, sadistic or sexually bent. They lack empathy, that's true, but sometimes being unemotionally involved can be an asset. Like if you're a surgeon operating on a child for a brain tumour. And another one of their attributes is they feel no fear. So they make top public speakers, or intrepid adventurers. Nature has no waste. Although what she was thinking by creating the Mama Pooter types of the world, I can't begin to understand. Total waste of space. (And such humongous space too.) But does that mean anyone could be a Psychopathic Sadist? And that I'd have no more advantage than the next person in spotting them? I'd always thought my monster insight could at least help to keep me and my friends safe. Now, I'm less than sure.

A text message buzzes my phone and I retrieve and open it before it wakes RP. It's a message from Kaleen. No surprise there. She wants to phone me. I text back, 'Give me five minutes.'

I head outside. The front door begins to squeak as I open it, but luckily the fridge judders into automatic defrost or something and covers up the noise.

I race out into the paddocks, stare down Sebby, who opens his mouth in an aborted bleat, and skid to a halt behind one of the ghost gums. I hope I'll still have a signal.

I'm relieved when my phone begins to ring.

'Hi, Vel. It's me, Kaleen,' Kaleen says unnecessarily.

I tell her I know who it is. That she's the only one who contacts me at such early hours. And besides, she just told me she was going to ring.

'Oh, sorry, Vel. What time is it?'

'3.30 a.m.'

'Oh, frick, Vel. Sorry again. Listen, I'm ringing to ask you about Willem. How's he going? Is he on the mend? It's just that I have a few days away from the parents. Now I'm nearly fifteen, they reckon I'm old enough. Isn't that cool?'

I've scraped down the side of the tree. I can feel the smooth cold bark on my back, through my pyjamas. The ground is gentle beneath me with fallen leaves. Their soft crackling sounds like the cornflakes I had for dinner. Seems so long ago now.

Kaleen doesn't let up. 'I'm in Germany, just got off the river cruiser. Do you know they even had a heated swimming pool on board? Everyone goes topless in Europe. It's called being sophisticated. Anyway, I could go and see Willem and say hello from you… Are you still there, Vel?'

I grasp the phone so hard it almost squeezes from my hand. 'Can you be quiet for a second, please, Kaleen.' I'm louder than I expected and for a moment I glance back at the house and hold my breath.

Kaleen shuts up.

My voice breaks as I tell her about Willem and I'm surprised I still manage to sound coherent. But I feel outside myself, like it's someone else doing the narrating, some hidden hand feeding the words which are coming from my mouth.

When I finish, the silence continues and then I hear Kaleen sobbing.

The last thing I'd said was, 'They're turning Willem's life support machine off on Saturday, at 10 a.m. Their time.'

Kaleen clears her throat and blows her nose. Now it's her voice which cracks. 'Oh gosh, Vel, I feel so…helpless. I'm so, so sorry.' There's a caught sob before she continues, 'What are you going to do now?'

'I'm coming to Holland,' I say. I sound so definite I almost believe it myself. Regardless that it will cost over three thousand dollars, regardless that I have to get someone to sign an unaccompanied minor form.

Kaleen is elated. She takes it as a given that I'll be able to come. In her world, money is never an issue, and her parents have always been more liberal than mine with whatever she does. Or wants to do. She barely got told off when we went TAOB. I nearly got grounded forever.

And even if I can get the money, I know Mum will never sign such a form. One which sends me winging thousands of kilometres around the earth, to unknown people and a strange country. All by myself. I tell Kaleen about that, the money, the form and also about a handling advice document that I'd need too, for when I arrived. It had to have the details of the designated person, for the stewardess to hand me over to. And the designated person had to be fifteen or older. I'd looked all this up earlier when I daydreamed, pre-accident, of visiting Willem in Holland.

Kaleen screeches down the phone. I hold it at arm's length from my ear but still hear her clearly. 'I'll be fifteen on Friday, Vel. Remember? That's your tomorrow, isn't it?' she adds quickly. 'It's just gone Thursday there, now, hasn't it? 3.30 a.m., you said? Still Wednesday here.' Finally she seems to have a grasp on our time differences.

'Oh god, Kaleen. I'd forgotten all about your birthday. I haven't got you anything yet.'

'You did already, Vel. Those Agatha Christie tickets. It's not your fault I wasn't home to use them. And actually, if you remember, the tickets were going to be my early Chrissy present. You made me that beautiful framed photo of Holmsey and me for my early birthday one.' I hear her draw a breath and let it out slowly. 'Anyway, you coming here will be the best birthday present ever. And I can be the designated person and sign the handling form thingy.'

For several long seconds we lose connection. Then there are three loud beeps and we're back on line. Strange that.

We talk some more about logistics, both getting stuck on the subject of cost. Kaleen hasn't got enough in her bank account to lend me the money. She suggests asking Brandon. He makes heaps selling apps. It's worth a thought.

Then Kaleen says, 'What about Old Ma Izzy? She has money.'

I tell her what happened. How Old Ma Izzy has cleared off to somewhere. Last known destination, Ceduna.

'Gee,' Kaleen says, 'that's almost in Western Australia. What's she doing there? It's the last township this side of the South Australian border. We passed through it a few years ago, when we drove to Perth. I sent you a postcard.'

I know the one she means. It's of Western Australia's capital city, Perth, lit up at night. Dusk-purpled backdrop, beautiful, like a fairy dream. I still have the postcard, among many others from Kaleen's travels, pinned to the corkboard above the fridge.

As Kaleen says goodbye with a promise of ringing tomorrow, I swear to myself that soon there'll be one on that board from Willem and me.

Thursday 1 November

I can't sleep. I'm too awake and hyped up about my plans. I'm also wondering what I'm going to do with Rosemary. And I still haven't told Kaleen that RP and I have become such great friends. I have more things to worry about than that. Such as time being not just 'of the essence', but of the main flavour. It's Thursday now. I don't have long to get to Holland. Or the Netherlands, as it's called on the KLM airlines website.

I keep my laptop facing away from the bed so the light won't disturb RP's sleep, but I think she's so exhausted even Sebby jumping on her wouldn't wake her now.

When I feel my head nodding forward, I climb back under the sheets and wait for my clock to chime its get-up call.

I wake before it has time to make me. Switch the alarm off and, in case someone comes in, cover RP's face with the sheet. Just as quickly, I rip it back. It looked like she was dead. I couldn't stand the thought of that.

Mum won't come in anyway. Last night she told me to have today off. That she would ring the school from work and tell them I wasn't well. In case she does look in on me, though, I decide to make an appearance.

No prizes for guessing it's cornflakes for breakfast. I don't feel like eating, but I have a strange feeling I'm going to need my strength. I have a small bowlful with lots of sugar. I pick up *The Advertiser* (everyone else has already read it) and start scanning through the pages, so I don't have to meet anyone's eyes.

One of the headlines catches my attention. I sit up straighter and carefully fold out the page. Then I take it, and three slices of buttered toast, into my room. I tell Mum I'm going back to bed. She glances at Dad. They share a sad sort of knowing smile, and nod at me in agreement.

When I get back in my room, Rosemary's sitting up in bed, with an odd look on her face. 'I need to pee, badly,' she says to my uplifted eyebrows.

I tell her not long now and the coast will be clear. Even Dad won't be home. Mr McManus is giving him a trial run. Dad has Danny to thank for that. (Or perhaps hate for that, going by the heaviness on Dad's face.)

I hand Rosemary two pieces of toast and the newspaper page. She reads some of the article out in a whisper. 'Massive hack. Over 800,000 Aussies involved. Bankcard and credit card details stolen. Police fraud squad is investigating.'

'Do you think the hacker might be Celestial Moonstone?' I say.

'Wouldn't surprise me, Vel.'

There's a double-quick knock. It's Mum. 'Velvet, darling,' she says, through a tiny sliver of open door, 'I'm sorry to disturb you, but Coral Lee's on the phone. Something about a horse.'

RP sends me a look of anguish and dives under the bedclothes. I shoot out to the phone.

When I get back, Rosemary takes one look at me and asks me what's going on. I feel so out of it, it's as if my body has gone numb. Like someone's hit me so hard the shock has overcome the pain.

'That was Coral Lee. The investigators have been there. They're going to Old Ma Izzy's next, and then coming here to have a talk with me.'

'Why would they think he's there, Vel? Or that you're involved.'

When I tell her that Coral Lee said there was some sort of leak from someone, RP goes as pale as dawn on a foggy day. 'Oh, shit, Vel. I think that might be my fault. Remember how I emailed you about the idea of taking Ganny to Old Ma Izzy's? It could be possible that your old computer is still infected with the Celestial Moonstone Fungus. CMF. That's what I've named the virus.'

'So she would have read your email.'

It's not really a question, but RP nods. 'And also seen the Stud Farm page. I saved it to favourites.'

I hear our cars outside starting up their engines, like they're heading off on a slow race.

'Safe to go to the loo now, RP.' I follow her out. 'It's good that Old Ma Izzy did refuse to have Ganny at her place, isn't it? Do you think that in some weird way she knew?'

'Yes, Vel, I reckon she might have.' Rosemary turns round and comes back into my room. 'I don't feel like going to the toilet now. Scared it away, I think.' She grins, but my face refuses to reciprocate.

'They're calling the hacker the Cash Drain Worm. CDW,' I say, picking up the paper. 'Some people in Australia have lost all their savings. And they say it's going global too.'

'It could be Celestial and co. I think we'll have to be super careful from now on, Vel. Even on the phone.' RP is still whispering.

Instantly I remember the three beeps and how Kaleen and I had been cut off. I suck in some air and bite my bottom lip.

Rosemary brings her plastered arm from under the sling. 'We need to get out of here,' she says, looking at the mobile number written there. 'Time to ring Brandon. He'll pick us up.'

I touch her shoulder. 'No, RP, if we clear out, that'd look suspicious and then the Ganymede investigators might turn up at school looking for us.'

We sit for a few minutes and then both speak at once.

'You first,' Rosemary says.

I sink back onto the bed. 'I don't think I can face them, RP. I really don't. I mean, look at me.' I hold up my hand. The shaking would be visible across a football field.

RP grabs my hand and squashes the trembling. 'I can do it, Vel. I'll talk to them. No problems.'

I'm not convinced she can. I know how honest RP is. But I also know that the way I am at the moment, I'll appear guilty before I've even been asked the first question.

'I'll just pretend I'm in a play,' Rosemary says, over-brightly. 'And they'll believe I'm you. I mean, why else would I be in your house?' Then she pauses. 'Oh, I do need to pee now, Vel. Back soon.'

While she's gone, I find some clothes which I've outgrown. One of my old T-shirts and a pair of not too worn-out jeans. I lay them on the bed and head out to the bathroom for a quick shower.

After I've finished, Rosemary showers and while she dresses I find the printout of the last email I received from Holland, and slip it into my pocket. RP needs to know about Willem, but not until after the investigators have been. That awful email doesn't have any power over me like it did. Now that I don't believe it.

Sebby bleats. Who needs a watchdog when you have a watchgoat?

I hear a car purr up into our driveway. It sounds expensive.

I pull back the curtain a half a drape. Suck in air like a whistle. 'I think they're here RP. Okay,' I say, "Break a leg."' Then I remember Rosemary's arm and murmur 'Sorry', in case she hasn't heard of the old theatrical way of wishing good luck, and thinks I'm being mean. But she's already gone and now I can hear loud knocking on the front door, like someone's trying to break in.

I think of how good it was of Coral Lee to let us know. At least we have a fighting chance. Maybe she doesn't dislike me as much as I thought she did.

I can't get near enough to eavesdrop, but RP's only gone for about fifteen minutes before she strides back into my room.

A smile dimple in one cheek, she raises her arm like the winner of the Tour de France. 'I convinced them, Vel. I did. They now believe that I, and my friend, Rosemary Pooter, had nothing to do with the stolen horse,' she says directly at me. 'The missing horse by the name of Tareek Hazzan Desert Starlight. Ganymede to us. Not that they know that.'

Rosemary also tells me that 'they', the two private detectives that Arabian Antiquity Arabs Stud hired had been on the case most of the year. They'd been sceptical about the email from Celestial Moonstone implicating us but had to check out any leads. I guess her name is a turn-off in the believability stakes. Thank God.

Rosemary has blossomed overnight. She's taken fate into her own hands and made her decision. There's no way she's going back to live with Mama. And there's this strength to her now, as if she knows she needs to be extra tough for my sake as well.

I give her the email without any word of explanation and sit down at my computer to wait for her to finish reading it. I'm expecting the tears, but once again Rosemary Pooter surprises me.

'I don't believe this email, Vel,' she says, her tone resolute.

For a second, I don't answer. I think like it too – the email doesn't seem real – but to hear her say it aloud confirms my conviction. But maybe she doesn't mean it like I do.

'Do you think it might be a bogus one, from the CMF?' I say.

RP shakes her head. 'No, Vel, nothing to do with the Celestial Moonstone Fungus. It's just a feeling I have that Willem's going to be fine. I really think I'd know if there was no hope left.' I hear her swallow. 'That's how I felt with Dada. I knew he wasn't going to make it. I mean, I didn't want to believe it, but I knew. With Willem, it's different.'

I manage a smile. 'That's how I feel exactly, RP.' I drag my suitcase from under my bed. 'Right, I'm going to pack, and then could you ring Brandon?' I gather my courage. 'I need to ask him for a loan.'

RP grabs my phone. She lays it on the bed, lifts her sling and reads out the numbers on her cast as she presses the buttons. 'I don't think he'll be able to help, Vel. He told me something yesterday on our way home. He picks up his new car tomorrow morning. He's been saving for ages. Wanted to buy it outright. But I'll ask anyway. How much do you want me to tell him?'

'How much money?'

'No, how much of what you're planning to do, silly.'

I chuckle. 'Tell him everything. I need every friend I can get.'

While I'm getting all my clothes, my passport and spare cash together, I can hear Rosemary chatting away. She sounds way happy. To save my phone credit, Brandon has called her back, so it won't matter how long they talk.

I have two hundred and fifty-six dollars from the tickets and from working for Old Ma Izzy. Kaleen said she can pay for anything I might need when I'm there, like food, so that should be plenty.

I try to go online and get the forms, but I find I can't. Shit, Danny must have switched his modem off. He hasn't done that for ages. Must have read about the hackers in the newspaper.

I try once more. No luck. Damn it! I swear out loud and Rosemary, with the phone to her ear, comes over closer and mouths, 'What's wrong?'

I point at my laptop and the little computer icon with no blue balls, which means it hasn't connected to the internet.

She tells Brandon she has to go, says something I can't quite hear, then hangs up. 'It's okay, Vel. Brandon's coming over. He was on his way home from dropping off the supplement feed for Ganny. He's got the farm's tray top, says he'll be at our disposal. His words.'

I slump back in my chair and sigh. 'It's no good, RP. I might as well give up. I can't even get online to download the forms. Not to mention having no money for the airfares.'

Rosemary puts her good arm around me and gives me an awkward hug. She's still holding my phone like she's unwilling to let go of the last connection with Brandon. But when it buzzes its familiar frenetic tune, she jumps and drops it. I catch it mid-fall, see it's Kaleen.

'Hi, Vel, don't talk. I don't have long before I have to catch this ferry and I'll probably lose the signal. Everything's okay. I've spoken to Aunty Margie, she's more than willing to help. Insists on it, actually. Did I tell you she and my uncle Eddie were childhood sweethearts? They were married for over thirty years. She's never got over losing him. She so believes in young lovers.'

I hear a huge engine noise and a nasal-sounding horn.

'Blurry heck, Vel. The ferry's here. I gotta go. I'll text you Aunty Margie's phone number and address. Seeya.'

I've put my phone on speaker, so Rosemary has heard it all. She smiles and rubs my arm.

A few minutes later, the text message arrives, like a bow wave from the ferry.

I feel heaps better knowing that Kaleen's rad Aunty Margie wants to help. I give her a ring but only get her answering machine saying she can't come to the phone but will be available around five. RP makes a call too. To the school, explaining why Rosemary Pooter will be absent today. She's right, she does sound like her mama.

Not long after RP's call, Brandon arrives. A loud crunching up the driveway in the tray top. I wonder what sort of car he's bought. If all goes well, I won't be here to see it, though. I have to leave for Holland – the Netherlands – soon, if I'm to make it in time.

I pack some more of my stuff: this diary, plus my new one that I got from Old Ma Izzy, and the framed pic of Willem and me. Then we're off to town. Rosemary wants to stop at her place and go on her computer, sort out (eradicate) the CMF and get some of her clothes. Also, she's going to print the forms I need. She'll have under an hour to do it. It's five minutes past nine now. The district nurse is due at ten.

'What about your mama, RP? Won't she hear you?'

'She'll be dead to the world, Vel. I bet she's been up most of the night trying to win her money back. She's often asleep when Jenny comes. She has all sorts of trouble waking her. Anyway, I'll be quiet.'

Brandon drops us off around the corner from RP's flat. We sneak like criminals along the street. Rosemary sighs with relief when she sees Mama's blind is still down.

As we enter the flat, the smell hits me like a palpable entity. Something with a life of its own. Splattered shit coats a wall in a fantastic pattern.

I whisper-hiss, 'Oh, God, RP. Why didn't your mama clean it up?'

Rosemary shrugs and disappears into the laundry. She returns with a large bucket and sponge and some old towels. 'I can't leave this for Jenny,' she says, her voice scratchy.

I have to go outside. I can't stand the stench. No wonder RP was dry retching last night. I feel my cornflakes swirling, but the fresh air revives me. I walk around the block, being extra careful as I approach the flat in case Mrs Pooter's blind is up.

It's still down, though. Still asleep, thank goodness. But the sooner we get out of here the better.

When I get inside, I find Rosemary at her desk. Her face is flushed and I can see she's having trouble with the old computer. And the printer's refusing to work.

'Don't worry about it, RP. I can ask Brandon to print out the forms. He won't mind.'

RP looks up, her eyes red. 'I'm not worried about that, Vel. I have to get rid of the Celestial Moonstone virus. I mean, Fungus. And I need to get Mama's computer too. Her laptop. It might be infected as well.'

I almost say, 'So bloody what?' but I don't have the heart to step on RP's integrity twice in one day. Having Rosemary pretend that she was me, to those investigators, would've been a big deal to her. Although in the end I think she did enjoy it.

RP steps into the main room, stops and stares long and hard at Mama's bedroom. She looks like one of those people statues you see performing in the streets. Not moving.

I whisper to her, 'I'll get your mama's laptop, RP. Don't worry. You talked to the investigators for me. I can do this for you.'

I sound more brave than I feel. The bull ants are drowning in the cornflakes and milk and they're threatening to come up for air.

Rosemary doesn't argue or try and talk me out of it.

I leave her standing there and tiptoe to Mama's door. I glance at my watch. Fifteen minutes before the district nurse gets here. I hope she's not one of those super-conscientious people who turn up early.

I take in a long breath and slowly, slowly, open the door. The laptop is glowing in the blind-darkened room. It's still on, but muted. Mrs Pooter doesn't say anything either. Still asleep. Thank God!

I let out the breath and begin to approach the bed. Such a huge bed. Must be double king-sized. I drag my consciousness away from the moment – Mum's self-help books be damned!

How the hell am I going to do this? What if Mama Pooter wakes when I try and take her computer away, and grabs me? I think of how she broke Rosemary's arm, and every hair on my body stands to attention.

I can't look at her, I won't look at her. I close my eyes and lean forward. Gently take the sides of the laptop.

It doesn't budge.

I tug a little more. It's as if it's become as heavy as Mama Pooter herself. I take another breath, feel as dizzy as I did last night on the sleeping tablet. My knees are buckling and, more than anything, I want to get out of here.

Finally I force open my eyes. A breath lumps in my throat. I meet a terrible sight. Mama Pooter's stare is fixed on the screen, her hands clamped to it in a grasp as stiff as steel.

I've seen a look like this before. The blue-glazed, locked-out look of one of Dad's sheep the morning after it was bitten by a copperhead snake. I know one thing for certain now: I don't have to worry about waking Mrs Pooter up. Ever.

I clench my teeth, lean forward again, prise cold unyielding fingers one by one from the laptop. They seem reluctant to release their treasure. Across the screen is a replay of what I saw the last time I was in her room. Exploding fireworks and gold-coloured lettering. The only differences being the amount, Twenty Thousand Dollars, flashing over and over, and the lack of reflection in Mama Pooter's piggy little eyes.

Karma does exist! Here's the proof. Mama Pooter, killed by the shock of her greed.

In a macabre twist of phrase, I recall what Rosemary had said. That her mother would be 'dead to the world'. She couldn't have been more right. And it couldn't have happened to a more deserving person.

I'm frozen for minutes, then I glance at my watch: five to ten.

Jenny will be here soon. I need to move. One last look at Mrs Pooter. I suck in air. I hadn't noticed it before, but with those porcine eyes and ginormous body, she looks like Jabba the Hutt from *Star Wars*. Worse even. Danny has a poster of him on his bedroom wall. Gross.

With quivering fingers, I reach out and shut Mrs Pooter's lids. I don't want Rosemary's last memory of her mother to be so horrific. Now she does look like she's asleep.

When I exit the room, RP dives forward, and with her good arm, takes the laptop from me. 'Thanks so much, Vel,' she whispers. She gasps when she sees the screen, shuffles the laptop onto the kitchen table and then, without looking into the bedroom, gently closes her mother's door.

I can't speak. What am I going to say? How do you tell someone their mother has died and now they're an orphan? Whatever Mrs Pooter has done, and even how terribly, terribly awful she has been, she's still Rosemary's mother. Her mama.

Rosemary's eyes are glittering. 'Twenty thousand dollars,' she says, pausing between the numbers. 'I wonder how come Mama hasn't transferred it to her bank account yet?' Then she answers her own question like I'm not here. 'Must have fallen asleep after she won it.'

I don't argue with her. It's sort of the truth. Well, 'asleep' in the biblical sense.

'RP, come and sit down.' I lead her over to the sofa. Isn't this what they do in movies? Make the 'soon-to-be bereaved' person sit down. I suppose it's to stop them from falling over with the shock. I might sit down too; my legs feel none too steady either.

RP keeps snatching looks at the screen. She's smiling and chuckling and whispering something which sounds like 'My system really works, my system really works.'

I push fingers into my temples. Bloody hell, I can't do this.

There's a knock on the front door and then the turning of a key. Jenny the district nurse (who else could it be) puts her head in the doorway and calls, 'Hi! Angela? Just me. You awake?'

Angela? I'd never thought of Mrs Pooter having a first name. And certainly not one as nice as Angela.

'Angela?' Louder now.

RP stiffens, looks towards her mama's bedroom. Of course I'm not worried that this will wake her, and thank God, now Jenny's here I won't have to tell Rosemary myself. She'll find Mrs Pooter dead and be able to explain everything better than I could. Nurses are trained for that.

RP jumps up, and I get up as well.

'Oh, Rosemary,' Jenny says, as she enters. 'You're home. Arm playing up?'

Rosemary nods.

Jenny's a large woman in her early sixties. Red face, frizzy hair. Pubic-permed, Kaleen would call it.

I introduce myself, tell her it's a student-free day. Well, it's sort of true. Student-free for us.

Rosemary starts talking. Her voice sounds so calm. It's like she's rehearsed what she wants to say. Maybe she's in acting mode again. 'You don't need to stay today, Jenny. Velvet will be helping me with Mama.'

Oh hell, RP, what are you saying? NOOO!

Jenny laughs. 'That's okay, Rosemary. You are a funny thing. That's what I'm here for. To help.'

'But Mama's had a terrible night,' Rosemary says earnestly. 'She's only just got to sleep. I don't think we should wake her.' She flickers a worried frown at her mama's bedroom.

Jenny puts down her nurse's bag. 'I was wondering why you were whispering. Is it her stomach again?'

'Yes, and her foot. You know, the gout.'

'Oh, I should go to her. I can give her something for that.'

As cool as spring water, Rosemary says, 'No need. I've given her something already. We had some Paramax left over from last time.'

Jenny sighs and collapses onto the sofa. 'Be a love, Velvet, and put the kettle on. I'm dying for a cuppa.'

I'm surprised my legs work at all. Especially after that last remark. I've shifted into autopilot. I've tried to signal 'no' several times to Rosemary, by shaking my head vigorously behind Jenny's back. But RP's been ignoring me.

'I'll just take a peek in at her, before I go,' Jenny says after she finishes her cup of tea.

As Jenny opens the door a crack, I hold my breath. I see RP doing the same, but for a different reason.

'Oh, bless. Sleeping peacefully,' Jenny says, firmly closing the bedroom door.

I'm furious! What short of nurse is she? 'There's a dead woman in there,' I feel like screeching. Then I remember how I'd shut Mrs Pooter's eyes. Damn it! Why had I done that?

I know why. Rosemary Pooter – my best friend – she's the one who matters. And, in that instant, I realise I can't be the one to tell her that her mother has died. Although it's not like something you can hide forever.

I slump back on the sofa. Jenny will be here again tomorrow. She'll find out then. And if I can get Rosemary away from here today, she doesn't need to know yet. Not right now anyway.

I think of Brandon. He's promised to pick us up as soon as we text him. Why shouldn't RP have one more day of happiness?

After Jenny leaves, Rosemary whizzes the laptop off to her bedroom. Before she closes her door, she touches a finger to her lips.

I lean back on the sofa. It's the most uncomfortable thing I've ever sat on. It keeps sagging and the bedspread covering is such a gross colour. Reminds me of Mrs Pooter's aura. Or what used to be her aura. Grey-green, like dirty beach foam. I close my eyes, bring up the blue, see my lovely Willem's eyes. Soon, Willem. I'll be there soon.

I must have dozed because it only seems seconds before RP's shaking me and holding her hand over my mouth so I don't call out. It wouldn't matter, but she doesn't know that. She's got a suitcase like mine, on wheels. The laptop is on the kitchen table again.

'I've got everything fixed now. Can you put the laptop back with Mama, Vel?' she says, with a 'sorry' creasing her brow.

I get up, stretch, check the time. Nearly eleven. I've been asleep. I make a pretence of being super-quiet. Actually I am super-quiet, opening the door crack by crack, closing it behind me with barely a swoosh and entering the room on shuffled feet.

I don't put the computer back on Mrs Pooter's lap, I sit it on her dresser. Already the air smells sour. Mama Pooter's wee accidents or bodily organics breakdown? I clamp my nose and re-swallow my breakfast.

Outside RP's flat, I text Brandon to get here asap. Rosemary and I lean against a galvanised fence to wait for him. The tin's warm on our backs. I think of decomposition and its acceleration by heat. I shake the thought away. I have to stay sane. Need to stay focused for both our sakes.

Rosemary touches my arm. 'What was all that about, in the flat, Vel? All that head shaking? And why weren't you whispering? You know I needed more time to get things done. You didn't want Jenny to wake Mama, did you?'

I feign a surprised look. 'Of course not, RP. Just not myself today.' Well, there was the truth again. I've never felt so out of it.

Rosemary rubs her brow. 'It's crazy she didn't wake up. Although last Sunday she slept till one. I hope she does that again today too.'

Rosemary takes out a long envelope from the front pocket of her suitcase. She opens it, unfolds several sheets of printouts and hands them to me. At first I think they're the unaccompanied minor forms, but on closer inspection I see it's airline travel stuff.

I hold them up like a salute. 'Bloody hell, RP. What have you done? These are airline tickets to the Netherlands. Returns and everything.'

Rosemary plucks them from me. Smiles broadly as she flips through them and puts them back into her suitcase's pocket. I get a glimpse of her passport in there too. I won't be going alone. There are two tickets. RP is coming with me!

'I've wanted to do something for you, for ages, Vel. You've done so much for me. Riding lessons and getting me to meet Brandon. And just being there for me.' She smiles again, but then, when I see her face cloud over sad, I know she's struggling with her ethics.

'You bought the tickets from your mama's bank account, didn't you, Rosemary?'

RP nods miserably, eyes creased to slits.

'Oh, RP, don't you dare feel bad. That money is yours really.'

Inwardly I think, well, as the last surviving member of your family, you've inherited it, so I'm right.

'Remember, it was your system which won it for your mama. And what about you being an unpaid carer for all those years? She owes you.'

Rosemary's face relaxes. 'I'm hoping Mama won't find out the money's missing for a while, Vel. She's not good with online banking. I usually do all the transactions for her. That's probably why she hadn't transferred the twenty thousand.'

'I'm sure she won't miss it, RP. In fact, I've never been so sure of anything so much in my life. Thanks heaps. And this will be awesome, you coming too.'

Now all we have to do is get to the airport.

Brandon pulls up in the truck and gets out. 'What's the story here?' he says, indicating RP's suitcase.

'Rosemary's going to Holland with me. Isn't that great?'

Brandon frowns. 'You girls ever travelled before? Do you know you have to be at the airport at least an hour before departure?' He eyes the suitcases again. 'There are weight limits on baggage as well. And have you got your passports? Visas?'

I'd done the research. 'Don't need a visa, we're only going to the Netherlands. And we both have our passports. And yeah, they're up to date.'

Rosemary retrieves the ticket printouts and hands them to Brandon.

He scans them and swears. 'Bloody hell, EST of departure is 8 a.m. I can't take you to the airport. I'm picking my car up at nine.' He pauses, teeth touching his lower lip. 'I suppose I could get my dad to pick it up.'

I smile in gratitude. He really is a good guy. 'Don't do that, Brandon. If you can get us to Adelaide tonight, I have another plan.'

'Absolutely no probs.' Brandon high fives me. 'I think you're both way cool. And to celebrate I'm buying some Mick the Greek's salad rolls, and a couple of those frogs a certain person I know loves so much.' He's not talking about me.

I glance at RP's face, it's lit to a bright crimson. She must have told him a lot on their bike ride back to town yesterday.

After getting our lunch, Brandon drives us to the park. We sit on a wooden bench under an old oak tree, unwrap our rolls and sip our bottled water.

Then I remember something. 'RP, how did it go with the computers? Did your mama's laptop have the CMF virus?'

Brandon's eyebrows furrow again but he doesn't say anything.

'No, Vel. I ran a complete Protectalot scan. Mama's was clean. And then I worked on your old computer. I managed to find the CMF hidden in an obsolete program. I must have missed it before.'

I can see her building up to explain it all, but I hold up my hand and her mouth shuts like a trapdoor.

She laughs. 'That's okay, Vel. I won't go into details. Let's just say I defeated it, cleaned it up. No more nasty CMF. Not in that computer anyway. Although it won't be as good as it was. It'll always be a little bit broken.'

'What the hell is CMF? A new virus?' Brandon asks mid-bite. 'I haven't heard of that one before.'

RP nods. Then she tells him about Celestial Moonstone and her new friend, and probably partner in cyber-crime, Kiss. Also about the ant fungus, and our comparing it to Celestial, as her being a fungus. CMF. Infecting and controlling anything she infiltrates.

'Wow,' Brandon says, hands behind his head. 'I know Kiss is a tosser. I've had enough to do with her on the show circuit. That poor mare of hers, Sylvania Star. Kiss knocked her about so much she was crazy. Took me ages after I bought her for her to come good. But I didn't known anything about Celestial Moonstone.' He takes a swig of water. 'I know her brother, Alan. He's in my class. A really nice guy, actually. Celestial mm…' He pauses. 'She's that weird pale-looking girl, isn't she? Nice boobs, but…'

There's that microsecond glance again at RP's bust. I sigh. Oh well, he's only a guy after all.

When I think about the Celestial Moonstone Fungus and how Rosemary has beaten it, I start to giggle. RP asks me what's so funny.

'I was thinking, RP, about the ant fungus and that yet-unnamed fungus scientists have recently discovered which attacks it and prevents it from taking over the poor ant.' I pause for effect. 'They should name it the TRPFF.'

Rosemary lifts one eyebrow to quizzical. 'Oh, I get it,' she says after a minute's thought. 'The Rosemary Pooter Fungus Fighter?'

I nod and we fall into laughter. It feels so good to let go.

Brandon sweeps our wrappers into a pile and deposits them in the bin.

'Thanks, Bran. That was a great meal,' RP says. 'Especially the company.'

She's not only talking about me. There's enough electricity between those two to light up a small town.

Great meal. Oh, damn it! That reminds me. Mum's going to put on the works for us tonight, dinner-wise. Roast beef, roast vegies, and her fabulous apple turnover. I have to let her know I won't be there. And I have to figure out something to tell her why I'll be away all night, as well, without raising suspicion. After tomorrow, when we're on the plane on our way to Holland, I don't care if the whole world is after us. It'll be too late to stop us. Then I think of Mama Pooter mouldering away in her bed until Jenny gets there, and start to shudder so much that RP asks if I'm cold, or coming down with the flu. I assure her I'm fine.

'Well, let's get going. My place next?' Brandon says.

I shake my head, try to smile. 'Can you drop me off at the hospital first, Brandon?' I say. 'I need to speak to my mum.'

I have to make this quick. Brandon and Rosemary are waiting for me. RP did say not to hurry but I'm a bit worried about the gleam in her eye. At least there's no back seat in a truck.

I find Mum in Ward Three – Cardiac. She's pushing one of those steel trolleys laden with water jugs, some empty, some full, and boxes of plastic bin bags. Hooked on the back of the trolley is a wide-fringed polishing mop and a huge tin of floor polish.

'Velvet,' she says with surprise in her voice. 'What are you doing here? I rang the school earlier and told them you weren't well enough to leave the house.'

I avoid Mum's eyes. 'I slept in and felt heaps better. Then Rosemary Pooter rang and said she needed help with her mama. She's got a broken arm, you know.'

Mum picks up one of the full jugs and carries it into room 5. There's a man in a white-clad bed with the sheet pulled up to his chin. He seems asleep. Although, in a hospital, you never know. Surely not twice in one day, I tell myself. I let out a breath of relief when his nose twitches and he brings out a skinny finger to scratch it.

'Mrs Pooter's got a broken arm?' Mum sits the jug on the man's bedside table, takes the empty one and refreshes his bin with a clean bag.

'No, not Mrs Pooter. Rosemary. Rosemary's got a broken arm, you know that. Her mama's got gout and an upset stomach. Rosemary asked me to help.'

Mum puts the empty jug on her trolley and stuffs the full plastic bag into a green garbage one. 'Mm…nasty, gout is. Uric acid in the big toe. That's what's usually affected.'

Mum knows heaps about medical stuff. Almost as much as a nurse, I reckon. She's been working at the hospital for over ten years.

'Yes, it is. Like I said, Mrs Pooter's pretty ill.'

Well, you can't get more ill than dead, I think to myself. God, what have I become? Stomping all over the truth like it doesn't matter to me any more. Then I realise it's not about that. It's because Willem's more important than not telling a few white lies.

'How did you get into town?'

'Taxi,' I say, without hesitation. 'I used some of my Old Ma Izzy money.'

Mum straightens and stretches, pushing a hand into the small of her back. 'I can give you a lift home. I knock off at four. You can help me with the shopping.'

I put my tone into plead mode. 'Can I stay at Rosemary's place tonight? Please? She really needs me.'

Mum stares at me with squinted eyes. 'How come you've gone all caring towards Mrs Pooter all of a sudden? I thought you didn't like her. Called her a fat cow, if I remember rightly. Most unkind, but I guess you have your reasons. Anyway, I'm making your favourite dinner tonight. Roast beef and everything.'

I'm squirming inside. If Mum doesn't agree to this, I'll be grounded in the literal sense. I won't be on the plane tomorrow.

We're back in the corridor, pushing the trolley to the next room. Mum scurries in with another jug and bag.

'Please, Mum, please,' I say, following her like a shadow, 'I'm doing this for Rosemary, really. She has such a hard time with her mama.' When Mum doesn't answer, I play the ace card. 'It'll take my mind off Willem. You know, being busy.'

Mum folds like the proverbial pack and gives her assent. 'I'll try and keep you some of the roast beef,' she says. 'If I can stop Danny from eating it all, that is.'

I give Mum a huge hug and she hugs me back like she did the other night. But I'm the first one to pull away.

'Seeya tomorrow then, after school,' Mum says.

I only answer 'Bye,' and shoot off, sliding to speed along Mum's newly polished hospital floors.

We get to Brandon's place at three-thirty, still too early to ring

Kaleen's rad Aunty Margie. I set aside my phone to charge and Brandon prints out the paperwork.

We need double the unaccompanied minor forms now that Rosemary's going too. Brandon's all set to sign them himself, but I think it'll be better if we can get Aunty Margie to do it for us. Hopefully, she'll be able to take us to the airport as well, and that should keep the airline authorities happy, or at least without suspicion.

In the pit of my stomach, the bull ants have been replaced with something lighter. Dragonflies? Yes, dragonflies, elusive and strong, shimmering with almost impossible colours, like the auras I see around the best sort of people. Multifaceted and bright. Like Willem's.

After Rosemary and I have showered, we round up all our gear and weigh our bags to make sure they don't go over the twenty-three-kilogram limit. Rosemary's doesn't come anywhere near that, even though she's taking every item of clothing she owns.

We set off for Adelaide. Brandon has managed to borrow his dad's Aston Martin. Well, he said he'd asked, but I haven't even seen his father around anywhere. I assume he's at work.

The car's silver-grey, reeking class and cash from every pore of its glossy metallic hide. Brandon pats the front passenger seat and Rosemary slides in beside him. I swear they'd have left without me if I hadn't moved fast. As it was, I almost forgot my phone.

On the way, we stop to check Ganymede. My phone rings, but keeps slipping out because of poor coverage. It's Kaleen. I send her a text to call me at her Aunty Margie's after five. Our time.

Ganny comes over towards the three of us but chooses Rosemary to nuzzle. They gaze at each other, girl and horse. I'm thinking Brandon might have a rival.

After several moments, Ganny walks a few metres away and lies down, legs tucked beneath him, head tipped towards Rosemary. Before I can stop her, RP, with a trance-like look in her eyes, climbs through the fence and onto his bare back.

Brandon scrambles through the wires, but Ganny has risen and, with Rosemary aboard, is cantering off as lightly as a firefly to the small end of the paddock.

I and Brandon stand in awe as Ganny figure-eights and circles, seemingly on his own accord, until I see the almost imperceptible flutter of RP's legs. Her balance is perfection itself.

'Wow, what a great seat,' murmurs Brandon.

I glance at him, follow his eyes. Tit and bum man, I think. Typical! But when Rosemary stops alongside him, he's only looking at her face. He stretches out strong arms to help her down. She falls into them and I walk away. I can see where it's going and I'm right. Several minutes later, when I turn round, they're still locked together in arms and lips and Ganny is standing, calmer than I've ever seen him, watching them. I think he approves.

When we get closer to Adelaide, I ring Aunty Margie again. It's not quite five so I'm not worried when she doesn't answer and I get her machine instead. I'm about to hang up when she comes on the line.

'Is that you, Velvet?' Her voice is breathless, but clear. 'Hang up and I'll ring you back.'

I hang up and my phone rings almost immediately.

'Velvet?' she says again. This time I answer yes, and she sighs audibly. 'Thank God. I've been trying to get in contact with Kaleen. To ask her your phone number. How are you doing, mate? Sorry, silly question. It's terrible about Willem. God, sorry again. I don't usually rabbit on like this.'

'It's okay,' I say. 'You talking. Thanks heaps for offering to help. You don't even know me. Us.'

'That's where you're wrong, Velvet. Is it okay to call you Velvet? I know Kaleen calls you Vel. You can call me Aunty Margie. Kaleen calls me her rad Aunty Margie. Not red, rad. Although in my university years…' She laughs. 'I know lots about you, and about your amazing horse, Spirit. And,' she pauses, 'I know about Old Ma Izzy and the riding and the training. Kaleen never stops talking about it. And about TAOB. See, I even know the acronym.'

I jump in before she starts talking again. 'Calling me Velvet's fine. Willem calls me Velvet. I like it. It's still good of you to help.'

'Us?' she says, in a delayed reaction.

'I'm sorry, Aunty…Margie. I haven't been able to contact Kaleen either. She doesn't know about Rosemary.'

'Rosemary? Another fugitive? Wonderful! I'm so looking forward to this. It reminds me of –'

At that moment, we pass under a bridge and the call is cut off.

I sweep a look at Brandon and RP. They've heard it all on speaker.

'Gee, she certainly is different,' they both say together, and then laugh. But it's for Aunty Margie, not against her.

I punch her address into the GPS system. It finds it quickly and begins telling Brandon where to go. I quickly text Aunty Margie that we'll be there, ASAP.

Ten minutes later, we pull up to a terraced house. Early Victorian. The paint is flaking from boards and window frames. Funnily enough, I'd thought it would be.

There's a neat garden of the cottage kind out the front, and a huge lilac bush growing along the wider side of the house, in the last flush of full flower. The perfume sends me dizzy and light. I breathe it in gratefully.

Aunty Margie opens the door before I have time to pull the little woodpecker door-knocker's string tail. Well, I think it's his tail.

She almost trips into our arms. It's the sort of greeting you might get from a well grown Labrador puppy or a large English sheepdog on steroids. She's blockily built, about sixty plus (I'm never good with old people's ages) and flushed with excitement or maybe the menopause. Mum's books are big on that stage of life too. I always skip those chapters. There's nothing old about Aunty Margie's grip, though, or the steely look in her eyes. I do a rethink about her age…early fifties? She's dressed in blue jeans and a bright red T-shirt.

After introductions and hearty handshakes, we're ushered into a dark hallway. We're blinded transitionally from the brightness outside. Now Aunty Margie becomes our seeing-eye dog. Follow the red. I mean rad. Sorry, I'm getting like RP in the joke department. I feel beyond hysterical, the give-in numb phase, like anything could happen to me now and I wouldn't blink an eyelid.

'Come and meet my dragons,' Aunty Margie says, detouring along an offshoot of the hallway, and entering a room.

Its interior glows like blue mist. Eerie. Okay, I do blink. Maybe I'm not at the totally numb phase after all.

Brandon and Rosemary come up behind me and we follow Aunty Margie in. What the hell. I'm beyond worrying.

Her 'dragons' turn out to be Australian bearded dragons of the lizard fraternity.

We're given a quick but fascinating dip into the 'world of the reptile'. Her favourite one is called Henry Lawson because of its lizard genus, *Pogona Henrylawsoni*, named after the famous Australian author and poet. He's a sweet little guy (the lizard, that is) with bright intelligent eyes and a neat spiky 'beard'.

We find out in a process of slithery shocks (they're extra active today because of the heat) that Aunty Margie has snakes as well. Thankfully non-venomous; you don't say poisonous, apparently. She tells us her huge free-range (of the house) anaconda, Sally, and not so huge but equally scary eight-foot carpet python, Shag (as in shag pile carpet; I know – RP humour, they'll get on well together) are still great deterrents to would-be burglars. Her neighbours on either side have had TVs and computers stolen, but Aunty Margie doesn't even bother with contents insurance. She does have Beware of the Snakes signs (her own design – complete with forked tongue and skull and crossbones) on every outside window, though. When she goes shopping, she takes Sally on the back seat of her car and never has to lock it. No sign necessary – they can't miss Sally.

Finally we make it to the relative cool of the kitchen. There's a fan going, and a big jug of orange juice on the table, clunking with ice cubes, circled by six glasses. In some bizarre way, the circle reminds me of Celestial and the ring of stones around the fire that night in the forest. Seems years ago now.

I flick through the pages of my diary and find it was on Sunday 14th, nearly midnight. Only eighteen days ago, would you believe? I quickly put my diary in my carry bag before the others notice it. I should have left it behind; there are just two pages left. Tomorrow feels like a new era, so I'm starting my new diary then. First entry.

After we've told Aunty Margie about what's going down – or, in our case, up – with the plane, I bring out the forms, which she signs with a flourish, filling in 'Guardian' as her status.

Brandon has to leave and I have time to speak with Aunty Margie on her own as RP sees him off. I tell her all about Rosemary Pooter's life, how she lost her dad at seven years old and how shockingly badly her mama has been treating her. Aunty Margie's all for going to the police straight away, and that's when I almost tell her about RP losing her mama recently (today actually) too, but I don't. I manage to convince her that I'll get my mum to do something about it when Rosemary and I return from Holland.

I also tell Aunty Margie about the Celestial Moonstone and Kiss (Clarissa) Rothchile ongoing hacking saga. She hardly says a word. She may be a great talker but she's a wonderful listener as well.

When RP gets back, her lips look bee-stung and her eyes dreamy. There's also a glint of a tear in each of their corners.

Aunty Margie looks at both of us in turn, slaps her thighs and proclaims. 'Right, what you girls need is a pie floater. Post-haste. I'll get out the chariot.'

Mm… A pie floater. I haven't had one of those for at least three years. The last time was when Mum and Dad took us to Adelaide to see the pageant.

A pie floater, another South Australian exclusive, is a meat pie, with mouth-watering pastry, floating in a bowl of thick pea soup and smothered in tomato sauce. The combination of flavours is heavenly. Many people are addicted. Especially the Adelaidians, who have easy access, the lucky things.

The last time RP had a pie floater was when she was five years old, so she hardly remembers it. 'I think I burnt my tongue and Dada got me a cold milkshake to sip, to make it better.'

We all sit quietly in a sort of reverence to Rosemary's father. He seems the antithesis of Mama Pooter. I wonder what he's saying to her now? Come to think of it, if the brimstone and the lightness of being places exist, she definitely won't be in the same one as him.

I look at RP's happy, flushed face. She's had a wonderful day. I'm pleased I haven't told her about her mama. And I won't until we get back. She deserves a holiday. But although I try to stamp it down with reason, I get this gut-churned conviction, like ice freezing me from the inside out, that one day and soon, my not telling Rosemary will come back to bite me harder than the bull ants ever did.

Aunty Margie's 'chariot' turns out to be a Mini Cooper, complete with dangling dice and nifty paintwork. Way awesome.

'This is nearly as cool as Brandon's dad's Aston Martin,' Rosemary says, as we cram in and spin off to the heart of the city.

Pie floaters, here we come.

Second Diary

Friday 2 November

It's Kaleen's fifteenth birthday today and in a few minutes RP and I are heading off to the airport. Two great events.

Last night, Aunty Margie gave us her double bed while she used the single one in her spare room. Rosemary and I slept until three-thirty, from sheer exhaustion, but then excitement woke us and we've been talking for ages. We have to get up soon, at five.

RP is worrying about her mama. 'She'll know I'm gone now, Vel. She would have known last night when I didn't get home from school.'

I start to tell her not to worry but then realise I should play along. 'What will she do?'

'That's what I'm scared of, Vel. She'll probably ring your place.'

Irrationally, for the briefest of seconds, I feel real panic, until I remember RP's mama will never be ringing anyone ever again.

'Shit, I hope not. Let's not think about it. Once we're on the plane, it'll be fine. They can't get to us there.'

RP flicks me a weird look. 'You don't seem worried at all, Vel. How come?'

That's where she's wrong. I am worried, not over her mama, but about my Willem. I twist my face into serious. 'I am concerned, RP. But I'm just trying to stay positive. Live in the moment.' I knew Mum's books would come in handy one day.

After a quick breakfast of strawberry smoothies and some Vegemite on toast, we triple check our bags and documents and Aunty Margie gets out the chariot. RP sits in the front with her. I was right: she and Aunty Margie have been getting on like budgies up a gum tree.

They start chattering away as soon as they get in the car. I'm left in the back seat trying to juggle one of the suitcases on my lap and strap the other one into the seatbelt next to me. God knows how twelve-foot-long Sally fits back here. She must coil her slippery self up at least three times.

When we get to the airport, Margie parks the car and we find the KLM Airlines gate. I've only ever been here before to pick up relatives with Mum and Dad. And once, when Kaleen came back from a UK holiday and Danny took me.

As Rosemary and I are under-age travellers, we can't use the electronic check-in. We have to go to the desk to have our documents and passports verified and our bags weighed in.

While we wait in the impossibly slow-moving line, I scan the many other passengers. I find several Category Two Angry at the Drop of a Rat Monsters, one Category One Up Your Own Arse Monster, four Category Three Away In the Clouds Monsters, and seven Category Four Head in the Sand Monsters. I try and calculate the odds. It's about one in forty at our school. Ten of the students are monsters. And one staff member, the newly suspended teacher, Hanker Wanker.

The ratio seems to be higher here. Lots of the auras, though, are prevalent in blue stroked with mauve, a classic sign of stress. So some might not be true monsters but have temporarily morphed into them.

I check the time, get out my phone and ring Mum. The answering service kicks in, as I hoped it would. She'd be driving, on her way to work. Good. I don't feel up to lying to her person to person. Much easier leaving a message. I keep it brief. 'I won't be home tonight either, Mum. Rosemary really needs me and it's…' I play the deciding card, hoping it will work as well the second time round. 'It's helping me keep my mind off…things.'

When we finally get to the desk, our tickets are scanned and then everything goes dead. No lights, even the boards with the departures and arrival times go blank. A sort of alarm sounds, like jangled bells, and in a few seconds all the computers spring back to life like they've just been switched on.

The check-in woman looks at us with dull eyes. 'Sorry about that, folks, we've been having computer glitches and micro-blackouts all morning.'

I feel a pang of sympathy for her. Airports are twenty-four/seven; her morning probably started a minute after midnight.

Rosemary and I and Aunty Margie share a trio of unspoken knowing. The same question in our eyes: 'Do Celestial Moonstone and Kiss have anything to do with it?' I think of my phone call from Kaleen, the line going dead, those three beeps. Had they bugged my phone? Do they know we're here?

The next thing we're being told is that our flight has been delayed. The woman checks and double-checks and then confirms it will now be leaving at midday instead of eight.

We go into the airport shopping complex. Aunty Margie buys us a cup of coffee and we slump into chairs that are not designed for slumping. I stir my cardboard-cupped coffee with the little white plastic stirrer without it raising a single ripple. Then I sit bolt upright. My subconscious has done the calculations.

'Oh no, this can't be happening,' I yell. 'We're not going to make it in time to see Willem, to stop them from...'

My mind and voice are struck dumb with another even more immediate problem. The district nurse is coming at ten. In two hours she'll discover Mrs Pooter and the next thing she'll do is try and find Rosemary. Crap! It would have been fine if we'd winged off at eight. But this delay spoils everything.

I grab Rosemary by her shirt sleeve. 'Have you got Jenny's mobile number? You need to stop her from going to your house.'

Rosemary looks at me like I've completely lost it. 'But you said...' Her face clears. 'Oh, I get it, Vel. Mama might get Jenny to search around for me.' Her face clouds over again. 'But Mama will probably be doing that already. Won't she?'

I don't have an answer for that, not one which will sound plausible. What I need is to employ some politician speak. 'Well, RP, at this time and stage it would not be judicious for us, in this circumstance, to follow this new endeavour to its end.'

Even the rad Aunty Margie is looking at me strangely now. Maybe

I've lost it. Damn it! I just want to get to the Netherlands. See my Willem. Make sure he'll be all right. I burst into tears.

'Okay, Vel. Please don't cry. I'll ring. What do you want me to say?'

I switch off my waterworks like someone closing a tap. No time for tears. Luckily, RP doesn't seem to notice.

'Just stall her a bit. Tell her your mama's had another bad night. Ask her to come after lunch. We'll be gone by then.'

RP gets out her address book and finds Jenny's details. I hand her my phone.

She keys in the numbers. 'Hi, Jenny. It's me, Rosemary. I wanted to let you know that Mama's had another bad night.'

RP holds the phone a little away from her ear so we can listen. I haven't put it on speaker. Not here.

'Oh, I'm sorry to hear that, dear. Do you want me to come early?'

'No, no. Don't come now.' Rosemary's voice rises to panic. 'I, we… I was thinking you should come after…after lunch.'

There's a few seconds of silence and when Jenny speaks again she sounds firm. 'Look, I don't know what you're playing at, Rosemary. Angela warned me about you. Your…strange ways. Put your mother on now. She won't mind you waking her up for me.' Rosemary puts her hand over the mouthpiece and shakes her head at us. Her eyes look huge. Then she straightens, takes a deep breath, removes her hand and visibly relaxes. Even her face changes, somehow appears older. 'Hi, Jenny. Yes, Rosemary can be a bit strange. No, I'm fine. Well, I've had a few bad nights.'

The receiver's clamped to RP's ear so we can't hear what Jenny's saying.

RP waits. 'Yes, come after lunch. About one, if you can. Not too inconvenient? Oh, you are a darling. Yes, that'll give me a few hours rest. See you then. Thanks, Jenny.'

I've lost all feeling in my arms and legs and I'm betting I've gone white. That was like a ghost voice from the grave. Rosemary really, really sounds like her mama. No wonder she'd convinced the teacher when she rang him about her being absent from school.

Rosemary has gone pale now. She hands the phone back to me and drains her coffee.

Margie gives her a round of applause. 'Bravo! Bravo!' she calls as she claps.

Some other travellers slant us odd looks and steer away from our table.

I have to admit that I think RP has missed her calling. Although she's still young enough. She'd make a brilliant actress. She is a brilliant actress!

Now, the problem of getting to Holland in time. Once again, I feel myself slump as I do the exact calculations. Twenty-one hours to get there. And then there are all the arrival delays. Customs, bag retrieval. And we have to get to the hospital. It's just not possible. I fall into crying again and this time the tears are very real.

My phone rings, but no one picks it up. Through a mist of tears, I see it's Kaleen. I may as well tell her I'm going to be too late.

'Hi, Vel.' Her voice holds the same excitement it always has. 'Sorry I didn't ring last night. Would it have been last night? I still can't get my head around these time differences. You are ahead of us, aren't you? Is Aunty Margie there? Are you at the airport yet?'

I swallow heavily and then, taking in what Kaleen has just said, gasp like a fish, newly beached. I feel like shooting myself for my idiocy. 'Time travel,' I shout down the phone.

The café staff are looking daggers at us now. Most of the tables have been abandoned and with this latest outburst, an old man picks up his newspaper and leaves without ordering anything.

I explain to Kaleen how Australia is nine hours ahead of the Netherlands and therefore even though the flight takes twenty-one hours to get there, we lose nine hours and arrive in twelve hours. 'Their time! Your time,' I shout again. 'Time travel! Travelling back in time. See what I mean?'

Kaleen's nonplussed. 'What happens to those nine hours?'

'Who cares!' I yell. 'I guess we pick them up on our way home. But it means I will be there in time.'

'I never thought you wouldn't,' Kaleen says, with a touch of the comical sliding up her voice.

'Hey,' I say, remembering something else. 'Happy birthday, Kaleen.'

Kaleen laughs loudly. 'Now who's confused, Vel? It's not my birthday day yet. It's still Thursday evening here. Eleven-ten to be exact.'

I hand the phone to Aunty Margie, and Kaleen and she exchange a few cheerful quips before Aunty Margie hands it back to me and whispers, 'Rosemary Pooter' and something which sounds like 'designated person.' Blurry heck (to use a Kaleen expression), another thing I'd temporarily forgotten.

'Kaleen,' I say in a quieter tone. 'Did you get the handling advice document? You need to put another name on it.'

'Another name? Who are you bringing? Brandon? Hold on, he wouldn't need it, he's way over fourteen.'

'Rosemary Pooter,' I say. The line goes static, it's like we've been cut off. 'Still there, Kaleen?'

After another couple of seconds, she answers. 'Rosemary Pooter? What the heck.' Her voice escalates. 'Why Rosemary blurry Pooter? Why is she coming?'

I clamp the phone to my ear. I don't want any of Kaleen's denigrating tone to reach RP. She's been so strong lately, and happy.

I walk a few metres away from the table. Glance back at Rosemary but, by the intense expressions on both their faces, she's caught in a depth-full conversation with Aunty Margie.

'Look, Kaleen,' I say, turning my head and keeping my mouth close to the phone, 'it's a long story. Rosemary Pooter's great. You'll really like her when you get to know her. Anyway, I'll explain it all when we get there.'

Inwardly I'm fuming. If it wasn't for Kaleen pairing up with Celestial Bloody Moonstone for the poetry project in the first place I wouldn't have even got to know RP. My mind pauses in its thinking. Moves into linear sequence. And then I wouldn't be going to the Netherlands… I have what our lit teacher would call a paradigm shift. In a sort of crazy way, I have Celestial Moonstone to thank for me being able to travel to Holland. As I've realised before, bad people do good sometimes, without even knowing.

'What are you laughing at, Vel?'

'Nothing and everything, Kaleen,' I say reflectively. 'Like I said, I'll tell you all about it when we get there.' My pitch dips to cajoling. 'Please, just put Rosemary Pooter's name on the form. For me?'

We have about three hours before our flight leaves for the Netherlands. We wander through all the airport shops and linger at the Book Nook for a free read. I go to the money exchange and convert my savings into euros. The Aussie dollar's strong, so I get a good rate. I give half of it to Rosemary. Only fair, seeing she paid for our trip. Eventually, at eleven o'clock, an hour before we have to go, we end up at the same café we were in before. Luckily, the staff don't remember us, or are no longer bothered. They're rushed off their feet by a herd of passengers in transit.

Aunty Margie queues up and we go and nab the last table available. All the others are occupied by people speaking a language I can't put a word to.

She returns surprisingly quickly with salad rolls and more bottles of water, all balanced on a green plastic tray with a white, purple-stained paper doily.

The rolls are not a patch on Mick the Greek's. Healthy enough to eat probably, but nowhere near as fit, if limp lettuce is anything to go by. They live up to our disappointment in taste as well.

I can see RP has something she really wants to tell me, she's radiating that bearer-of-exciting-news look.

After she finishes eating, she finally lets it out. 'Guess what Aunty Margie is, Vel?'

I begin to open my mouth to answer, but the excitement of her newly found discovery rushes RP on. 'She's a suffragette. She's missing her meeting today, because of our time glitch.' Rosemary looks at my watch. 'It's on now, actually.'

Aunty Margie nods in agreement, but doesn't look upset.

RP continues, 'Would you believe there's still a suffragette movement here in Adelaide. How cool is that?'

I have no idea how cool that is because I have no idea what, or who, suffragettes are. Suffragette movement? Sounds painful.

Aunty Margie seems to notice my uncertainty. She explains that suffragettes were a radical (is that where Kaleen gets rad from?) feminist movement group established over a century ago and instrumental in legalising women's personal freedom, equal rights, and even the right to vote. Rad Aunty Margie's exact words. They sound a little rehearsed. From a long-ago speech?

'Men helped our cause too. Lots of women's liberationists forget that.' She swigs some water and clears her throat. 'If it wasn't for some prominent and freethinking men, we would've had a much harder struggle.' She's talking like she was back there. But I know she's not that old.

Aunty Margie leans forward and stabs a finger at the now empty tray with the stained doily. 'Look at this for synchronicity,' she says, her voice escalating to almost the same excitement level as Rosemary's. 'These are the suffragettes' colours: white, green, and purple.'

RP stares reverently at the tray like it was a religious relic, then grabs my arm. 'And did you also know, Vel,' she says, with eyes wide, 'that South Australia was the first state in Australia to bring in women's right to vote.' She pauses for effect, or perhaps dramatics. 'And the first in the world to allow women to stand for parliament.'

I'm not sure how I should react. All this talk is a lot like a history lesson. But thinking about it, I am pretty impressed. Women's right to become prime minister. Wow. Way cool!

We're finally on the plane. The blue beneath our wings is translucent with 'clouds like lost spectral waifs'. I think I read that somewhere when we were doing our poetry project, but I can't put a poet to the line. But it's so true.

I turned off my phone before we got on the plane (I know there will soon be hysterical messages in my message bank from Mum and Dad) and I'm not turning it on again until after I've seen Willem. I'm not checking my emails either, for the same reason. I need to stay focused. The dragonflies are winging around merrily.

I've given RP the window seat, even though it was mine according to my ticket, and the woman in the middle seat was kind enough to exchange with me, so that I could sit next to Rosemary. The seats are three across and in four aisles. I'm glad we didn't get the centre aisles. It would have been hard to look out of the window from there.

We've got over our initial excitement over all the free things you find, waiting like Christmas presents, on your seat. A half-sized blanket, an eye mask for sleeping, earphones in plastic wrap, and even a packet of salted pretzels. The little TV screen in front of each seat is intriguing too. At the moment, it's showing our altitude and speed. Both sound impossibly high to me. Also, it's apparently many degrees below zero out there. We're nearer to the sun, so how does that figure? But some things in life sound implausible until you know the facts. In a dim recollection of a science lesson, I recall something about altitude and getting beyond the blanketing effect of the lower atmosphere.

I lean back in my seat. It only goes so far back, but I know I'll be able to sleep, especially now that we're on our way. I glance at my watch. One-thirty already. I try to imagine what would have happened when Jenny got to Mama Pooter's place. But I switch off my thoughts; they're too horrific for me to view.

I close my eyes. The humming of the engines and the cool air-conditioned confines are so relaxing after the hot weather we've been having. I conjure up a soft green; it floods the back of my eyelids and becomes a forest-coloured sea. Willem is floating there in a fantasy bubble of clarity. I merge into the bubble with him and we embrace and are lifted higher and higher…

There are several bumps, and the woman next to me is rubbing my arm. 'Dear, we have to fasten our seatbelts again.'

I open my eyes. The seatbelt sign has come on.

'What's happening?'

'Turbulence, I think,' she says. 'Is this your first flight? You and your friend?'

Rosemary stretches out her good arm. 'Rosemary,' she says. Then, with a half-nod at me, she adds, 'This is Velvet.'

After the woman has shaken RP's hand, I extend mine as well

'Emily,' she says, smiling broadly. She reminds me of Old Ma Izzy. Same age and weight. Also there's something vaguely familiar about her aura.

RP launches into her newly acquired knowledge of all things suffragette, which includes the most famous of all suffragettes, Emmeline Pankhurst.

Rosemary and Emily get so involved in a conversation that RP asks to swap seats with me again, which I do gladly. With relief has come exhaustion, and all I want to do is sleep.

When I wake again, it's because a little tray of compartmented food is being thrust in front of me. Rosemary's already brought down my tray-holder from the back of the seat.

'I got you the chicken, Vel. Instead of the beef. We had a choice, but I thought you'd like the chicken.'

Emily smiles benevolently. 'We couldn't wake you. You are a sleepy head.'

I try and look around Rosemary to get a better picture of Emily, but she's quite a slender woman and, even as small as RP is, I can't see her properly. But she's not a monster. Their conversation continues. Rosemary seems to be doing all the talking. Emily is listening and nodding and sometimes repeating in confirmation what RP has told her.

'So, you've had to look after your mother? Oh, that's too bad. Your father dying when you were so young.'

She seems caring and RP is enjoying the attention, so as soon as the air stewardess has taken away my empty tray, I lie back and try to sleep. I figure the journey will go quicker if I can be out of it.

It seems only minutes, but I'm sure it's a lot longer, when Rosemary nudges me awake. 'There are four movies on,' she says. 'Which one do you want to watch? Come on, Vel, you're missing all the fun.' RP's eyes are as bright as a rabbit's.

I stretch out and scan through the films. I remember Kaleen telling me they always have ship disaster movies on planes, and plane crash movies on ship cruises. It figures; lots of the passengers are nervous enough already. I haven't felt scared at all, and going by the way Rosemary's been acting, she's as far removed from frightened as she could be.

I look at my watch again. Even though we're going to be in Holland behind our time by nine hours, it doesn't mean we don't have to pass the twenty-one hours on board. To stay focused, I've decided to keep on Australian time until we arrive and then put back my clock the nine hours. We've been flying for six hours already. Fifteen to go. I take out the picture of me and Willem. The one I framed. Press it to my lips and briefly close my eyes. The dragonflies hum their fluttering colours. Thank God, the bull ants have gone.

Soon, I hear the heavy steel trolleys trundling down the aisles. More food. Awesome.

Two movies later, they're feeding us again. It does break the boredom and the strange thing is I feel hungry enough to keep eating. The meals are pretty small, though, sort of toy tea party sized.

After this one, they turn down all the lights and we're supposed to sleep. Now that I'm expected to, I can't. Mum would put that down to my contrary nature. But the sleep I've had has re-energised me and I can't help the excitement bubbling me up, like froth in a Jacuzzi. I'm closer to Willem now, in both senses, than I have been for over the past six months.

I scan the cabin, note the other non-sleepers. Personal lights on, they're watching their screens, or rustling magazines. Probably doing crosswords or sudoku.

RP has talked herself to sleep. (I'll never, ever say 'Dead to the world' again.) Emily is leaning sideways towards the aisle, her face averted, but by the rhythmic lifting of her chest, she seems to be sleeping as well.

After another hour, I feel my eyelids droop. I keep opening them, trying to fight sleep, like a child on her first late night out.

Next thing, I'm being shaken again.

'Seat belt on, Vel,' Rosemary says, sounding very awake. 'We're about to land in a few minutes.'

The cabin around me is in full silence. Collective breaths being held. I read somewhere that landing and taking off are the two most dangerous times of air travel. I can't wait for the plane to land, though, which it does in a perfectly ladylike fashion (I'm guessing planes are the same as ships, all of the female gender), like someone tripping lightly down a catwalk. Although the engines do make odd noises, as if they're trying to go backwards or something.

'Reverse thrusters,' RP says loudly, confirming my thoughts.

When all the engines are silent and the 'Unfasten seatbelts' signs have come on, the mood around us turns quietly festive or desperately relieved, one or the other, I'm not quite sure which. I think our section must have been reserved for the bulk of people with flying phobias.

Emily gets up and retrieves her carry bag from the overhead compartment. She appears in a hurry to get off. Lots of others are doing the same and soon there are queues three abreast in all the aisles. Emily, mobile phone to her ear, pushes past some people in front of her. Momentarily, she seems to remember us, mouths a goodbye over her shoulder and then she's gone, merging in with the steadily growing exodus.

Rosemary and I exchange a glance. 'Gee, Emily is in a hurry to get off, RP,' I say. 'Maybe she's more nervous than she looks.'

The stewardess assigned to us because of our unaccompanied minor status is great. She helps retrieve our bags from the carousel and then takes us through Customs.

The Customs man is nice as well, and when he says, 'Welcome to the Nederlands' (which is how you say it in Dutch) I'm so reminded of Willem's gorgeous accent that when the man asks, 'Do you have something to declare?' in a moment of lame excitement I say, 'Yes, I do! I'm in love with Willem Van Den Hoven.'

The Dutch people must have an easy-going attitude, for all he says, as he smiles, stamps my passport and waves me through is, 'Well, dat guy is one lucky fellow.'

Soon we're entering the arrivals lounge and there's Kaleen with a welcome balloon and a grin, nearly as big, on her face. She hugs me for many minutes (her eyes are wet when she lets me go) and then passes the handling advice form to the stewardess, along with some ID. The stewardess checks it with her paperwork then bids us a friendly 'Take care.'

All Kaleen says when she sees Rosemary is a short 'Hello.'

Rosemary throws herself into reluctant arms. 'Hi, Kaleen. Thanks so much for helping. And for your rad Aunty Margie too. She's such a hoot.'

'We couldn't have done it without her,' I say, cutting in. I can see Kaleen's eyes misting over green. The envy monster everyone morphs into from time to time. What's Rosemary Pooter doing here, with my best friend and worming her way into the good books of my Aunty Margie? I can almost hear her thoughts.

'Hey,' Rosemary says. 'Isn't that Emily?'

I follow her gaze and see that it is Emily. Walking about fifty metres away. She's staring in our direction and she's flanked by two men, both in black like proverbial bad guys and towering over her. But she's definitely in charge. They follow like puppies as she glides towards us, a saccharine smile stretching the lipstick on her mouth and a finger held aloft like she's hailing us to stop. Then as she gets closer, I can see that what I thought was vaguely familiar about Emily has now become as clear as air.

I grab my bag and yell, 'Run!' I have no idea where I'm going, or if my friends are following me. I'm trusting they know me well enough to take me seriously.

Soon I'm outside the airport. I hail the first taxi I find, throw my bags in and hold open the door for Kaleen and Rosemary, who come puffing up behind me. They pull their bags in as well. It's one of those taxis which has room for baggage along with passenger space.

'Gee,' Kaleen says, 'what's the blurry hurry, Vel? I was going to catch the train to Amsterdam. I have to be a bit careful about finances. I've used up a lot on the hotel room.'

'I'll pay. Can you lock the doors?' I say to the taxi driver.

He rolls his eyes and I hear a click. 'You girls on the run?' he says, with a wink and perfect English. 'Where are you off to?'

I think of the piece of paper I've had in my pocket for over twenty-four hours. I know the address written on it off by heart. 'Lucas Andrew Medical Centre in Jan Doorop Street, please,' I say breathlessly.

Then I flick a glance back over my shoulder at the terminus. They're still there, Emily and the two men, no more than ten paces away, now approaching fast, with matching frowns as black as the guys' clothes.

RP's face is ashen. 'Is Emily a monster then?' she whispers, near my ear.

I feel Kaleen stiffen beside me. Then she hisses, the last word lifting intonation. 'Rosemary knows about the monsters?'

This is going badly, really, really badly. And with the taxi driver listening, I can't explain anything to Kaleen.

I nod 'Yes' to both my friends and slump back into my seat, just so pleased we're moving. And when I look back through the windscreen, see the distance we're making, putting between us and them, I feel my lungs sucking up air like I've been drowning and it's only now that I can breathe.

Emily is watching the taxi. Her hand is clenched, two fingers up now. Punching the air. Her aura has become so pronounced that even from this far I can see its grimy colours. Like dirty foam washed up on a beach after a storm. Beyond my monster categories. But an aura exactly like Mama Pooter's.

Now I have a new evaluation. Sadistic Psychopathic Aura Category – Off the Screen.

Saturday 3 November

On the way to Amsterdam, Kaleen talks me into going to our hotel room first. She's booked us into a place called the Ramada Apollo. It's gone 1 a.m. in Holland, so it's a bit late, or early (take your pick), to visit Willem. Kaleen assures me we'll go to the hospital first thing in the morning. It's a short ten-minute walk from the hotel.

In a half trance, I unpack my clothes, hang up my T-shirts. I feel as tired as if I'd run a marathon. And not just from jet lag. I don't want to think about despicably rotten people like Emily and her ilk, or deal with friend issues right now. Willem is my priority.

Both Kaleen and Rosemary have gone quiet, Kaleen because she's pissed off and Rosemary most likely because she knows Kaleen's pissed off.

When I come out of the bedroom, RP's the first to speak.

'So, Vel. Emily's a monster? Why didn't you say something earlier? And what's the deal with her heavies? Were they going to abduct us?'

I nod. It's good when people answer their own questions. I still have to answer her first one, though. 'I didn't recognise her as a monster, RP,' I say quietly. 'Not in the beginning. But her aura was familiar, though.' So far, the truth. I don't explain why it was familiar. 'And now I know that sort of aura is very, very bad news.'

Kaleen speaks up. 'What? Worse than a Category One?' She glares at Rosemary, like a challenge. I guess she's hoping RP will ask what a Category One is. But of course she doesn't.

'Much worse. Off my monster radar, actually,' I say with conviction. I fill up the kettle and switch it on. Put camomile teabags into three cups.

'Gee, I had no idea,' RP says. 'I told Emily heaps about myself. She seemed so nice. I really liked her. Do you think they'll come after us?'

I shake my head, pour in the hot water, jiggle the bags. 'Opportunists,' I say. 'Three young girls on their own. Emily thought we'd be easy pickings. She's probably a pimp for some sort of prostitution gang.'

Kaleen visibly shudders. RP turns bloodless. They both stare at me with a look I can't decipher.

Kaleen, ever practical, says, 'But they couldn't have grabbed us off the street. People would've noticed.'

'They wouldn't have had to,' I say, my voice flat. 'Probably would've offered us a lift. Emily would be hoping that she'd been nice enough on the flight for us to have trusted her fully. And she would've introduced the heavies as her brothers or sons.'

'Just as well we have you, then,' RP says, with a shining smile. She picks up her cup of tea and clinks it against Kaleen's. 'Here's to Velvet Brown and her amazing gift.'

'Yes, to my best friend, Velvet Brown,' Kaleen intones, clinking back a little too hard.

I feel a warm glow, like you get on a freezing cold day when you first come in and sit by the fire. My ability is useful. But, as I've felt before, it's changing. Growing like a muscle. I just have to know when, or how, to throw my weight. One thing's for sure: from now on I'll be taking a lot more notice of everyone's auras.

I wake at six in the morning. There's a breeze stuttering the windows and even though I forgot to pull the blind, it's gloomy in here. A cold day out there, by the look of it. It's autumn in Holland, only a few more weeks to go till winter.

I'm actually in another country. It feels odd, but I feel safe despite the Emily episode. Or maybe because of it. It proved that my ability's not crap. And the reason why we've not all been drugged and dragged to another foreign country and forced to be the sex slaves of some megalomaniac or worse.

I stretch. Only now, I allow myself time to think about what I'm going to do to get to see Willem. I know, from ringing up the hospital when I was back in Australia, that only family and designated friends are given updates of his condition over the phone. Hospital policy. I can't blame them. My only hope is that now I'm here, I can talk my way in to seeing him.

'Turning off his life support at ten a.m.' That terribly cold email. They're lying words. I don't believe them. I won't believe them. I clamp my hands over my ears, even though the words are coming from inside my head.

When I enter the kitchenette, Kaleen's there, trying to be quiet but dropping things and generally making more noise than if she was trying to be noisy.

After breakfast of toast and jam and extra strong coffee (three teaspoons each), Kaleen and I leave RP, who's still sleeping, and go for a walk along the canals. Luckily, I remember to bring my jacket, but even so I'm surprised how cold it is. A sort of cold that seems to bite through every pore of the material of the coat, and me. Kaleen sees me shiver and hands me her scarf. I wrap it around my neck and pull it up over my chin, grateful for the borrowed warmth.

The brisk walking warms us too and soon I'm so involved in updating Kaleen, especially about Rosemary Pooter, that I forget the cold. I explain everything that's happened, except about dead Mrs Pooter.

Kaleen's pretty non-committal and I can tell she doesn't really understand about the abuse. But then you had to be there. See Mrs Pooter in action, see poor RP struggling with all her mama duties and her own deprivation.

All she does say in the end, when we're nearly back at our hotel, is 'Well, Rosemary Pooter can't think much of herself to put up with all that. I'm just surprised it took her so long to run away. I would've run as soon as my father had died.'

I think about this as we enter our hotel. Kaleen's right in a way. But I know how some people can become so depolarised by a domineering influence in their lives that they lose their sense of self. They start to lean towards the one who's destroying them. You read about it in kidnap situations. Although in RP's case I feel there's something more. Something she hasn't told me.

Could she have killed her mother? Before she walked to my place? But no, that can't be true. For one thing, Rosemary Pooter's not that sort of person; she's as morally and ethically straight as Mrs Pooter was bent. There's no bad aura, nothing monsterish about RP. And those deathbed eyes of Mama Pooter's, they were openly staring in their greed. I'm putting my money on a heart attack.

Rosemary's not in the hotel room. Before we have a chance to get worried, she returns, pink and frosted, blowing on her hands.

'Gee, freezing out there. Feels weird after all our hot weather.'

She's carrying some choc chip muffins so fat they're almost bursting out of their bags. There's something else in her old-fashioned string shopping bag too, but it's wrapped in white paper.

'McDonald's,' she says gleefully, handing over the muffins. 'I saw the arches when the taxi was bringing us here.'

Kaleen keeps looking at me and Rosemary in a strange fashion. Eyes half-hooded in a way which denotes she doesn't understand what's going on.

In the end, I ask her, 'What's up, Kaleen? Why the look?'

She flushes pink right down to her chest. 'Oh, I don't know. I can't understand it. You two seem really…fine. It's just that…that with Willem and…today being…the last…' Her voice trails off. She hiccups a sob.

I lean over and hug her. 'Kaleen, it's not going to happen. That's why we're like this.'

She pulls back, brings her hand across her eyes. 'What?' she says, her voice strained. 'Like this? Like what? In denial?'

Rosemary's eyes meet mine. She moves closer and grabs my hand. Now we're both looking at Kaleen and I've no idea what our expressions are saying. I don't what to think about anything else, except getting to the hospital and seeing Willem.

My new plan is to go about nine o'clock and arrive at the hospital as his family's getting there. Somehow talk my way into going in with them. And then my mind draws a blank, like a page which is too greasy to write on, where your pen keeps slipping and only making the odd undecipherable mark no matter how hard you try.

Kaleen's phone buzzes and makes us all jump. It's Brandon with a text for Rosemary. 'Hi K, is RP there? Culd u tell her I say hello, thnx.'

Now Kaleen's eyes are blazing. Behind them I know she's thinking, What the heck? Brandon and Rosemary? Has this girl taken over my life?

Brandon and Kaleen aren't really an item, though. I mean, there is something between them, but I think it's just good old mateship. I don't think anything happened between them on that night we went TAOB.

In the end, we leave the muffins.

'Lunch, they'll make a good lunch,' Kaleen says, putting them under a paper towel.

Rosemary's looking guilty. I think she's picked up the vibe and decided she's to blame. I can see both my friends are struggling to hold back for my sake. They know anything they're going through pales to insignificance in the light of what I might be facing. I feel cold now, as if somehow part of me has gone to sleep. Willem's only a moment's step from all my thoughts.

I watch in a sort of detached way as RP picks up her string shopping bag and takes out the white-wrapped bundle. She hands it over to Kaleen, who glances at it like it's something else to eat. Something as distasteful as the muffins have become. She unwraps it and almost drops what turns out to be the most exquisite hand-blown glass horse.

'There's an indoor market on this morning,' RP says. 'Lots of stalls. Only a block away. This guy was making these. You could ask for what you wanted.'

Kaleen holds it up to the light. 'It's beautiful, Rosemary. How did he do it?' She traces a fingertip down the hind legs. 'It's amazingly perfect.'

'I thought you'd like it.' Rosemary smiles her shining smile again. 'Happy birthday for yesterday, Kaleen.'

Kaleen visibly melts. The water comes out as tears. I watch, moist-eyed myself, as the two most important people in the world to me, apart from Willem, embrace in a long hug. Afterwards it's like they're trying to make up for lost time. They can't stop talking. I knew they'd get along eventually.

It's eight-twenty.

I take a huge breath and say what I'd rehearsed overnight. 'I'm off soon. I need to do this on my own, guys.'

Kaleen and Rosemary look up mid-sentence. 'Are you sure you want to do this by yourself?' Kaleen asks, soft-voiced.

I shake my head, let out the breath in a sigh. 'No, I'm not. But I feel I have to. Why don't you two go to the market? Hey, get me one of those horses.'

Both my friends nod mutely. Standing with arms linked, they watch me get ready.

I carefully fix my make-up and hair, put on Willem's favourite top, pick up my bag and Kaleen's phone (she's lent it to me to use the GPS), and head off. I'm hopeless with directions. I'm going earlier than I thought I would, but I can't wait. Last night I had a dream where I got to the hospital too late and Willem was... Even now I won't bring up 'that' thought. I've stuck it firmly into the parallel universe back at home.

I've borrowed Kaleen's scarf too and, outside, the wind whips it around my face like a wrap. I leave it where nature has placed it and walk on. I'm striding now. I check the GPS. I'm going in the right direction. I'm on Doroop Street already.

And here it is. The hospital, it's not scary or monsterish. It holds my Willem somewhere, like a cradle holds a baby. So precious – life. (I realise I'm sounding like Old Ma Izzy.) And Willem is still alive. I know he is.

The doors open automatically and I step into a warm downward breeze from the overhead air ducts. I take off my jacket and scarf. There are unfamiliar words written up on a board. But in English as well. There are figures too, but numbers are the same in Dutch as they are for us.

I find an arrow directing me to Enquiries. It's almost right in front of me.

The woman behind the counter is no-nonsense large, and busy on the phone. She acknowledges me with a micro-nod, but continues unabated. Finally she says, '*Tot ziens*,' and hangs up.

I try my Dutch. She lifts an eyebrow and then starts talking to me in German. Well, I think it's German. In another time or circumstance it would be funny. But as it is, it makes me feel tired. I try English.

'Oh, I'm so sorry,' she says, in such good English I can't detect an accent. 'I thought you were German.'

So, I was right. It brings no joy.

'It's just my bad Dutch,' I say, trying to smile but failing. I tell her Willem's full name and mine, and what's happened to him. Then I ask if she could tell me where he is.

The woman consults her computer. She begins to frown. Clicks up some more information. Her frown deepens, reaches her eyes. 'I'm so sorry. Your name's not here. Not on Willem Van Den Hoven's visiting list. I can't give out any details. I'm sorry.'

I fall forward on the counter. Crumple into my elbows. 'But I've come all the way from Australia.' I swallow hard. 'Please give me…his room number. Just his…room num…ber.' My voice is breaking up like a faulty transmission. 'I have to see him. I need to see him now.' My voice escalates. 'We're in love.'

Even in this state of anguish I realise how pathetic that sounds. But it's true. I'm dying inside the longer it takes. I've been chipped away by time ever since I heard of Willem's accident. Soon there'll be nothing left of me at all.

The phone rings again. The woman answers it, slips back into Dutch as fluid as a waterfall. A slight shrug in my direction shows me her powerlessness to change the rules. But her eyes are soft with sympathy.

I walk slowly out to the front of the hospital. I'm hoping Rita and her family will be coming along soon. I can't miss seeing them. The car park's exit and entry is off the same road. Then I get a terrible thought. They're here already. Maybe the teacher friend lied to me in his email. It's all happening earlier. Happened. Oh. God. No!

With a start, I realise I've actually said that aloud, and loudly. Several people veer past me like I'm drunk or insane.

I see Kaleen and Rosemary coming towards me. They say they've been touring the block and were on their way to the market. I manage to explain what's happened. I sound strange, even to me.

'Is that the information counter there?' Rosemary asks, pointing through the glass doors.

When I say yes, she spins off as quick as a fox, almost too fast for the doors to open in time.

Kaleen helps me over to a low brick fence surrounding some tatty shrubs. I hope they're better doctors than they are gardeners, I think, uncharitably and a little illogically.

I sit down. Kaleen next to me. She holds my hand. For several minutes we don't speak.

I'm the first to talk. 'I wonder what Rosemary's doing in there?' I say, swivelling around in time to see RP rushing out through the hospital doors.

Once again they open just in time. She's clutching a piece of paper and I've never seen her so happy. Well maybe once, when she first rode Spirit. And maybe that last time, when she rode Ganymede. Oh, and after, when Brandon had kissed her.

'Here it is, Vel. Willem's room number. He wasn't in the Intensive Care Unit. They must have brought him back to you know...turn off...' Rosemary's face clouds over. She stops talking.

I take the paper, read, 'Ward 10 NW Room 342C.'

'How?' The one word a croak.

Rosemary bounces excitement. 'When I looked through the doors, Vel, I saw that woman leaving her post. Probably going to the toilet. I snuck behind the counter and got onto the computer. Easy really.' RP looks proud of herself. She closes my hand around the paper. 'Anyway, Vel, get going.'

I'm surprised to find my legs are working and soon I'm back inside the hospital, checking out the board to find where the ward is. The woman's come back, but her eyes are locked onto the computer screen. She doesn't notice me.

It's like a maze in here. I'm soon wishing I'd brought Kaleen and Rosemary. But they'd be at the market by now.

After many minutes, I find the right floor, ward and room. The door's closed, and I can't hear any voices. I feel paralysed.

A cleaner woman, she reminds me of Mum, parks her steel trolley, zips past me and swishes open the door. I follow her in. I stand at the entrance, the door pushing on my back. Watch as she pulls away the bedspread, strips off the sheets and empties the bin bag. Lots of used tissues in there. So many tears, I think numbly.

I check the number on the door again, to make sure I have the right room. There's no mistake, it's room 342C. And it's definitely Ward 10. When the cleaner turns around to pick up the bedclothes, she sees me standing there, does a little jump and clutches her chest. Says something I can't understand, in Dutch.

I'm frozen again. 'Where's the boy who was in here?' I struggle with my limited Dutch, scrabble up a word for boy. 'Jongen?' I say my voice intoning the question. Then I point to the empty bed.

She shakes her head sadly and brings a hand to her mouth. When I keep staring she swipes closed fingers, like a knife, across her throat. The gesture is macabre but its meaning is clear. 'Kaput,' she says.

I don't know how, but I'm out in the corridor again. I'm on the floor. The cleaner makes sympathetic noises and touches my arm as she goes past. For a moment, I hate her. Hate everyone, even myself. And I'm furious at Willem. Why did he have to die? Why couldn't he have waited until I got here? I glance at my watch, wonder at my dry eyes. Am I beyond tears, or am I afraid that when I start crying I won't be able to stop?

It's only nine twenty-five. It wasn't supposed to happen until ten! More than anyone now, I hate the Van Den Hovens' teacher friend. Although it doesn't make sense. Did he really believe I'd come all the way here, so much so that he had to cover for the family by lying? And did they really believe I'd make a scene? Make the impossible even worse?

I fall back against the wall. None of it makes sense.

I close my eyes. Try and bring up the colours, but all I see is black. For a moment I feel myself falling, spiralling down. I don't fight it. Then I hear my name being called. It's in an accent, so it can't be Rosemary or Kaleen.

Willem?

I open my eyes, see a fair-haired girl approaching from the other end of the corridor. She's carrying a can of Coke and what looks like a bar of chocolate.

'Velvet?' she says again. She keeps walking slowly towards me.

I stand up, my eyes fixed on hers, like you do on the horizon, when you're on a ship and trying to avoid seasickness. It's Rita; I know her face. It's almost as familiar as Willem's, even though it's so different. She's taller than I thought she'd be, but apart from that, looks exactly like she does on Skype.

Rita comes closer, leans down and lifts me up with her handshake. Then we hug and I'm crying and crying and she's patting my back and making the same sort of noises the cleaner woman was making. Universal I'm-so-sorry language.

'Velvet?' she says softly. 'What are you here, doing? *Verloren?*'

Verloren. I remember this word, it means lost. Willem was always saying he could get lost, '*Verloren*', in my eyes and then laughing at his lameness. Oh God. No! I don't want to remember. It hurts too much.

'*Verloren?* Velvet?'

Is Rita saying that I'm lost? I show her the paper with the room and ward number.

She reads it and gives a wan smile, then stares into my eyes. 'You are not knowing? Oh, Velvet, it is what you call great...' Her voice stops; she seems to be having some internal struggle. 'Come,' Rita says, rushing me back along the corridor.

When we get to the end, she points at the signs where the two wards dissect. One says Ward 10 NW and the other says Ward 10 NE. I had been in Ward 10 NE. There's North East and North West. I hadn't checked it properly. I assumed there was only one Ward 10. I didn't think the NW was a direction. Maybe just an acronym of some famous doctor.

I pull in short breaths. 'Does this mean there's another room 342C?' I gasp. 'Does this mean...I'm not too late?'

Rita puts down what she'd been carrying, grabs my other hand, spins me around, then draws me in and hugs me hard. 'Willem is alive,' she says, laughing. 'He is awake. He wanted dis Coke and dis chocolate.' She holds them up like proof. 'He's going to be fine.'

Then we're running and running, holding onto each other's hands like it's a matter of life or death not to let go. Dashing down the corridor to Ward 10NW, to room 342C. To where my Willem is. I'm laughing so much and so loud I'm sure the whole world can hear me. And I'm not giving a damn if they do.

When we get to the room, Rita puts a finger to her mouth. 'I go first,' she says, making a surprised face and pointing in the direction of Willem's bed.

I get it. She wants to surprise Willem with me.

I can see the shape of his toes holding up the bed covers. My heart's fluttering like a sparrow's and I'm prickling all over in tiny bumps.

I hear them exchanging lines in Dutch. Willem's voice sounds strained and broken. I recall how I'd had a croaky voice and sore throat after I'd had my ankle set. The nurse told me it was something to do with the breathing tube. The one they use when you're under anaesthetic. That was only for an hour. Willem had been on a respirator for weeks.

The conversation seems to go on for ages. Several times I hear my name, Velvet Brown, being mentioned. There's concern in Rita's tone.

What's happening? Why is it taking so long? I was certain Willem would call me in as soon as he knew I was here. Maybe he doesn't want me to see him in this state? So weak. But that doesn't seem right. Willem's not like that.

I can't wait any longer. Without Rita inviting me, I enter the room. They both look up with shock on their faces. Rita's eyes are filling with tears. She glances from Willem to me and shakes her head. In that moment I know. Willem doesn't recognise me. He doesn't know who I am. He has forgotten me.

I feel a wrenching blow, as if I've been knocked off my sanity by some unseen force. That hidden hand writing away my life.

But I'd read about this. That brain injury victims sometimes have specific memory loss. I just hadn't believed it could be true of Willem. Surely what we meant to each other would be strong enough to shine through any darkness? Weren't we the star-crossed lovers destined to come through anything, even death or this near death, with love intact forever?

Then, with a slap across my consciousness, I realise this is not about me and what I want. What's really important here is Willem. That he's alive. My Willem's alive! Living and breathing and looking as sexy as ever.

I walk over to the bed and touch Willem's hand. Not the reunion I'd imagined, with kisses and hugs and talk of love. But it's enough. Willem smiles at me with a light of interest in his eyes. Suddenly I'm glad I took so much trouble with my appearance this morning. And that I'm wearing the low-cut top he loved so much. Men are such visual things. Thank God.

Perhaps this won't be hard after all. My heart's leaping at the possibilities. Not an ending. Another beginning. All the fun of fresh courtship.

'Are you willing?' my eyes ask.

He replies by pulling me to him and kissing me gently with a reverence as soft as dew touching the first light of a pristine dawn.

Three hours later, after I've been ushered off by the nursing sister, and with promises to Willem to return this evening, I enter the outside world once more. It seems so changed now, even though no sun's shining it's brighter and the air's not as cold. I don't need my jacket, and with mild consternation I realise I've left Kaleen's scarf back in Willem's room. I'm scatterbrainedly in love. I know it, I'm even humming a silly tune, one I can't put a song to.

I see Kaleen and Rosemary coming towards me again. They pull up next to me and make a confession. They haven't been to the market, they've been walking around and around the hospital block, waiting for me to come out.

My friends look at me with concerned eyes and downturned faces. I smile at them, grab their hands. 'Willem's fine,' I shout, bouncing them up and down with me on the spot. 'He started to wake up last night.' I stop for breath. 'Apparently he became agitated and tried to pull out the tube. He's breathing for himself. And all his other injuries, his broken collarbone and fractured skull are healing great.' I don't say anything about his memory loss. I'll tell them about that later.

'That's absolutely brill news, Vel,' Kaleen screams, still jumping up and down.

'Oh my God, that's so awesome,' Rosemary says, her voice reaching screech pitch. 'But we knew he'd be okay. Didn't we, Vel?'

We end up in a group hug and for many, many minutes we don't let go. People have to walk around us to get past. Then we skip back towards the hotel, arm in arm, three across, just like Dorothy and the Lion and the Scarecrow in the *Wizard of Oz*. I know, so not cool, but we don't care. Willem's alive, he's going to be fine and at this moment that's all that matters.

There's a strange car parked out the front of our hotel. It has the ominous lines of officialdom. Black, this year's model, and unfashionable. Two men in suits and a woman in a lady suit are watching us.

The woman gets out, takes something from her pocket and

approaches us before we can enter the foyer. A flash of silver, and black print on parchment, leather-clad, gives us her name and status. Wilhelmina Rika Karstens. KLPD. She repeats her name and says she's from the Netherlands Police Agency.

I'd been expecting this. By now we would have been missed in Australia. But once again, I don't care. I've seen Willem, which is what we came for. What's the worst thing they can do? Send us back?

She brings out two photos, one of Rosemary and one of me. 'Rosemary Pooter? Velvet Brown?' She doesn't like wasting words.

We nod, and Kaleen, not wanting to be left out, adds. 'And I'm Kaleen Pingelly.'

Wilhelmina Rika Karstens barely skims her a glance. But equally she doesn't seem interested in me either. It's Rosemary she's locked eyes with.

'Rosemary Pooter, I have to inform you of your rights.'

I've heard this a thousand times before on TV, except they now include the new proviso, that what you don't say may be taken against you as well.

I can feel the now very cold air touching my tongue. I snap my mouth shut. Try to make sense of what's happening.

I can't believe this. Rosemary is 'a person of interest' over her mother's death. What do they think RP did? Bash her mother over her head with her plastered arm? Then I remember how Rosemary had told Jenny about giving her mama the painkilling tablets. Bloody hell.

We've been at the Netherlands Police Agency for over an hour, stuck in this room. Me and Kaleen. I'm so glad Kaleen insisted they take her along too. At least I have someone to talk to. Being a crime writer, she's bristling interest in everything around us, but I can tell she's as confused as I am about this. More so, because at least I have an idea about what's going on. Surely it's a misunderstanding?

Poor Rosemary was crying so much when I last saw her, before they took her away to another room, I can't imagine they've had much luck in getting any answers. What a terrible, terrible way for her to find out about her mama. I mean, is there ever a good way to find out about someone who's died? But to be accused…

Guilt's churning my insides to acid. Oh my God, I should have told her. I'm waiting and hoping the police come for me soon. But I'm dreading it too.

Kaleen takes me by the shoulders. 'Vel,' she says. 'You know more about this than you're letting on.' Her tone turns to 'no nonsense' as she shakes me gently. 'Come on. Out with it.'

I spill all I know about Mrs Pooter's death and for once Kaleen is lost for words. Totally '*verloren*'.

Soon, though, she begins to speak, quietly at first and then with conviction filling out her words. 'Blurry heck, Vel. Frick! No wonder they believe Rosemary has something to do with her mother's death. Think about it.' She pushes back a strand of hair which has fallen across her face. Starts talking almost like a narrator at a play. 'After being fobbed off twice, once while she was at Mrs Pooter's, and once by phone, Jenny finds Mrs Pooter dead. Rosemary Pooter missing. The police check out the last phone call to Jenny. Find out it was made from the airport. Realise it must be Rosemary. Impersonating. Oh sheeze. The more I think about it…'

Kaleen leans forward, hands rubbing down her face and then, in a higher voice, 'They get Mrs Pooter's laptop, discover the win. All that money. The motive. They see the airport bookings. Find out that Rosemary and a friend have done a runner. Skipped the country. The only thing that surprises me, Vel, is that they didn't get you two sooner.'

I don't answer. Wilhelmina Rika Karstens has come for me. I leave Kaleen sitting there alone with only a TV for company, its volume so soft it doesn't matter if the programme's in another language.

I'm taken to a different room, with television surveillance of the interrogating kind, and Rosemary Pooter slumped over a table, a cup of tea near her hand and a woman stroking her back. Making those noises again. Universal I'm-so-sorry noises.

Oh God, Rosemary, I'm so sorry too. What the hell have I done? Will you ever forgive me?

Wilhelmina sits down alongside the other two detectives, facing us, like they're on a TV show panel. She fills me in with what's happened in Australia. Reads me my rights. Begins to ask the questions I knew I'd have to answer one day. Although I thought I'd only be telling them to RP.

When I finish, Rosemary lifts her head, eyes red and swollen and staring. Directly at me. I wish she'd yell. Do something. Demand why hadn't I told her? Why had I let this happen? But she looks like a puppy that's just been kicked and has no idea of what it's done wrong. And there's something else in Rosemary's eyes. Betrayal, and far worse still, resignation, like this is all she deserves.

Rosemary straightens and the woman, a social worker, from what I read on her name tag, stops rubbing her back and lets her stand.

'I want to confess,' Rosemary says, scanning the room like she's giving a speech. 'Yes, I did kill Mama.'

'No!' I scream. 'You didn't. She was dead when I got there, like I told the police. Please, Rosemary, don't do this.'

Rosemary slides back down into the chair. 'And I killed Dada too.'

Everyone is staring at her. I start to say 'No' again, but something stops me. She needs to do this, she needs to talk.

There's a second of silence, like suspense, before she begins. 'The night before Dada went back to Iraq, he and Mama had this argument.' She catches my eyes. 'I know I told you, Vel, that I didn't know what it was about, but I did. It was about me. Dada had seen the burn marks on the soles of my feet. He'd been tickling my toes, doing the little piggy thing.' Rosemary's face curls up to a small smile and for a moment she seems as far away as the recall. 'This little piggy went to market… This little piggy stayed a…' She sucks in a long, slow breath. 'He wanted to know how it happened. Did I do it? Burn myself? I couldn't lie, could I? I could never lie to Dada.' Her voice sounds like a seven-year-old's, plaintive and sad.

I look around. Even the male detectives have damp eyes. And the social worker is weeping openly.

I go over to Rosemary. No one stops me. I hold her in my arms. Wipe the wet from her cheeks. 'Go on, RP,' I say softly.

As I hoped it would, the use of her nickname seems to make her rally. Her voice becomes clear. 'When I told Dada that Mama did it, he was furious. So angry. I'd never seen him like that. I mean, at first he didn't believe me. But then he did. And they had this terrible, terrible fight. He said he'd take me away as soon as he got back from Iraq. He had to go the next morning. Dada only had a few more months of duty. He threatened Mama with prosecution if she treated me badly while he was gone. And…and…' Rosemary stops and swallows. She's crying too now, those tears without sound. 'Mama was okay for a while. Until Dada was killed. After that, she got even worse than before. And then I heard a report from his fellow soldiers. Dada had been unusually inattentive. I knew that was why the insurgent sniper got him. Then I didn't care any more about Mama being worse. I wanted the pain. I deserved it. I killed Dada. It was my fault he wasn't paying attention. He was worried about me. I shouldn't have told him.'

She's sobbing into my arms, big huge gasping sobs, like someone regaining their breath after being winded. And now she's making noise. It's amplified by the complete silence of the room. Like an echo of all her tears unshed and all the cries unspoken.

Sometime later, I get back to Kaleen in the other room. She knows me well enough not to ask questions when I look like this. I've just got off the phone to Mum and Dad. I'm grounded beyond infinity. All I could say in reply to their many 'Do you know how worried we've been? Do you know how crazy we've been going? Do you know how…?' was 'Yes, I know. Yes, I know. Yes, I know,' like a broken record.

I don't blame them for being mad, but I can't be sorry. I can't. I'd do it all again if I had to. For my Willem.

I've got strict instructions from them which I have to stick to until I board the plane for my return trip in two days' time.

Rule One: I'm not to go anywhere on my own. Rule Two: I have to stay in the hotel room at night. And Rule Three: If I have to go anywhere further than ten metres, I have to catch a taxi. Mum actually specified the distance. Ten metres. Why didn't she just say I can't go out at all? But of course I'm going to. I want to see Willem again this evening.

Oh God, I wish I could put reverse thrusters on, like the plane did, to slow down my life. I realise I still have to tell Kaleen that Willem doesn't remember me. Also all about the things which have happened in Australia. She's got lots of it right, but not everything. And something from the coroner's office came in while Wilhelmina was walking me back to this room. I hope the other detectives have told Rosemary.

They'd discovered how Mrs Pooter died. A stroke. I was wrong about the heart attack. But I guess you have to have a heart to get one of those.

The detectives have the go-ahead from my parents to let me stay at the hotel with Kaleen, so they give us a lift back there. As they drop us off, they tell me they need to keep in touch, so could I please turn on my iPhone. Wilhelmina has given me her contact number. And said that Rosemary's still being looked after by the social worker, Ruth Kensington, but all going well, we should be able to catch up with her tomorrow.

I flop down on my bed and listen as Kaleen puts on the kettle. We're like an old married couple. I'm sure we know each other almost as well.

Presently she brings in some cups of coffee and the choc chip muffins. I burst into tears when I see them, remembering how happy RP was when she bought them for us. God, I didn't think I had any tears left. I must be severely dehydrated by now. I do a slow blink, and for a second imagine a scene, me in hospital on an intravenous drip to replace my fluids, in the same room as Willem and in the bed next to him.

'Gee, Vel. You're smiling now. Make up your mind.' Kaleen gives a nervous chuckle, puts one of the muffins on a plate and cuts it in half.

Like I said, an old married couple.

She props the pillow behind my head and scrapes a chair to the bed, just as if I'd been in hospital.

'Don't think I don't know what you're doing, Kaleen Pingelly,' I say. 'You want me to be comfortable enough to start talking. You're busting to know what's gone down with Mrs Pooter. And how the police found us here.'

Kaleen chuckles again. 'Just tell me one thing, Vel. Did Celestial Moonstone and Kiss Clarissa blurry Rothchile have anything to do with it?'

I put up my hand with the muffin in it. 'All in good time, Kaleen. You'll just have to let me eat this delicious muffin.'

And I am hungry. I hadn't realised it until now. I haven't eaten since early this morning. I'm also feeling so tired. The jet lag has finally caught up with me. And it's the sort of exhaustion where you feel like you're going to pass out into full unconsciousness.

After I've finished my muffin, I close my eyes. I can't manage the coffee.

When I wake, it's dark. Kaleen has pulled the doona over me. But my foot's been sticking out and now it's almost frozen. I can't feel it. I pull it under the covers and try and rub some life back into it. Then I switch on my bedside lamp. Bloody hell. It's eleven-thirty. Why has Kaleen let me sleep for so long? I jump up and nearly trip over the chair. Kaleen's still in it and has her doona wrapped around her like an Egyptian mummy. She jolts awake and squints at me with bleary eyes.

I shake her. 'Look at the time, Kaleen,' I say, putting my watch under her nose. 'I was supposed to see Willem ages ago. How come you're asleep anyway? You don't have jet lag.'

'I'm sorry, Vel,' Kaleen says, yawning. 'I was so excited having you here that I stayed awake most of last night. Well, morning. I did pick you up from the airport at one o'clock, remember.'

'Shit, I can't go to the hospital now to see Willem. It's too late.'

I hobble (my foot hasn't woken up yet) over to my travel bag, pull out my phone, switch it on and pray the battery hasn't gone dead. It was one of the reasons Danny gave it to me and bought a new one. This one didn't keep the charge. The little box holding my sun pendant falls out as well, and I retrieve it and open the lid. I'd promised myself that when I'd seen Willem was all right, I'd wear it again.

I slip it around my neck and fasten the clasp. My phone is flashing thirty-two messages and forty-five missed calls. I ignore them and text Willem, 'Sorry, fell asleep. Jet lag. Love u, c u t'morrow morn.'

Kaleen is all bouncy awake and I have to admit I feel heaps fresher myself. She reheats our coffee and sits back down in the chair, her face like an expectant father's. Then she waves her hand in a 'go on' motion, which threatens to turn theatrical if I don't tell her more soon.

'Well, Kaleen. What happened is this. Friday, at one o'clock, as RP had asked her to, Jenny the district nurse was supposed to be at Mrs Pooter's. But she was held up at another patient's place. He'd had a fall and she had to wait until the ambulance got there. Then, because he was a big bloke, Jenny helped them get him on board. She rang Mrs Pooter, got no answer but put it down to Angela still being asleep. By the time she arrived, it was two o'clock. She knew there was something wrong straight away because of the smell. It got to forty-one degrees on Friday. A real stinker.'

Kaleen looks at me with eyebrows half-raised, probably wondering if I'm joking, but I assure her that just slipped out. This is far from a joking matter. Although I must admit I do feel slight hysteria rising, the sort you get when things keep getting stranger and stranger and you have zero control.

'Anyway,' I continue. 'You wouldn't need any medical training to know that Mrs Pooter was deceased. The first thing Jenny did was ring an ambulance. And then she thought of Rosemary and rang the school.'

I lean over to get my coffee. Kaleen grabs it and hands it to me. I take a long sip.

'It got really crazy then, for Jenny anyway. She discovered Rosemary hadn't gone to school, that her mother rang in earlier to say she was sick. Then she remembered how Rosemary had been keeping her away from Mrs Pooter. Those excuses about her being ill. And she knew by looking at the body that Mama Pooter had been dead much longer than a few hours.'

'Yeah, I know, there are signs,' Kaleen says. 'Like mottled skin and stuff. I had to do research for *Death Does Not Innocence Make*.' She pauses. 'Geez, that title would be so true in this case.'

I nod, take another sip of coffee. 'Well, next the police are called. They still don't check the computer. No one is thinking murder. I mean, even at this stage Jenny's suspicious, but she doesn't really believe Rosemary has actually killed her mother. The police get to the school at afternoon recess. An assembly's called. The constable tells everyone Rosemary Pooter is missing. They don't tie me into it yet. There's no reason why they would.'

It seems to be getting colder. Kaleen pulls her knees up under her chin. I pick up the doona, which has fallen away a bit, and tuck it around her. Then I switch on the heater with the remote.

'Go on,' Kaleen whispers.

'They asked if anyone knew anything, and that's when…'

'Don't tell me,' Kaleen says, sarcasm twisting her lips, 'Kiss and Celestial came forward.'

'No, they didn't actually, Kaleen. Kiss and Celestial were absent from school as well. But Cheryl wasn't. Later on, Cheryl got in contact with Kiss and Celestial and then they phoned the police and told them how they'd "overheard" Rosemary Pooter and Velvet Brown talking about getting away. Going off somewhere. To Holland, they thought. The police knew I was involved then. That's when Mum and Dad found out I was missing too.'

'I suppose, Vel,' Kaleen says, 'it's also when they found all the information on Mama Pooter's laptop.'

'Well, not straight away. They took it to their computer expert. Rosemary has tight security on there. Only she and her mother knew the password and she'd done something else too to keep it from being hacked into again. I think their experts had a lot of trouble, took hours before they discovered anything. The really incriminating stuff. Mrs Pooter's twenty-thousand-dollar win. And Rosemary's airline bookings.'

'Well, that explains why they weren't there when you two got off the plane. But I'd have thought they'd ring the airports straight away, though. Even before they looked at the laptop. That's what my detectives, in my novel, would have done.'

I roll my eyes. 'Fact is a bit different from fiction, you know, Kaleen. And things don't move as fast as they do on those crime shows you watch, either. They get the forensics back in two minutes. In real life, everything takes a lot longer.' I tell her how the police agency has only just been informed that Mrs Pooter died from a stroke. Kaleen leans back and releases a sigh. Relief if ever I heard it.

'Bloody hell, Kaleen, you didn't think Rosemary really topped her mother, did you?'

Kaleen looks sheepish. Reminds me of one of my dad's favourite merinos. 'Well, Vel. I don't know RP like you do. And it's the quiet ones you always have to be careful of. I mean, if she had killed her mother, I wouldn't have blamed her. Rosemary was a saint or a martyr, one of the two, to have put up with it for so long.'

I draw in air, like sucking a straw. 'I'll tell you all about it one day, Kaleen. More of RP's story. What I learned this afternoon.'

'Yesterday afternoon,' Kaleen says, looking at her watch. 'It's Sunday morning now.'

'Pedantic,' I snort. 'Anyway, I've left the gory bit until last.'

Kaleen leans forward again, 'Should I get out my Clues Folder?'

'God, have you brought that along too?'

'Don't go anywhere without it.' Kaleen smirks. 'I've got heaps written down from yesterday.'

I sense my anger rising, lava-like. I know it's sort of irrational, but I can't help it. 'Glad we can be of some entertainment, Kaleen,' I say.

Kaleen back-steps. 'I didn't mean that I was enjoying it.' She looks like the merino sheep again.

I feel all kinds of rotten. I reach out and touch her arm. It's warm outside the bedclothes now, with the heater going.

'I'm sorry, Kaleen, I think it's the jet lag still, and it's been such a long day.'

Kaleen goes quiet for about two seconds, but then she can't help herself. 'The gory bit…please, Vel.' Definite excitement escalating her voice.

Although, if I had to be perfectly honest, I like this part too. While I was hearing it from Wilhelmina Karstens, it was difficult to keep my face from showing 'inappropriate' feelings, as the school's nurse would say.

'Well, Kaleen, when the first ambulance got there, they realised they were up against something too big for them to handle. Sorry about the pun. Don't laugh, Kaleen.'

I stop and soft punch her. She stifles her laughter, almost choking on it.

'Anyway, they had to get the super mega-sized ambulance from Adelaide, and the fire brigade and the rescue police too.'

Kaleen is stunned mute.

'And,' I say, drawing out my pause, '…a demolition crew.'

'What the heck for?' Kaleen goes quiet again, thinking. 'Oh,' she says, opening her eyes to huge. 'They had to knock down the wall, didn't they?'

'Yes, they did. To get her out. There was no way, apart from dissection, to fit her through the door. She was so bloated she almost took up the entire room.'

I don't say anything about her exploding in the morgue during the autopsy. My mind can't bring that image to words. Somehow it doesn't seem funny any more. I've seen shows on TV where some large people are having so much trouble just trying to live a normal life. And they can't really; a lot of them are housebound or bedridden.

Kaleen and I sit in a moment of silence, not for Mama Pooter – we could never feel sorry for her – but for all those others. And most of the large people I've met have been truly lovely. It wasn't her size which made Mrs Pooter dreadful, but her evil selfish mind.

'Wilhelmina didn't tell you this in front of Rosemary, did she, Vel?'

'No, of course not, Kaleen. All of the NPA officials were really nice to Rosemary. I don't think they ever believed she had anything to do with her mother's death. Even before they brought us in.'

My phone buzzes. It's Willem: 'Sweet dreams. C u in morn.' There's no 'love, Willem,' but I hadn't expected that. Not yet.

Sunday 4 November

I wake at five-thirty and can't go back to sleep. Kaleen says it takes a few days to get over jet lag, but we'll be leaving by then. Finally I get up and check my phone. I've got it on the charger in case it decides to go flat. Luckily, Kaleen had an adapter plug. European sockets are different from Australian ones.

All those texts and missed calls. Some have even gone to message bank. I skip through the ones from Mum and Dad and Danny. I didn't think Danny would be worried about me. But, like I said, he has changed. There's a voice message from Kaleen's rad Aunty Margie asking if we arrived safely and to get back to her as soon as possible. Crap, I should have rung her yesterday. Without checking the time difference, I press Call. It rings through to her answering service. I leave a message saying how we got here okay and that Willem has recovered and is doing well. I even start to cry. I didn't think I'd do that. Jet lag.

There are two missed calls from Brandon, and his voice message asking about RP.

Through more tears, I read a text sent by Rita: 'Willem beter! Skype u soon.' I work out by the date that it would have been sent when our plane was about five hours from arriving. If only I'd turned on my phone.

There are three missed calls from Wilhelmina's number. I muse for a second on how her name is the feminine form of Willem. Synchronicity? Coincidence? Then I open up a text from an unknown caller. Instantly, I guess who it's from, though. There's only one person I know dumb enough to get the spelling wrong even in texts: 'Yaw four it!! Poelice cumming two get ewe.'

Clarissa bloody 'Kiss' Rothchile. There are four such texts, almost in a row. Quite entertaining, really, if you want a laugh. Then I listen to a voice message from the same number, which shuts off my laughter as quickly as if someone had stomped on my mouth. I play it through twice. Even though the words are muffled, it's definitely Kiss – I recognise her voice, and anyway, only she would be stupid enough to do this. Talk about self-incrimination. Now I'm smiling again.

I ring Wilhelmina and tell her I have a voicemail message on my phone, one I think she'll be very interested in hearing. She tells me she'll be over to the hotel around nine-thirty.

When I hang up, my phone rings out its tune so loudly I almost drop it. I turn down the sound. It's from Rita.

'Velvet? I'm sorry to be early ringing. Nurse from *zickenhouse* rang, said Willem is *vermoeid*…er…tired.' She pauses for words. 'Says no visit dis morning. Come dis afternoon. Okay?'

I barely get 'Okay' out, when Rita says. 'Meet de parents?' She chuckles, 'I see dat fillem.'

At first I think she's just making conversation then I realise she's also saying I'm going to meet Willem's parents. OMG.

Kaleen and I break Mum's Rule Number Three and walk to McDonald's. We have the Big Breakfast with extra everything. And I order two cups of coffee. I'm determined to beat this jet lag.

I tell Kaleen about Kiss's texts and she insists on reading them. Soon she's almost falling off her chair with laughter and the staff are looking at us like the ones back in Australia at the airport did when it was Aunty Margie, RP and me. She sobers up when she listens to the voicemail one, though.

'Hell, Velvet. That's so bizarre.'

'Hey, Kaleen,' I say, 'do you realise you just swore?'

'Desperate circumstances. I'm allowed to.'

I take another bite of my bacon and egg muffin. 'Not our desperate circumstances, Kaleen. But if I'm right and Celestial Moonstone is involved too, pretty bad for them. Or at the very least, some serious explaining to do.'

Kaleen shudders. 'And Hanker Wanker? That was his voice in the background, wasn't it?'

I nod. 'It definitely sounded like him.'

On the way back to the hotel, we take a walk along the canals, stop to watch the canal boats picking up tourists and locals. Amsterdam's water buses. I lose count of the many bikes which glide past us. Feel tempted by the coffee houses, where they sell anything but coffee according to Kaleen. She tells me the Dutch are getting stricter, though. Cracking down on drugs. We both laugh at the pun. Okay, I can't blame the jet lag for that one. It's only us, being lame.

I tell Kaleen about Willem's memory loss. Her eyes get misty, but she doesn't seem surprised. Said she's heard of that happening with those types of accidents. When I tell her Willem and I are going to start again, though, rekindle it all, and even brighter this time if that's possible, she's so stoked she high-fives me and does a little skip up the road and back. No one seems to notice; probably think we're high.

Two official cars are waiting at the front of our hotel. When I see Rosemary Pooter and the social worker, Ruth Kensington, getting out of the first one, I speed up my step. Wilhelmina, who's been driving the other car, gets out after them, and slides a briefcase from the front seat.

Back in the hotel, and for the next hour, she quizzes me on everything I know about Celestial Moonstone, Clarissa Rothchile and Mr Hanker, whose first name turns out to be Bruce. Bruce Hanker? Who would have thought? Wilhelmina even gets Kaleen to answer some questions too. Kaleen's tripping over herself in excitement and I bet anything that as soon as Wilhelmina leaves, everything we've talked about will be going down in her Clues Folder. Especially now Interpol and the National Central Bureau, which is part of IPOL and specialises in organised crime, are also getting involved.

Of course, we say nothing about my monsters. Or about Celestial Moonstone's crazy aura mirror-imaging. I think I know what that is now. And why I'm seeing it. My sight is changing and growing (perhaps puberty has something to do with it?). I'm seeing another side and depth of wrongness or extremeness. And in the case of Mama Pooter (and maybe Celestial, I don't know yet), perhaps pure psychopathic sadistic evil, the worst of the worst, stands alone in aura only without the lines, jagged or blurry.

I have no idea why I've been given my monster-seeing ability, or how it works. But I have to learn to adapt and accept. Know the auras I see are very important too. With or without the monster shapes. And after our near-fatal miss with that horrible woman on the plane, Emily, I do accept it now. I do.

After Wilhelmina has left, Kaleen leaves me alone with Rosemary. I tell her sorry once again and start to explain why I didn't tell her about her mama being gone. I can't bring myself to say 'dead' in front of RP. It sounds so final.

She peers at me over her glasses, such a familiar look. She hasn't worn them for ages, mainly needs them for reading. 'That's okay, Vel. I know why you did it. And I've had some time to think. You know, come to terms with my parents' deaths. Also Ruth's been wonderful. She's helped me so much.'

It seems Rosemary doesn't mind using the D word. 'Closure,' I say, remembering Mum's self-help books again.

Rosemary nods. 'Yes, well…sort of. But I don't feel so guilty now. Just telling someone about it seemed to help. And Ruth made me look at it from a different angle. You know, laterally.'

Thank god for RP's practical side. That's where she and Kaleen are alike, even though Kaleen can be pretty rash or radical at times. Probably inherited that from her Aunty Margie.

I look at my watch; it's almost midday. I have to get to the hospital, but I don't want to leave Rosemary on her own.

'I have to go and see Willem, RP. Come with me.' I grab her hand. 'He really wants to meet you. I told him I wouldn't have made it here without you.'

RP peers at me again. 'Oh, I don't know, Vel. You'd want to be alone with him, wouldn't you?'

I say about Willem's parents. How they're going to be there too. How I could do with some moral support. It's only then she agrees to come with me.

I rush around getting ready. Ruth's offered to drive us to the hospital. She's staying the night in the same hotel as ours. We have to be at the airport tomorrow. Our plane leaves at four-twenty in the afternoon.

I take special care with my make-up, but not too much; I'm keeping it natural. I change my clothes, put on the top I wore yesterday.

RP comes back, wearing some make-up too and looking a little less pale.

I walk in front of her, like a model. 'Do you think this top's okay, RP? Not too revealing? You know, for Willem's parentals.'

'It looks fine, Vel. It's not like you have big…' She stops, the rest of her face goes as pink as the blusher she's put on her cheeks. I look down. I know what she means. I have 'teacup titties', while RP's are more like soup bowls. Puberty might be dealing me more in the monster-seeing department but not in the mammaries.

Ruth drops us off at the hospital at the same time as Rita and her family are getting out of their car. It's beautiful and sleek, the colour of an otter when it's just slipped out of a river. I don't know what type the car is, but it looks classy.

I gasp a breath when I see Willem's parents. His father is an older version of Willem and his mother is an older version of Rita. So that's where they get their different looks. It figures.

Rita runs over to us and I introduce her to Rosemary. When her parents catch up, Rita introduces us all to each other. The mother and father shake our hands and both have friendly smiles which reach their eyes. They look paler than RP before the make-up, though. I hadn't thought about Willem's parents, how worried they must have been.

Willem is sitting up in bed, finishing his lunch. Rosemary and I stand in the background and let his parents do the talking. I have no idea what they're saying, but I don't hear our names being used, so we don't interrupt.

After what feels like hours, Willem's parents tell us they're leaving. They say goodbye with light hugs and promises to catch up soon.

When they've left the room, Rita leads us over to Willem, gives us each a quick kiss on the cheek, then rushes off to catch up with them.

Willem shakes RP's hand and I see his eyes travel to her chest. Blast these teacup titties of mine. But I can't feel envious of RP, not with what she's been through. And anyway, I know how deeply she feels about Brandon. I can't even blame Willem. He hardly knows me now. Loyalty doesn't come into it.

Rosemary and Willem chat for a few minutes and then RP picks up a magazine, goes over to the other side of the room and sits on one of the visitors' chairs. I feel like hugging her. She's letting me and Willem have some private time.

I sit on the bed, take his hand. He looks at my face and then, I can't believe it, he's looking at my chest too. Without thinking, I stick out my front. Willem's eyes open wide. His hand leaves mine and comes forward. I start to pull back, but then stop. He wasn't looking at my breasts. He's touching my sun pendant and his face is glowing. For several long seconds he doesn't speak.

'Velvet, I gave dis to you, didn't I?' He sounds incredulous, like he can't believe his own words.

I squeeze his other hand tight and hang on.

He continues, his voice almost a whisper. 'And der is a horse? A white horse? Has eyes like…' He opens the pendant and reveals the blue ribbon entwined with Spirit's mane.

I nod vigorously, tears cascading down my cheeks.

'Oh my God, Velvet. I remember. I remember! It's as if I've been walking in a dark forest wid only little glimpses of you and den we come to a clearing. I see dis pendant and…' Willem pulls me to him. His embrace is so strong. He's saying again and again how sorry he is.

And I'm telling him, in between his long kisses, that it's not his fault. How everything will be in bright colours from now on, no more dark paths. And all our nightmares forgotten.

Thursday 8 November

I'm back in Australia, in my bed, staring at the crack in my ceiling and wondering if I'll ever sleep normally again. It's 2 a.m. and I have jet lag in reverse. Rosemary and I got home on Tuesday night, at eleven o'clock. It took the twenty-one hours travelling time, plus we picked up the nine hours somewhere as well (I think they were waiting for us at the equator) and sped ahead to the future.

At this time of the morning, it makes my brain ache thinking about it. And my body clock is so shot to confusion, it's not sure if it's night or day even when I try convincing it by pointing out the moon or the sun.

As Kaleen said, you can't explain jet lag to anyone; they have to experience it to know what it's like. At the moment, I feel wide awake, as if it's time to get up. But a lot of the time I feel sort of spacey and out of it.

So much has happened. But there's lots I don't know about, not yet.

I managed to soften Mum and Dad up a bit with some gifts I bought for them in Holland. Two little white and blue porcelain Dutch clogs, and a hand-carved windmill. I know – clichéd, but they liked them. Not enough to unground my infinity-and-beyond grounding, but enough to stop them from lecturing me for days. I still had to listen to them all the way back from the airport. And fair enough too. I do understand how worried they've been. And what made it all worse for my parents was hearing about Hanker Bruce Wanker being involved in some dodgy thing on the internet and his strange (I'm still not sure what this is yet) connection with Celestial Moonstone and Clarissa 'Kiss' Rothchile.

Of course we weren't part of that. But after it came out, accusations were running through our small town like the shits. Stuff like Rosemary Pooter had murdered her mother with a blunt butter knife. And that me, Kaleen, Rosemary, Kiss, Hanker Wanker and Celestial were part of a huge drug and gambling cartel about to take over the world.

The truth is even worse. Well, about Hanker Wanker at least. It appears he was a big knob in an international paedophile ring. (Pun unintentional. Anyway, it would be a minuscule knob, the pervert.) Which is why Interpol and the National Central Bureau, NCB, in the Netherlands, were so interested in Kiss's voice message. It wasn't only what Kiss said but what Hanker Wanker was yelling in the background: 'Get your gear off… Get your gear off…' repeated like a mantra. And you could hear loud rhythmic clapping as well. He was already a suspect and on their list; this just put him at the top of it.

What Kiss said in the voice message to me (in a puke-inducing tone) was 'If the police don't get you, we'll get you.' And then a string of words which sounded like an incantation. Although what that has to do with a paedophile ring, I don't know. Maybe she's in one of those different religions who speak in tongues.

Maybe I'll find out more about it all when I get back to school next week.

On the good news front, Old Ma Izzy is home. She rang me last night and told me where she'd gone. All the way to Western Australia, to Arabian Antiquity Arabs stud farm. It took her three days to get there. (I should have guessed where she was heading when I received her parcel, postmarked Ceduna, near the SA/WA border.)

I'm not sure what she did, but there's another serious investigation happening, which involves AAACL (Australian Anti Animal Cruelty League) and the RSPCA (Royal Society for the Prevention of Cruelty to Animals), who have reopened their files on the case.

So, the owners won't come looking for Ganymede again any time soon; they have enough to contend with. It seems Old Ma Izzy knows people in high places. Lofty places, I think. Still, that doesn't surprise me. I'm so relieved that she's the person I thought she was. She even explained why she couldn't hide Ganymede on her place. If he'd been found (and he would have been), she would've lost all credibility and might not have been able to pull off her plan. Still I'm the tiniest, tiniest bit put out that Old Ma Izzy didn't confide in me before she left.

I'm going to ring Brandon this morning and ask him to take Ganymede back to Kaleen's. RP and I have been worried about Ganny, although Brandon texted me the day we got back to say that Ganny was fine.

Rita's been keeping in touch with texts as well, and yesterday morning she wheeled Willem outside the hospital and he phoned me. (They've both been told off for using their phones inside.) It was brill talking to him again. He sounds so much stronger. And he's remembering more and more as the days go by. He said he also remembered Brandon, and had got Rita to let him know on Facebook that he was fine. (I'd already updated Brandon on Willem's condition as soon as I'd got home, in reply to his text about Ganny. But Willem didn't know that.)

Rosemary has gone into care in Adelaide and is currently being looked after by another social worker, Grace Pender, the twin sister of Ruth Kensington, which is a really strange kind of coincidence. Originally from England, both loved travelling, both became social workers and now both have had the privilege of caring for Rosemary Pooter. The only difference is that Grace was the sister who got married. I'm hoping she's as nice as Ruth. She looked exactly like her, and seemed okay when she met Rosemary at the airport.

I haven't been able to talk to RP; she still doesn't have a phone, and no one's given me a contact number. But I'm going to keep an eye on my emails in case the police give Rosemary back her mama's laptop. I really miss her and Kaleen. Kaleen will be back this weekend. But God knows when I'll see RP again.

It's no good, I can't sleep, I'm going to go through the one hundred and twenty-seven emails in spam to see if there are any that don't belong there. Luckily once again, Danny is not turning off his computer at night, so I get in quickly and open my Gmail account. Dozens of emails offering me a bigger penis. What do they think I have? Penis envy? There are lots and lots of gambling ones as well, obviously the Spam Mail Powers That Be don't know that (a) I'm a girl and (b) I'm under-age for gambling.

I'm almost at the end when I see one from Tarrant Moselle, Kaleen's publisher from Wanda-Willow Press. How that ended up in spam I don't know. For a second I have a cold flush (is that the opposite to the hot flushes Mum's self-help books are always banging on about?) that I may have missed an email from Tarrant before this, if it had ended up here. Spam is deleted automatically every so often and I don't always check it.

I needn't have worried.

Tarrant Moselle – Wanda-Willow Press to Brown Velvet Nov 7th

Dear Velvet Brown,

As you are Kaleen Pingelly's agent, I thought it judicious of me to enlighten you that Kaleen Pingelly's aforesaid novel, *Bitter the Taste of Murder*, now known as *Murder Does not Innocence Make*, will be published in ebook format on, or around, late February next year.

It will be available on Amazon.com.au and all Amazon sites worldwide. Royalties will be determined at a later date when pricing is agreed upon by yourself and Kaleen Pingelly.

I earnestly hope this meets with you and your client's approval.

Always yours sincerely,

Tarrant Moselle. Publisher @Wanda-Willow Press

What a cop-out. An ebook? I almost feel like printing the email out so I can have the satisfaction of screwing it up and throwing it, with force, into my waste-paper basket. It deserved to be in spam. Maybe the Spam Mail Powers That Be aren't so stupid after all.

I'm sure this is not what the book contract specified. I rummage through the paperwork on my desk. Find a copy of the contract, flick through the pages and then check them again more slowly. I sink back into my chair. Crap! There's nothing saying Kaleen's novel was going to be in printed form. Just that it would be published at an unspecified date, but within the next two years.

In Tarrant's email there's also no answer to my question about what he was going to do about promotion. But maybe he's got something up his publishing sleeve and perhaps I'm being too hard on all of this. There are ebooks bestselling to great heights. You just have to have the right marketing. And hit the right demographic.

Now I do feel tired. I forward the email to Kaleen and climb back into bed.

I'm woken by Mum asking if I'd like some lunch. I scrunch a look at my watch, through slits for eyes, and see it's almost midday. Bloody hell.

'What?' Mum asks, her voice muffled by the door.

I sit up and then fall back against my pillows. 'I'll be out in fifteen,' I croak through parched throat and lips. I pour myself a drink of water. I don't care if this jug has sat there from before I left for Holland. I need something wet.

Later, I stumble into the kitchen. This will be the first meal I've had in here since I returned from Holland. I've been having my meals in bed, reheated at random hours. The meals that is, not the bed. Mum is home today as she's working shift tonight. Dad's nowhere in sight; he's still on the job trial. It's going well, apparently. He's even thinking of taking up the caber in a sort of boss bonding with Mr McManus. Mum said he'd been contemplating the bagpipes, but luckily she was able to nip that in the sporran. Sorry, her joke.

I sit at the table, face flat on my hands. Then, through my fingers, I smell eggs and fritz on the sizzle. It perks my appetite and makes me look up. There on the corkboard above the fridge is my postcard, resplendent with windmills, blue sky-backed sails in full spread, atop the grassy green of pastures. The contrast of Friesian cows, sharp black and white, grazing out of it. I sent the card from Holland on Sunday, the day Willem remembered me. Us.

Mum sees me looking. 'That arrived here this morning,' she says, smiling.

It's so good to see her happy.

She straightens the postcard, by moving the thumb tacks and stands back, admiration flooding her eyes. 'Looks like a very beautiful place, Velvet. And I'm so pleased Willem is on the mend. It's unusual for them to make a recovery like that. Particularly when the tests were so negative.' She keeps staring. 'Still, I have heard of it happening. Especially when the patient has so much to live for.' Then she's back at the stove turning over the slices of fritz, and humming a distorted little tune.

It's good to be home. God, the Dorothy of bloody Oz again. I have to stop being so lame.

Friday 9 November

Finally I feel better. Last night I forced myself to stay up till eleven o'clock and then get up at my normal hour of seven o'clock. It seems to have done the trick. Body clock reset.

I'm going to ring Brandon. I didn't do it yesterday. I wouldn't have made much sense. And he did text me again that Ganny was doing fine, so I wasn't worried. It's eight o'clock now, I hope I catch him before he goes off on his bike. He's training pretty hard at the moment as he has a time trial on Sunday. I know all about time trials. Willem told me. They sound awful. Basically, you have to ride flat out over forty or fifty kilometres, I can't remember which. Then your time is compared with other riders in your group. Your aim is to beat your previous best and also go up the ranks. Or, if you're as good as Brandon and Willem, aim to get the winning time.

Brandon answers on the second ring. 'Hi, Vel, what's up?' then before I can answer with what is up, he cuts me off. 'Listen, Vel, I don't have time. We're doing the Willunga Hill ride today. And Crow's Nest. Can I ring you back?' I'm about to say yes when he does it again, talks over me. 'Look, could I wing past your place this afternoon around…' There's a short pause. 'Around one?'

I answer, 'That's fine.' But he's already gone.

Speaking of hill climbs makes me remember the misunderstanding I'd had with Willem and Kaleen, when Kaleen and I were heading home from TAOB. I'd overheard Brandon talking about a Category One with Willem and jumped to the conclusion that Kaleen had told them about my monster-seeing ability. I'd been wrong. They were talking about hill climbs. In the world of competitive cycling, a Category One is a very steep ascent.

I draw in a breath, recalling my last conversation with Willem on Monday, a few hours before Rosemary and I had to leave for the airport.

I told him all about my monster sight and, just like RP, he didn't raise an eyebrow. He knew me enough, I think, to trust what I was telling him was the truth. He squeezed me tight and his eyes sparkled as he called me his clever brilliant special lady. Saying how he'd always known I was gifted, a cut above the rest.

I'd baulked at that. 'No, Willem,' I'd said. 'I'm not special, or better, just different.' Then I'd gone on to tell him how I was still learning more about my gift, how it was always changing.

I told him about Mama Pooter, her peculiar aura, and how I'd only picked up for sure on what it meant when I'd come up against Emily. Their type of auras were categories way above, and way worse, than any of my known ones.

He grinned and almost laughed. 'Oh, Velvet. It's like wid us racing cyclists. We say category *Hors*, which is French. De hardest of climbs. It's a category beyond categories.' Then he'd laughed. 'Not many hills here, in de Nederlands. Hard or easy.'

The truth lifts my lips to a smile as I think, But Willem, you've climbed the tallest of mountains to get back to be with me.

It's almost one o'clock. I have the house to myself. Mum's on day shift and Dad's still working. Hooray. Hopefully, soon we won't be so poor. Maybe we'll get to have a holiday this year after all. There's still time. The last family holiday we had was when I was only four-years old. I have this mist-like memory of an old woman, her hair white in stark contrast to her dark skin. I know now it was my Pitjantjatjara great grandmother and the three other women with her, and equally old – the aunties.

Until Dad got this job, there'd even been talk about him and Mum selling the property. I can't begin to think of that. Not living near Kaleen and my beautiful Spirit any more, or Old Ma Izzy. And what would I do with my darling Sebby? Secretly, though, I think it was what spurred Dad on to keep working. Contemplating losing his precious Merino sheep was too much for him to bear.

Brandon arrives in a blur of Lycra-clad muscles and bulging well…you know. I avert my eyes. I guess this is what it's like for guys looking at our boobs. It's hard not to, when they're sticking out in an encouraging 'Look at me! Look at me!' fashion. It's good to have the other side of the gender perspective sometimes.

I'm sure Brandon has noticed me noticing, but he doesn't say anything.

'How did the hill climbs go?' I ask, staring directly into his face, but finding my gaze slipping downwards again.

Brandon props his bike up against the house. Why don't those bikes have stands, I wonder? Then I remember how weight is an issue. They want to keep them as light as they can for maximum speed.

'Awesome, Vel,' he answers. 'I had a great day.' His tone doesn't match his words, and now he has his sunglasses off I see his eyes.

He's a different Brandon from the one I saw last time, when he took me and Rosemary Pooter to see Ganny on the way to Aunty Margie's.

We sit at the table. He swigs from his water bottle, and I sip a cup of green tea I'd made myself to have with lunch. I ask if he wants something to eat but he shakes his head.

A minute later he speaks. 'What's the deal with Rosemary? When is she coming back? Have you heard anything more about her, Vel?'

This time I shake my head. 'Sorry, Brandon. I'll let you know when I do, though.'

He takes another long swig. 'Thanks,' he says, his lips barely moving.

OMG. I think Brandon's met his match. What I mean is, women are always falling head over tit for him and I think he's had lots of fun at times, never being serious and breaking all those hearts. I've heard things from other girls. Not that it was malicious intent; he was only being a guy. But now he's on the other side of the gender too. Only difference is RP won't do to him what he's done to others (even how unintentionally). She's not like that.

He tells me how he's brought Ganymede back to his place and that he can stay there for as long as we like. He talks with dreams in his eyes about RP, how amazing she was on Ganny and what a honey she is. He even says he's never met anyone like her. (That's way up the uncool scale. But it's what love does to you.) I assure him she feels the same way about him, too.

'Why didn't you tell me she didn't have a phone, Vel? I could have given her my old one.'

I know his old one is less than six months new; he's always updating.

I smile. 'I thought you'd guess when she didn't phone you.'

He slumps down on the table, sweat marking the tablecloth. 'Oh God,' he says, 'I thought she was trying not to be pushy and then when you went to Holland I knew you both had other things on your mind. I did try and ring you.'

I grab his arm and shake it. 'Anyway, Brandon. What have you heard? Of course, you know about RP and her mama, that it wasn't her fault. But what about Celestial Moonstone and Kiss and the revolting Hanker Bruce Wanker? What's been happening with them? What's it all about?' Now I can't stop to let him talk. 'Brandon, you know Alan Moonstone. Has he told you anything?'

Brandon gives a low laugh and puts up his hand. 'Hang on, Velvet. Give a guy a chance to answer. Okay, first Hanker Wanker. He's involved with a worldwide paedophile ring which operated on the net, exchanging videos and images. It's only what I've heard. It hasn't come on the news yet.'

I sigh in frustration. 'I know about that, Brandon. But what's it to do with Celestial Moonstone and Kiss? Were they a part of it too? The paedophile ring?'

Brandon screws up his bottom lip. 'No, not in that way. Hanker Wanker got involved with them to take photos. You know, nude shots of them and worse. Look, it's all a bit complicated, but simple when you actually know what went on.'

I stare at him with annoyance creasing my brow. 'I've also got this wacky voicemail from Kiss. I haven't been able to make sense of that either.'

'The "Get your gear off" one?' Brandon says. 'Yeah, Vel, Kaleen told me about it yesterday when she rang. And about all those dumb text messages from Kiss.' He gets up and refills his bottle at the sink. Takes a long drink.

I fling him an impatient look.

'Okay, Vel,' he says, sitting down again. 'First you have to understand the Moonstones. Where they're coming from. What they believe.' Brandon clears his throat. 'Well, how can I put this? Fundamentally they're Wicca followers. Witches. Not fairytale horrible, more new age earthy. Mother nature worshippers really. White witches.'

I'd heard of modern-day witches before. There's even a small coven in our town. Old Ma Izzy told me and Kaleen about it ages ago.

'I'm not surprised, Brandon,' I say, my voice resigned. 'I knew there was something odd about the Moonstones. But white witches aren't evil, so why is Celestial so dire?'

Brandon smiles. 'You've heard of the black sheep of the family? Well, she's the black witch of the family. Although, from what Alan Moonstone told me, there's no such thing as black or white witches. Just rogue witches who use their powers wrongly. Like trying to take control over other people's lives. Manipulating them.'

I begin to tell him what I saw that night in the forest with Celestial and her two brothers, but Brandon interrupts.

'Yeah, Vel. Alan told me they saw you there. What they were trying to do was to bring her back to good witch. It was a ritual to make her stop doing all that evil shit.'

I sniff. 'Well, it didn't work.' I look at Brandon. He has his eyebrows up. 'Oh my God, did I ruin it for them, Brandon? Break the spell or whatever it was?'

No wonder Alan Moonstone had morphed into an Angry at the Drop of a Rat Monster. He was pissed off at me for interrupting them.

We sit quietly for a few minutes.

Brandon's the first to speak. 'I wouldn't worry about it, Vel. I think Celestial was pretty far gone. The sad thing is, while she was trying to control Hanker Wanker, all the time he was taking advantage of her and Kiss. And what happened on the night when Kiss left that voice message on your phone was another ritual.' Brandon pauses, looks grave. 'A sacrifice… Of Kiss.'

I gasp a breath and almost choke on a mouthful of tea that I hadn't swallowed. Brandon looks bemused, but still half serious. 'Not that sort of sacrifice, Vel. Not killing Kiss. Sacrificing her virginity.'

I never thought I would, but I actually feel a bit sorry for Kiss at this moment. She's like the poor dumb cow going to the slaughter. No idea. And Celestial and her weird aura mirror image? That's going on my '*hors*' categories – my Beyond Monster Categories List. I just have to find another definition for it.

I shudder at Celestial Moonstone's vileness. She's so contemptible, only wanted Hanker Wanker for her sick ritual to take Kiss's virginity, and add to her own personal power. But then I chuckle. The joke's on them, if you could call it such. According to a very good source (my brother Danny), Kiss had no virginity left to sacrifice.

Saturday 10 November – late afternoon

What a fabulously awesome day it's been. Way, way cool, but a little bit sad too. I'd better explain.

To start the day, Willem Skyped me. I couldn't believe it. He's out of hospital and home now. We talked until 12.30 p.m. (Australian time.) Stuff my cleaning chores.

He's been doing some light exercise on his stationary bike. He hopes to be back competing in three months. He's not doing boxing any more, though – doctor's orders. He said he doesn't mind. It's the cycling he's always loved most anyway.

Rita has started a campaign to stop mopeds and other motorised vehicles using the bike tracks. There's been a lot of fatalities recently and many people are signing her FB petitions and donating to the cause. She's put up posters and has written to the politicians and everything. Her YouTube vid of 'Why it's Dangerous on our Bike Paths' (with poignant pics of Willem on life support) has had over two hundred thousand hits already.

Then, just after lunch, Kaleen arrived with her rad Aunty Margie. And Kaleen is so incredible – not a trace of jet lag. She was her usual bubbling self – even more so, if that's possible – but also infuriating, as she kept saying she had some totally off the scale, coolest news that I was not going to believe. Then when I'd ask 'What?' she'd clam up like, well, a clam, and refuse to speak. Like I said, infuriating.

Mum got on with Aunty Margie like a rabbit-hole full of bunnies, and they talked of Old Days, brimming with Hippy and Woodstock and weed-laced brownies. And when Aunty Margie told Mum about the suffragette movement group she belonged to, Mum was way interested. I reckon Aunty Margie might have another convert. Mum even forgave Aunty Margie for signing the form so I could go to Holland. I think Mum's got softer on all that. She knows what Willem means to me now. How committed we are.

Finally, Aunty Margie nudged Kaleen and said, 'Go on. Tell them our news.'

Kaleen sat up straight and, almost like she was giving a toast, said, 'My very rad and wonderful Aunty Margie's going to become a mother.' There was, dare I say, a pregnant pause where even the silence seemed embarrassed. Aunty Margie's well past her fertility date and besides, there's the question of a guy needing to be involved. Aunty Margie's been a widow for years.

Kaleen and Aunty Margie dissolved into laughter. Mum and I sat on, waiting for the punchline.

Kaleen delivered it. 'Oh, your faces!' she said, and then snapped a pic of us. She caught her breath and her next words came out in fluid lines. 'Aunty Margie's going to foster Rosemary. Isn't that the coolest thing you've ever heard?'

And it was, but that's where the sad part comes in. I mean, I was absolutely over the stars with happiness for RP; it was the very best thing that could have happened to her. But it means she has to move to Adelaide. She won't be living here any more.

I think Kaleen's more than the tiniest bit pleased she'll have me all to herself again, though. Not that she'll admit it. Mum was overjoyed as well and Aunty Margie assured us she'd let Rosemary come and stay here as often as we liked. And even let RP stay at Brandon's if she wants. Mum sucked in a stiff breath when she said that. I know she doesn't approve, but not everyone can be as rad as Kaleen's Aunty Margie. Lucky, lucky RP.

Then the next cool thing Aunty Margie told us was that she was picking RP up in the morning and they'd be here around ten. Kaleen got super-excited and said we'd be able to go for a picnic ride, the three of us – herself, Rosemary, and me. Then she even talked Mum into ungrounding me for tomorrow.

I'll ride Zeus, Kaleen will ride Watson, and RP can take my gorgeously magic horse, Spirit.

Like I said, what a fabulously awesome day it's been. And what an incredible way, way cool year it's turned out to be after all.

235

22 December

This is my last entry in this diary I got from Old Ma Izzy. It's full already, so much has happened. (It's one of those diaries without dates – only month headings – but some of my days filled up a month's pages.)

The picnic ride went better than anything we could have imagined, except RP didn't ride Spirit, I rode him. Kaleen of course was mounted on Watson. And as a surprise for RP, Brandon (I phoned him the night before) rolled up in his new car, a bright red latest model Holden, towing a gleaming new horse trailer. On it was the mare he'd bought from Kiss, Sylvania Star, and also Ganymede.

RP and Ganny got along like a dream, their kindred union of shared past suffering (Rosemary's plastered arm a physical reminder) ever strengthening their bond. And Kaleen had me all to herself when RP and Brandon rode off together into the proverbial sunset (well, into the depths of the forest) for most of the afternoon and didn't even turn up to eat any of the picnic lunch. Which was a bit of a bummer because we had frog cakes, Yoyo biscuits and fritz sandwiches with lashings of tomato sauce. (Sorry, Enid Blyton.)

Spirit was his usual wonderful self. I still don't know why he took off with me that night when I saw Celestial Moonstone and her two brothers. Perhaps he wanted me to see that something was up with Celestial? I should have asked her brothers what they were doing. Maybe they would have told me. Although I'm beginning to believe nothing can be done for people like Celestial Moonstone, Hanker Wanker, and Emily. Except their incarceration to protect the innocent.

The Moonstone family has left town. Celestial has to do three hundred and forty hours of community service wherever they end up, and has to attend counselling as well. Not that I think either will help.

I still haven't got a definition for her. Cracked mirror aura psycho-megalomaniac? Seven years bad luck for anyone who gets close to her?

Celestial wasn't the global hacker, but she had been hacking various people's (including ours and Spider Johnson's) computers and even tapping some phones (once again ours) as well. The police got onto her because RP forwarded Celestial's information to them after she'd cleared the virus from our old computer. Celestial had been hacking Hanker Wanker's computer too, and it was through that, in a sort of bad accidentally does good type of way again, that the police discovered his paedophile connection.

Kiss has changed schools, which is another good thing to have come out of this. That, and Hanker Bruce Wanker having to serve fifteen years jail without parole. The student teacher's accusation of him grabbing her breast (what is it with guys and our boobs?) was only a small part of the sentence.

Kaleen isn't upset about her book going digital, she's all for it actually, and she's looking forward to seeing it on Amazon. She's still hush hush about her new book so I have no idea what that's going to be about.

Me? I'm jumping out of myself excited, waiting for January to rock up, when my Willem will be getting off the plane from Holland. We're staying at Kaleen's rad Aunty Margie's, and going to watch the cycling race the Tour Down Under. What a blast. I can't wait. Bring on next year!

PS: Just to further prove how amazing Rosemary Pooter is, remember when she was fixing up my computer? Well, when she was checking out the deleted trash (I knew there was some way to access it) she came across my I See Monster Files. She loved them, formatted them into a manuscript and sent it off to an Australian publisher. And guess what? They're going to publish it! And they want more. I was pretty mortified at first and a bit pissed off with RP for reading it, but now I've got used to the idea. YOLO.

The only thing is, how the hell do I tell Kaleen?